Locked Down
The Locked Trilogy Book 3

By GB Williams

Published by HanWill Publishing

Also By GB Williams

Locked Up (The Locked Series Book 1)
Locked Up (The Locked Series Book 2)

Last Cut Casebook

Chapter 1

What's he doing here?

Seen him loads at the Dance School. Not seen him at the park before. Loads of people here today though, he must be someone's daddy. He did pick that Denise up that time she tripped over. Mind, she trips over a lot. Nana says she's a clumsy clod now, but she'll grow into her feet eventually. She'll have to hurry it up or ballet won't help her.

Oh, that's Rosa just gone over to him. He hugs and kisses her head, like Daddy does with me. Oh, so he's Rosa's daddy! Weird kid. Comes to tap but is always early, always sitting waiting, goes home in her dance gear. Won't even do the recitals because she don't want to get changed in front of other people. Maybe she's got that anorexia or Body Disagreement Disorder thing that cousin Thelma's always on about.

What's he giving her?

Ping!

Oh look! Someone new's joined the network. ChinaDoll. Better get her on my team or the girls are going to beat me. Some of these monsters are just too fast to catch them all. Yes – ChinaDoll got one! Hell, I missed. ChinaDoll got another one. She's good.

'Hello.'

What's Rosa doing here? Since when does she have a Game Boy?

'Are you PrincessMads?'

Oh, she's not, is she? 'Yeah.'

'I'm ChinaDoll. Can I sit with you?'

'Yeah, guess so.'

Mum says it's a free world and this is a park, so I can't really stop her sitting on the grass. Oh, she doesn't smell after all. Two more monsters caught - she really is good at this.

'Gotta go.'

Already? Stacey and Jen didn't make it today because of the dentist, and now Keisha's going early too.

'Okay, Keish. See you tomorrow.'

Only me and ChinaDoll now in the game. I'm not playing her, she too good. Keisha's already run out of the park.

'I better go to,' I say.

'Why don't you carry on playing in the car.'

Rosa's daddy is standing by us now.

'I can drive you home and you can carry on the game a while.'

Don't really want to.

'Oh, that would be great!' Rosa said. 'I'd like to play a bit more, please.'

She looks so hopeful. Like I can save her or something. I like this feeling. maybe it's time PrincessMads had a ChinaDoll to play with.

'Okay, but I don't live that far away.'

We scramble to our feet and get in the car. It's a nice car. Rosa's Daddy holds the back door for us and we scramble in, sit down and put the belts on. Then we start playing again. 'All secure ladies?'

We nod, but I'm catching another monster. The door closes carefully, and the car starts moving. This game is getting good. Oh, and a match opportunity, me and ChinaDoll against Hebbie and the ScottyDog. Yes, we're showing them. That's good. Great. ChinaDoll beats Hebbie. Yes, we won!

Must be home by now.

Hang on. I don't recognise these streets.

'Hey, I think you missed the turning, I live by the school!'

And the school is well behind us now.

Chapter 2

'You don't have to do this.'

His knuckles were white as he gripped the steering wheel and spoke to his companion.

Her perfectly shaped eyebrows rose in query. 'Respectfully, sir, neither do you.'

'Oh, yes I do.' He probably shouldn't be dragging her into this. Flushing his own already teetering career was one thing, he didn't want to drag her prospects down the pan too. DCI Piper turned to look at the house two doors down from where he had parked.

'Why?'

'Because all too often, bad things happen to good people, and if I can't give some sort of help to those people, what good am I?'

'Then I have to do this too.'

Piper turned to look at the woman at his side. PC Siddig was too serious, it was clear in her dark eyes and it kept her from being written off as overly pretty. She was never going to get away from looking exotic though, not with her Middle-Eastern heritage. She was young and still keen.

Considering Siddig, he knew she wanted to be a career copper. He wasn't convinced that at 21 she realised just what that might mean.

'Sir, this is exactly what I got into police work to do.'

His brows raised. 'Work against the boss's orders?'

'Work to solve cases, protect the innocent, give families closure. Besides, we're not working against DCS Broughton's orders. He restricted you to cold cases, but he didn't say anything about me.'

That amused Piper, given he was CID and she was uniform. 'He doesn't know you're working with me. Neither does your sergeant, come to that. We could both get into trouble doing this.'

'Yes, sir. That is a risk. But if we find what we both think we're going to find, then not doing this is an even bigger risk. Besides, one, it's my day off, I can do what I want, and two, DCS Broughton didn't tell you which cases to reopen, or which ones to avoid.'

'True, but I doubt he meant this one.'

'I doubt he *knows* about this one, sir.'

That was one of the factors Piper was relying on for his defence. And if he was going to do this, he had to do it now. Pulling the key from the ignition, he opened the door and stepped into the street. The air was fresher; May had brought warmth with it, but also an unseasonable north wind that would appear unexpectedly, mug its victim and bite through the lighter layers the temperature otherwise demanded.

His footsteps sounded too loud as Piper joined Siddig on the pavement. Without a word, he led the way to the house.

The door was a heavy wooden block, painted white, though a dark scuff on the bottom suggested it stuck in winter and had to be persuaded with foot as well as hand. There was a polished brass knocker. Piper discretely pulled in a steadying breath as he reached for the brass and used it, instantly feeling guilty for the finger marks. His stomach knotted as he waited for an answer.

The woman who answered was five two, had a comfortable layer of years around the middle, apart from the natural progression of facial lines, she was otherwise well preserved. She also wasn't the woman he was hoping would answer. And the door hadn't stuck.

'Mrs Whittaker,' he greeted the older woman.

Her brief smile paled as she went white, the furrows gathering on her brows. 'Inspector?' The word was slightly breathy, her hand rose to her chest, lined fingers clutching at the simple gold cross she wore. 'Oh God, what's happened? Is Addy...?'

The surprise of the question nearly robbed Piper of his senses. 'Addy' was Mrs Whittaker's daughter, a woman for whom Piper had a great deal of respect, a woman he had dealt with on two occasions. Unfortunately, each occasion that had brought him to Mrs Whittaker's door was with bad news. Little wonder she was worried now, even though it was Addy, or rather Ariadne, Teddington he had actually come to see.

'It's nothing like that. No problem. May we come in?'

Mrs Whittaker swallowed and nodded, stepping back to admit them, indicating the first door on the left. It led into the lounge. Only once the three of them were inside did Piper introduce the two women. He was too tense, so he tried to look natural as he stood before the fireplace.

'So, this isn't about Ariadne?'

Piper shook his head. 'No. Have you decorated?'

Mrs Whittaker nodded. 'Well, Luke did it really.'

Now Piper was frowning. 'Luke?'

'Our new lodger. He's been a Godsend. So helpful with everything. With Addy not here, I was struggling with the painting, and he just took over. Did almost all of it, even fixed the new light and helped with the furniture.'

Which was also new.

'No family photographs?'

'I've kept them in my bedroom for the moment. Till Addy's back anyway. Won't you sit down?'

Piper looked to Siddig, who sat and thanked Mrs Whittaker, though Piper remained on his feet. He wasn't here to talk décor, he was just being a coward not getting directly to the point. He took a breath. 'Actually, it was your daughter I wanted to speak to. Is she around?'

'Sorry, no. She's gone to stay at a friend's. To recover. She was in a car accident a few weeks ago, you know?' She looked at him. 'Of course you know.'

Piper nodded - that accident was part of the reason he was restricted to cold cases. 'I knew about the accident, I hadn't realised she was recuperating away from home.'

Mrs Whittaker was nodding. 'It's the stairs. She can't handle the stairs with the broken leg and arm. Her friend has a bungalow.'

'Do you have an address? Perhaps I could visit her there.'

'It's in Northumbria.'

Other end of the country.

'She took her mobile with her. Give her a call. Though I couldn't guarantee a response. The place where she's staying is rather beyond the reach of most signals. You can try emailing her. I think she has internet access.'

Mrs Whittaker stood up, moved to the side and pulled out an address book.

'Here, try this.'

As Mrs Whittaker read the email address, Siddig wrote it down. It wouldn't be the best way to contact anyone in this situation, but it was better than nothing. At a prompt, Mrs Whittaker also gave them the address. It would be difficult to swing such a trip, but Piper figured he could do it in his own time if he had to. Siddig was putting the hours in.

'May I ask what this is about?'

It wasn't that Piper didn't want to tell her, she had a right to know. It was simply that it would be better if Mrs Whittaker had family around to support her through the aftermath. He swallowed; this was a hard reality that had to be dealt with.

'I'm here about Terrence.'

Not only did all colour drain from Mrs Whittaker's face, her whole body was shaking as she reached an unsteady hand to the nearest chair and carefully lowered herself in.

'I've reopened the case.'

Her hands were over her nose and mouth, underlining how wide her eyes were as she looked up at him. 'Why?'

He couldn't give the real answer to that one. He couldn't even give the *official* answer to that one. And there wasn't any other logical explanation.

'Cases go cold, Mrs Whittaker, but that doesn't mean that the police forget about them. We have various review processes, and this is one. I'm looking at a number of missing persons from around the time of Terrence's disappearance; I'm looking for crossovers and any possible links that might have been missed.'

'But it's been twenty years.'

And clearly the pain of that hadn't lessened, judging by the tears gathering, indeed falling from Mrs Whittaker's eyes. This was the part of his job Piper hated the most. As a father himself, he knew the desperate pain that children could bring to a parent's heart, and he was lucky to have all three of his at home safe and well.

'I know, and I'm sorry to drag all this up again. I appreciate that this can't be easy for you. I was actually hoping to see your daughter, she was, according to the case file, the last person known to see Terrence-' He cut himself off before saying the word *alive*. While the most likely reality was that the boy was dead, until they were able to prove it, he couldn't say such things in front of a worried mother.

Nodding, Mrs Whittaker turned away, wiped her eyes. 'She was.' A sniff and a swallow come before she could continue.

'Mrs Whittaker, I'm sorry to have to ask this, but have you kept hold of any of Terrence's belongings?'

The question seemed to confuse her. He wasn't surprised; he felt terrible for having to ask.

'There are a few bits and bobs in the box room. Why? What are you after?'

Piper looked away. This really was embarrassing. 'When I looked at the file, there was record of a DNA sample. But when I went looking for the records on that, it seemed the thing had been deleted. When the police take DNA samples, we're only allowed to keep them for a certain length of time. Any suspect who hasn't been convicted within three years has their DNA removed from the database. It appears that there was an issue a few years ago when they had a purge, someone got a little enthusiastic. They didn't just delete suspect records but removed a few victim records too. Terrence was one of those records. Because of the age of the case, no one has asked for additional samples.'

'But now you are?' She held her head high.

Piper couldn't blame her for the accusation in her tone. 'I'm sorry, Mrs Whittaker. I realise every time I come to your door, I come with trouble, but in this case I really do want to help.'

For a moment she simply scrutinised him. 'There are things up there. I doubt you'd get much DNA, not after all this time. But you're welcome to try. I would like to know what happened to my boy.'

Chapter 3

'Dammit,' he swore as he put the phone down. More misplaced evidence was the last thing he needed.

'Problem, sir?'

Piper looked up, surprised to see the young man darkening his door. 'Carlisle!' Piper was still surprised the man was out of hospital just five weeks after taking a bullet in the back; he certainly shouldn't be back in the station. To be fair, Carlisle still looked pale, though he was recovering the weight he'd lost on hospital food. Maybe even putting a bit on, thought Piper. That'd be with not being able to exercise. It was unlikely that he'd ever make it back to active duty though, not after having had part of his lung removed. Piper forced himself to stand up and shake the offered hand. 'Good to see you.'

Carlisle was grinning. 'Good to be back in the station again.'

That made Piper frown. 'Why? I'd take all the time I could to get away from this place.'

'Oh, come off it, sir. You know you love it.'

He did. He loved his job, which was why he was working so hard to keep it. 'Speaking of which -' He turned to grab his coat off the back of the chair. '- I need to go get on with it.' He signalled for Carlisle to precede him out of the office. It was a small office, a desk, two chairs and a filing cabinet. But it was his office and he didn't want Carlisle in it while he wasn't. Carlisle registered surprise, and for a moment looked like he would object, but there were really no grounds to, so he led the way out.

'Anything juicy in the mix?'

'Not really.' Piper locked the office door, something he was doing more religiously these days. 'The usual stuff, though thankfully quite quiet. Doing some cold case reviews. You know.' Piper shrugged. 'Routine. Excuse me.'

Door secure, he turned away from Carlisle and towards the back of the station. The weight of Carlisle watching him walk away was like a ball and chain at his ankles. If he was wrong, he was doing a major disservice to a man and his career. Thankfully the ball melted away with the certainty that he wasn't wrong, he just had to prove it. He used the Dallas key fob to release the back door and stepped out, stopped short, surprised to come face to face with Broughton. Well, face to broad chest, Piper tipped his chin to look the man in the eye.

'Superintendent!'

In his immaculate black uniform, Broughton frowned down. 'Is that what this has come to? Cold recognition of my rank and forget the friendship? I slapped you down, I didn't demote you.'

Didn't hurt any less, he'd trusted a civilian to do the right thing. He'd been right to. Her risk. Her choice. If he'd acted by the book he probably would have got her killed. It was better this way. 'No, sir. Sorry, it's just-'

Broughton's scowl didn't ease. 'Just what, Matthew?'

'Carlisle's in the station.'

'And?' Broughton straightened his shoulder. 'He might not be on active duty, but he's still one of us.' The scowl turned into a distinct glower. 'Unlike certain others.'

Piper knew exactly which *certain other* Broughton was referring to, but that was a problem for another day.

'Sir?' It was a risk, but if he asked, he might get, and if Broughton refused, he hadn't lost out. 'You told me to look into some cold cases, and I have been. There are some questions I have for the family of one victim, only they've moved up to Newcastle.'

'Then for God's sake go north for a couple of nights. If it saves me seeing your miserable mug around here, it'll be worth it. Just make sure you file all the paperwork first. When?'

'Probably Monday, sir.'

'Not sooner?'

For the first time in weeks, Piper smiled about his job as Broughton walked into the building.

* * *

Twenty-five minutes later, Piper parked outside the Central County Library and Archive. Two minutes later still, he was standing in the back of the archive rooms with Siddig, a buff file with not a lot in it, a pad and some rough notes. There were a few photocopies, one a copy of the front pages the day after Carlisle was shot in the Invicta Bank raid.

'What is all this?'

Siddig sighed and sat back. 'Pretty much nothing.'

That wasn't what Piper wanted to hear, but he couldn't fault the girl for her efforts.

She closed the paper she was looking at and put it back on pile at her side. 'Look, we were looking for any indication of the two usual catch points, cash or cock.'

Just because he knew the two reasons for most failures in the Force, didn't mean he was ready to hear it so blatantly from Siddig. However, he might admire her capability, she still looked too young and refined to be so coarse. *Or maybe I'm just getting old.* Besides, if she really was intending to be a career cop, they would both have to get comfortable with a lot worse than that.

'But I can't find anything on Carlisle. Over the last three years, he's had a few girlfriends.' She shifted in her seat, for a moment looked away. 'And I should say, I'm one of them.'

Piper nodded. 'I got that impression.'

'It was only a few weeks and -'

Piper raised his hand to stop her. 'It's okay. I asked a couple of those that know.' There were always *those that know* types in every office, he'd picked the most discrete of them.

'You're not going to stop me working on the case like it was a conflict of interest?'

'Siddig, I knew *before* I asked you to help me with this. I have considered all angles, the possibility of how it might influence your judgement, for good or ill. And I've had to question my own motivations for the same reason. Remember, I've known Carlisle a lot longer than you have. Hell, I've worked with him longer than you've been in the Force. So no, I don't see you as having a conflict of interest in this. What I do need you to do is to be open and honest about the fact that you had a relationship with him. If this goes higher, that statement will need to be made clear from the get-go. Understand?'

She nodded.

'Good. So, the girlfriends?'

'I've spoken to several of them. The relationships lasted between two weeks, and that was because she got a job overseas and left unexpectedly, and seven months. The exes have nothing bad to say about it, other than he's a bit selfish, but that's hardly new.'

Piper raised his brows. 'That's a little sexist.'

This time she pinned him with a look. 'Your interpretation is what's sexist. I didn't say him, or men general being selfish was hardly new, I said selfishness was hardly new.'

Suitably castigated, Piper tipped his head in acknowledgement of the point.

'None of them gave any inclination of any sexual behaviour that might be used against him or construed as deviant. Just to be clear, yes, that does include me. All his actions are in your *normal* range. So if there's anything of that nature in his nature that could be used against him, I haven't found any indication of it. I've no evidence of his being bisexual or of frequenting brothels, other than in the normal course of his job, and there are no rumours about his using prostitutes or rent boys. The only gripe a couple of the girls had was that he was, and I quote, "tight as arseholes." And he is, though again, nothing beyond the usual course of events for those who aren't terribly well-paid and who are just being careful with their money. But I looked into his finances anyway.'

'Tell me you found something there.'

'Nope.' She shook her head. 'I've got to tell you that Carlisle might be the only person I know who actually lives within his means. He has a reasonable one-bed flat that he can comfortably afford on his wages. His car is average, his bills are covered, he lives modestly, his phone is way off the latest model, and it's on a basic plan, his watch is a model that costs a ton, but he's had it since he was eighteen - I spotted it and asked him once. His clothes are prêt-à-porter, shoes from your standard high street retailer. He puts away between fifty and a hundred quid each month. Gotta say, he actually looks to be a nice guy, an actual catch.'

Piper wanted to catch Carlisle alright, but he needed to catch him in the act. 'If he's that good a guy, why did you stop going out with him?'

The shrug was eloquent, but he gave her a look that told her she wasn't getting away with that. Her eye roll was only just caught in time.

'It was nothing major. I just didn't feel that it was *going* anywhere. He's a better catch on paper than in real life. At least as far as I'm concerned. Though I did find the exes with the axes were the ones who got dumped rather than did the dumping.'

That was usually the way. 'Did you find anything that might be of use to us?'

'In this lot, no. But I've been looking at the locations of where the kids went missing and it struck me how we've not only got a load of missing kids, we've also got a three-year-old case where those bones were found. The ones where they don't seem to be the same body or even age and DNA traces have given us nothing to go on, other than the fact that there were seven different DNA sets; five boys, two girls.'

Piper was nodding. 'The Joskins Field case?'

Siddig confirmed it.

'I didn't work that myself, but I remember the incident. I think Wilson was SIO.'

Siddig was nodding as she stood. 'DCI Kyle Wilson. He's retired now.'

'Yeah, I was at his leaving do. Odd affair.'

'Why?'

Switching his attention from the past to the present, Piper shook his head. 'Nothing much, just an odd atmosphere. I take it you found out something on the case?'

'Not exactly. It's more what I didn't find. I went through Wilson's notes. There's a comment, rushed over and no detail, but the comment indicates concern about the number of missing forensics records. Now all three of the cases you picked for investigation are missing their DNA records.'

'Seems like-' Piper didn't finish the thought, as a bespectacled lady in a bright sari came up to the table.

'You finished wi' them papers now, love?'

Piper chastised himself for being surprised that a woman who looked so traditionally Indian should have a London accent.

'Yes, thanks. And thanks for all your help today. You were brilliant.'

The woman positively glowed at the praise while she gathered up the papers and took them to wherever they belonged.

'What was in the papers?'

'Background mostly, but don't worry, I copied the interesting parts for you.' Her hand went to the slim file. 'The other thing that I didn't find was a record of anyone reopening that case, and with cases of that nature, we're supposed to look at them every two years.'

Ideally that was true, but it wasn't always possible. He nodded. 'Seems like I need to open some other cases.'

'Yeah and I think Wilson can tell us which cases. I should go talk to him.'

The memory of the oddities he had seen at the retirement party nagged at Piper. Wilson avoiding Broughton after decades of friendship had been unusual. But he remembered the look Wilson had thrown him. He hadn't understood it at the time and still didn't now. The only difference was that he couldn't ignore it any longer.

'No.' He made it as gentle as he could, but he had to refuse the idea. 'Thing is, I've known Wilson for a long time, it wouldn't be completely beyond the realms of reality for me to pop over a see an old colleague. If you go, it'll look like someone rooting around.'

The way her lips pressed together told Piper everything. 'Yeah. I see the sense in that.'

'Good. I get you don't like it. You don't have to. As long as you understand it.'

The faint buzzing turned out to be Siddig's watch. 'I have to go. Got a shift.'

As she started pulling together all her belongings, Piper knew he had to say something.

'I appreciate you doing all this, Siddig. Especially outside of work.'

'Well, we can't very well do it inside the station, can we?'

Investigate a potential traitor in the ranks? No, not really. Not without getting internal affairs involved and he wasn't ready to go there - not yet.

'No, but I just want you to know that I'm grateful for your help.'

Her smile was brilliant; she had the whitest teeth of any person he knew. 'Remember that then when you're supporting my application to CID.'

Chapter 4

Charlie faced Rhys over the chasm of the empty dance floor. Lights, necessary for the cleaners, betrayed all the secret damage and degradation hidden during opening hours by coloured lights, smoke machines and an undulating crowd of people who didn't come here for the decor.

On sight of Charlie, Rhys had ordered all his men out, so now only the two of them stood in the large space. Though Charlie realised they weren't that alone - two heavies with more muscle than brainpower flanked the door he had just been escorted through.

'You've got some balls showing up here.'

Charlie wasn't surprised by the venom in Rhys' tone, except perhaps that there wasn't more of it. 'I didn't come here to fight.'

'I'll consider myself lucky, given that the last time you visited any member of my family, you killed my brother.'

Charlie didn't react. It was true and he had never denied it. And even the years in prison, a discharged sentence, and the mess of a life he now lead didn't make him regret the action. He looked at Rhys evenly.

'Two weeks ago I found this at a boot fair.' He pulled a watch from his pocket and held it toward the other man. It wasn't an obviously valuable watch, just a well-made one with a quality leather strap. 'Took me a while to realise that the inscription might mean something to you. *R Best Brother P.*'

Rhys' body tightened, his lips flattened, and his eyes narrowed.

'I heard you lost some stuff in that raid on the Invicta Bank last month, figured if it was yours, you might want it back.'

Rhys said nothing.

'Not yours?' Charlie asked.

No response.

'Okay then.' He turned the watch towards him, looked at the face. Eight minutes past seven exactly. Odd that an analogue stopped exactly on the minute, but there again, a one in sixty chance, he supposed. 'Sorry I bothered you.' He shrugged, turned slowly, aware that too sudden a movement might get misinterpreted.

'If-'

Charlie stopped, having taken one step.

'If it is my watch, what do you want?'

He considered turning but didn't. Instead, he shrugged. 'A watch that works would be good.' He had to play this carefully. While he didn't share his father's love of fishing, he remembered the old man's advice to tempt the fish in before going for the catch. 'That's how I ended up with this.' He momentarily lifted the watch, then carefully placed it on the nearest table, a tall round thing that punters could rest a drink on as they stood around.

Charlie walked out.

* * *

That two-week-old memory would not leave Charlie in peace, but it wasn't the only thing weighing him down. His feet were dragging as he walked from work. The burden of just too many memories dragged at him and there was little to look forward to.

Oh, get over yourself.

Easier said than done.

All he'd ever wanted to be was a policeman. Being in uniform, and more, working as a DC, then DS, had been everything he wanted it to be. Except for the disillusionment that came with realising that for every bad guy they took down, at least one more popped up. Then there was Phillip Mansel-Jones. Not exactly Don Corleone but getting there. And when they'd realised he was getting there while abducting and abusing kids, and probably killing them, it quickly became clear that they were never going to stop Mansel-Jones legally.

Charlie had not gone out that night intending to kill, just to find the truth. The fact that he'd found a terrified kid had surprised him because of the way he'd reacted to the discovery. It was then that he'd made the choice to go back and stop Mansel-Jones in the only way he could be sure of. He put a bullet through the man's chest. And he had served his time in jail for it. And in the process, he'd lost everything he had ever worked for.

When he'd been released, he'd felt lost, uncertain. Turning informant and getting involved in an investigation hadn't exactly turned out well.

So now he was in a rut with a job he hated, just about surviving financially, and banned from going anywhere near the only thing in his life that made him happy. The woman he wanted to be with.

Oh, stop being such a wuss, and figure out why it sounds like a car is following you.

He'd noticed it as soon as he'd stepped beyond the parameter of the paper mills where he worked. It was that extra weight of being watched. His muscles bunched across his shoulders. If he was being watched, the last thing he could do was look over his shoulder, let them know he was getting paranoid.

He reached out with his other senses. Carefully he swept his eyes from the periphery of his left to the far right of his vision. Nothing. He concentrated on his hearing, trying to decipher each noise, the story of the sound.

The wind rustled in the trees planted to mask the worst carbuncles of this now aging industrial estate - aging badly. The dual carriageway rumbled a couple of dozen metres away. The tone of the rumble changed with the size of vehicle, the tempo of their wheels thumping across the expansion joints. The engine that he focussed on was the one softly purring behind him. As he walked, he moved further away from the curb, not to be caught out by an opening car door.

Breathing deeply, forcing the regularity, he schooled his body to calm, yet his heart beat faster, preparing for fight or flight. Thank God he'd got back into running since his release; he couldn't outrun a car, but he could get to enough places a car couldn't go.

The slow-moving vehicle moved up beside him. A black - light caught on the wing - a very dark blue Jaguar was pulling up alongside him.

Charlie tried not the react, though tension pulled at every muscle. He kept his head down and forward, his pace regular and steady.

'Oi, copper!'

Frank Beard. Small time crook; a thief and fence, once under suspicion of being a getaway driver. Frank had loved that, right up to the moment they'd found the right guy. Then all his bragging went up like an unknotted balloon and those who had started to rate him suddenly had nothing to offer but contempt.

Charlie stopped. He turned to the car.

The front passenger window was down and Frank was leaning over the cream leather seats. Frank couldn't afford a car like this. Rhys Mansel-Jones, yes, but not Frank Beard. Frank was smiling at him, an unsettling experience. Last time Charlie had seen Frank, the man had crooked yellow teeth, one was black. Now his teeth were white, straight, perfect. Dentures or veneers. Impossible to tell which. What he did know was that neither came cheap. Maybe Frank wasn't so small time any more.

'What do you want, Frank?'

'Get in.'

'Why?'

'Just get in.'

Life was all about risks, but on the other hand, leaping without looking - not a great idea. Charlie rolled his shoulders, turned and started walking again. He heard Frank's grumble, then the engine gunned too high. The way it revved told Charlie this car wasn't quite as good as it looked.

The car rolled up beside him again, but this time Charlie didn't stop, forcing Frank to keep pace. Thankfully the road was wide and straight, and not busy at just gone two in the afternoon, so what few cars there were could easily bypass Frank.

'Oh, come on Charlie,' Frank called through the open window. 'It ain't like you've got the lifestyle to be picky anymore, mate. Get in the car. It'd be to your advant-idge.'

Now Charlie did stop. Frank stopped a little further on. The car door was pushed open. Getting in that car was probably a mistake, but as Frank had hinted, he had nothing left to lose. He got in the car.

Chapter 5

Kyle Wilson lived in a respectable part of town. It was all late 1950s council houses which were now largely owner-occupied. It was obvious which were still council, or rather housing association now. They just weren't loved in the same way. The new uPVC windows had been bulk purchased, rather than chosen to fit in with the aesthetics of the rest of the house. Wilson owned his property - it was well maintained, with an immaculate garden and original features. No hideous pebble-dashing or facia-bricks. Piper looked at the house as he spoke to Sheila on the phone.

'I won't be late late, love. About an hour. You don't have to wait dinner for me if you and Josh are hungry.'

Even as he said it he knew that typically, Sheila would wait. He loved her for it, but sometimes it felt problematic. Not today though. Today he would only be an hour late at most. There was no reason for this visit to take longer.

The iron gate opened without hitch or squeak, the pavers to the front door were regimentally aligned and there was not a sign of moss, lichen or weed. The narrow patch of lawn was bowling green immaculate and the perennial borders a slash of spring colour.

His knock was answered quickly enough. Kyle Wilson looked cordial, until he recognised Piper standing there. Then he looked worried.

'Matt? What are you doing here?'

The reserve was unexpected. 'Can I come? I need a word.'

Wilson didn't move. 'Is this official?'

Piper's throat started to dry. 'No. Should it be?'

A myriad of emotions ran over the other man's face until he decided to front it out and smile. 'No, of course not. Come in, come in.'

It was a false welcome; Wilson had never been much of a poker player, or an actor, and he wasn't fooling Piper as the serving DCI stepped inside.

'Come into the kitchen, I'll make us a brew.'

A brew. Piper was overcome by a moment of nostalgia. Wilson was the only one in the station who offered a brew. Most offers were tea or coffee, often a cuppa. But only Wilson called it a brew. And it was always tea. Tea so strong you could stand a spoon up in it.

Five minutes of inconsequentials and catching up later, they were sitting at the kitchen table with two mugs of very strong tea.

'Why are you afraid of an official visit?'

'I'm not.'

'Then why are you suddenly so interested in your tea you can't look me in the eye?'

When Wilson looked up, his eyes were wary, almost aggressive. 'Is this an interrogation, Chief Inspector?'

For a moment, Piper just looked at Wilson. He was fifteen years older than Piper, he hadn't needed to retire when he did, and the decision had come about suddenly. Something was wrong. Very wrong.

'I remember your leaving do.' Piper watched the reaction, *en garde* was the best description he could come up with. 'I remember thinking at the time that there was an odd atmosphere, but I got called away to an active case that night and didn't have time to sort it out. There's no talk about the station of you leaving under a cloud. No indication of any wrongdoing on your part. In fact, I still hear people wishing you were back.'

'I wish I'd been back there when that Charlie Bell crud blew up last year.' The anger in Wilson was obvious. He'd once supported Bell to the hilt, but Bell had condemned himself by his own actions. 'I'd love to give that bastard a piece of my mind. Not to mention a boot up the jacksie.'

'Charlie made his mistakes, but he's not the monster people make out. Besides, I didn't come to talk about him. I came to ask you about the Joskins Field case.'

Wilson sat back, clearly wary. Piper figured if he wanted to gain some trust, he should show some.

'Broughton is, well, pissed off with me at the moment. He's ordered me onto some cold cases. I picked up three from seventeen to twenty years ago, missing kids. Terry Whittaker, Frankie Hall and Alex Butler.'

Wilson's eyes narrowed, like someone had jabbed him with a needle.

'What have any of them got to do with the Joskins Field find?'

Piper shrugged. 'As far as I know, absolutely nothing.'

'Then why are you here?'

This was where he was on shaky ground.

'Do you have much to do with anyone from the station these days?'

'I got friends.'

'After all the years you served, I'd hope so. So who was the first to come see you?'

Wilson's eyes slipped away. He took a sip of the tea. Then he looked Piper straight in the eye. 'You are.'

Realising that his jaw had gone slack, Piper remembered to breathe again and think. Time to take a risk. 'The Don keeps them away?'

Wilson scowled at him. 'What do you know about the Don?'

'Not enough to do anything with.' Piper shifted to his relaxed position and sat forward, speaking low as if to guard a secret, even though there was no one else in the house. 'Look I've heard vague mentions, but no one talks about it. I haven't found anything that's substantial enough to do anything about, but I'm looking. I'm not entirely sure where to look or what I'm looking for, but I'm looking.'

'Is this why Broughton's pissed with you?'

Piper shook his head. 'Broughton doesn't know.'

'Don't let him find out.'

Now Piper was the one frowning. 'You think he's…'

'I think he's a politician. In that uniform and behind that desk, he's the best bloody DCS I ever worked for. But he's got friends too, and them I don't trust. When I started asking questions, I went to him with them. Two days later it was pointed out to me that I was retiring age. Don't go to Broughton, not unless you've really got something.'

'Then help me get something. I've been through your Joskins Field file. There's a mention of missing evidence, but no indication of what's missing or from where.'

For a moment Wilson looked into his mug, like a fortune teller trying to divine the future. 'Seems to me you're not going far wrong as ya are.'

Piper wouldn't leave it like that, he continued to watch Wilson in silence until the older man looked up and rolled his eyes.

'Cassidy. Smith. Possibly Talbot. But that's all you get.' Wilson stood and took Piper's mug, though it was barely touched. The two brews got emptied into the sink.

It wasn't much. Piper stood and headed for the front door. Wilson followed to see him out.

'Oh, I heard that young lad you were training up got shot during that bank robbery last month. What happened to him?'

Piper was a step down the path when Wilson asked. He turned to answer.

'Carlisle? Lost a section of his lung, but he's recovering.'
Wilson nodded, but the expression wasn't positive. 'Shame.'
'That he got shot?'
'Yeah,' Wilson muttered, shutting the door. 'That's what I meant.'

Chapter 6

'Sorry to interrupt, but I need I word,' Small said.

Looking up from the notes he was making after last night's call on Wilson, Piper saw DCI Linda Small at his office door. Possibly the most ill named individual he'd ever met. While slim and athletic, she was anything but small. A blond Amazonian was a better description. She worked Missing Persons and while they knew each other well enough, there wasn't much cross over to bring them working together.

'No problem, come in.' He slipped the notebook into his drawer to concentrate on the woman.

Small closed the door after the DC and came to sit in the chair opposite Piper. 'I was talking to Broughton and he said that I should chat with you because a couple of cases of mine echo cold cases you're working on.'

Interesting. 'Go on.'

'I've two on-going investigations, Steven Pearson and Madeline Stolz. Stephen went missing three weeks ago and Madeline, on Monday afternoon. Both were seen getting into cars the descriptions of which seem to match, a dark blue Mondeo saloon. We don't think they were taken by the same man. Stephen was with a shorter chubby guy, dark brown hair, while the man Madeline was seen with an athletic individual around five nine, five ten, dark blond, clean shaven.'

Piper nodded. The general public were notoriously bad with descriptions of both people and cars. 'Tell me about the boy.'

'Stephen was nine years old, dark blond, and something of a loner. His last know whereabouts were Woodland Walk Park.'

Stomach sinking Piper understood why Broughton had sent Small to see him.

'He was seen talking to one of the guys fishing on the riverbank.'

Piper turned away.

'I know. The inevitable jokes about rods and tackle and the rest, really feel unpleasant in this case.'

'Very, and inappropriate. A dark sense of humour is often what gets us through the day, but it's just not funny when kids are involved. However, I was actually thinking was what about fishing licence, maybe-'

'Five active for that day. Two match the description one was in work and one in a job seekers interview.'

Piper nodded and smiled. 'Of course you've already checked. Didn't mean to insult.' She accepted the unspoken apology. 'Madeline?'

'Eight years old, brunette, outgoing and friendly. She stopped in Harriot Gardens most days after school to play with her friends on the way home from school. The friends say that on Monday, two of them couldn't stop, one had a dental appointment and the other is her cousin and the mum wanted both back for logistical reasons. The other friend, Keshia Troy, said that they were playing on their Game Boys, all synced up to play some Pokémon group game, then another girl turned up and linked in. Madeline knew the girl, but Keshia didn't. Keisha left first, and no one's seen Madeline since, and no one knows who the other girl is.'

'There's CCTV around Harriot Gardens, did you manage to get anything?'

Linda nodded, but didn't look hopeful. 'There's a possible; adult male, with two girls of about the right height getting into a car. It's difficult to be entirely sure because they're only in a corner of the shot since the camera was actually being trained on a bunch of kids getting in a fight on the other side of the road. I've shown the video to the Stolzes and even they can't be sure it's their daughter because of the limited view.'

'Anything on the car?'

'Older bodywork, mark three, so early 2000s, but we only got the top of reg plate, nothing we can be certain about.'

'What about the kids in the fight? Were you able to track them down?'

She frowned now. 'Haven't tried, you thinking they'd be reliable witnesses?'

'It's more that I'm wondering if they were an arranged diversion. If someone knew the CCTV there was monitored, which is fairly common knowledge, maybe they were paid to draw attention away from where the car was parked.'

Linda didn't look happy at that idea. 'I hadn't thought of that. Not sure I want to think about it.'

Hands flat Piper rubbed them together his mind ticking through the facts Small had supplied. 'No, me either, but use of the same car would tie them together.'

'Multiple men suggested an organised ring too.'

Something else was no one wanted to think about, but if Yewtree had taught them anything it was that sometimes they had to think the unthinkable.

'Do your cases seem to be from a ring too?'

Piper shock his head. 'It's not obvious from what we've got, but then there's the Joskins Field case, that spread of body part is unusual, and that suggests organisation.'

'Did you get any more DNA matches?'

'I've requested tests, but you know how long these things can take and no one's prioritising cold cases.' There simply weren't enough resources. Piper pressed his palms together, rubbed them as he considered what was happening. 'Do we have a particular issue with missing kids in this area?'

'Not really, not in comparison. I mean too many kids do go missing but in league tables of cases we're not out of obvious kilter. Unfortunately, we head the same tables for overseas kids missing and found but given the county's proximity to the continent and the general influx of people through the county and down from London, that probably shouldn't be considered a surprise. What are you thinking?'

'Nothing useful really. One of the cases I've reopened, the boy, same general description as Stephen, was also taken from the Woodlands Walk Park.'

'How old's the case?'

'Twenty years.'

Small's brows rose. 'Then no offence but I'm hoping for a coincidence now. Two cases linked that far apart suggests an organisation that knows too well how to stay hidden.'

Or people prepared to keep it hidden. 'True, but tastes don't change much, it's possible that one person could be in the same area over that length of time and pick a couple of matching boys from the same place. I have no idea if my cases and yours are actually linked, but I think we should keep it in mind.'

Chapter 7

'I think I've fucked up.'

However Piper had expected Charlie to greet him, that hadn't been it. Twenty-four hours after his meeting with Wilson, Piper was still bothered by what the older man had said. But as he joined Charlie at a small table, he accepted the pint that had been bought in anticipation of his arrival. Charlie was a fair way through his own.

'Why?'

Piper tried the pint. Bitter, one he didn't recognise so probably this week's "guest pint". He appreciated that Charlie had not only remembered he favoured bitters; but had gone to the expense of buying a guest beer, which being from microbreweries were always expensive.

Charlie placed a box on the beaten copper table top.

'Good pint,' Piper said as he put it back on the Guinness beer mat. 'What's this?' Even as he asked about it, he was taking the box, opening it. 'Wow.' The watch was polished steel, large, and impressive. He closed the box and put it back on the table. 'You can't afford that either.'

'Present.'

Piper would have liked to have smiled and cracked a joke, but that felt inappropriate. 'Who from?'

'RMJ,' it was barely audible.

Rhys Mansel-Jones. Piper reached for the pint. Drained most of it. 'Another?' He stood and went to the bar before Charlie could answer.

Charlie was frowning at him when Piper sat back down with two additional pints.

'I'm getting a bus back, what's your excuse?'

'You don't want to know.' Thoughts of missing kids, bent coppers and a lost pension didn't do anything to relieve Piper's tension.

'Now I really do.'

'Tough. Why would RMJ give you such a present?'

He listened in horror as Charlie recounted his visit to the Den of Angels. When the younger man stopped, all Piper could do was watch him.

'What were you thinking?'

At least he had the good grace to look embarrassed as he scrapped back his blond hair. It needed cutting. 'I don't know.' He sighed. 'I probably wasn't thinking. Not clearly, anyway.'

'You said it yourself, the guy wants you dead because you killed his brother. Giving his watch back won't give him back his brother.'

'That's almost exactly what he said,' Charlie acknowledged.

'Then why give you a watch?'

'That's where I fucked up. By accepting it. Frankly I was a bit worried about getting out of there intact if I didn't. Besides, don't be too impressed by the watch, it's a knock-off.'

'How can you tell?'

'It's supposed to be a TAG Heuer, it says TAC.'

'That's still not a reason.' Piper muttered as he looked more closely at the watch, Charlie was right. A knock-off.

'It's because I said-'

'No. No. I get that.' Piper put the watch back down and pushed it towards Charlie. 'That doesn't explain it.'

Charlie shrugged. 'Keep your friends close, your enemies closer?'

'Maybe it's a lend and you're on borrowed time.'

The blood drained from Charlie's face at that thought. Piper considered apologising, but it the man wanted to play dangerous games, he had to live with the consequences – or die with them.

'What did he ask for?'

'Nothing. Yet.'

Piper sipped the second pint. Bolting the first one hadn't done him any favours. Sheila's fish pie would soak up a fair amount, but he still had to drive home. He was already risking it. Maybe he'd get a taxi back - it wasn't that far.

Right now he had to figure out the implications of what he could hardly describe as Charlie's finest hour. 'Why did you do it? Why go see RMJ at all?'

Charlie didn't squirm, but Piper knew the man well enough to see that he wanted to. Blue eyes studied the pint, lips pressed together. One long index finger traced a bead of condensation down the tulip curve of the glass.

26

'It's stupid,' Charlie said. 'But RMJ is almost as bad as his brother. I kind of thought that maybe, if I had an in, and I did have an in, then...'

'Then what?'

Charlie closed his eyes, shook his head. 'I thought I could...' He sighed. 'It was stupid and arrogant, but I thought I could maybe...' Charlie rolled his eyes, saving Piper the need to. 'Blow up the organisation from the inside.' The bigger man slumped in his chair like a truculent teenager.

'Did you get beaten up a lot in jail?'

Misunderstanding was written all over Charlie's expression as he looked up at Piper. 'Eh?'

'Well I was just wondering if you'd suffered some form of brain damage to explain the apparent drop in your IQ.'

The muscles in Charlie's jaw clamped. Piper had distinctly meant to insult, but he hadn't meant to hurt.

'Wow, I'm guessing the thing you don't want me to know about in work is really stressing you out.'

One problem of associating with intelligent people was the chance that they'd see right through you. 'There are things in the station that I'd rather weren't there.'

Ears pricking up were obvious even if Charlie didn't move. His eyes swept the room, before the ex-officer sat up and leaned over, keeping his voice low. 'The Don?'

God Lord! Charlie hadn't been active in the station for nearly five years, yet he'd heard of the Don? 'What have you heard?'

'Not a lot,' Charlie virtually whispered. 'When I was in situ, there was a rumour or two, but in Whitewalk -' Piper recognised the nickname for HMP Blackmarch, where Charlie had served his time. '- there were more, talk about how the chosen few could get off if the Don was onside.'

'Any indication of who the Don is?'

A headshake. 'Only someone inside the station. But with some of the things I heard were being done, it would have to be a serving officer, couldn't be a civilian, they wouldn't have the access.'

'Anything concrete?'

Again the headshake.

'That's the problem. It's all whisper and rumour and if I can't find something to take to Broughton, I've got no chance of getting any real investigation going.'

Charlie rubbed his hands over his face. 'Not sure if I can help you there, but I can try.'

Piper rubbed his temples then shook his head. 'Christ this stuff is dangerous.' He looked at the bitter.

'Yeah, it's 6.2 percent, that's why I was surprised you bolted the first. Fancy something to eat to soak it up?'

He didn't, but it was about the best option he had. They ordered and eat without significant conversation. Though Charlie did pick at the wound of wanting a certain woman's phone number he knew he couldn't have.

'Oh,' Piper said as they headed for the door forty minutes later, 'don't forget you're supposed to register your change of address with CHIS.' Covert Human Intelligence Source needed to be very clear in their details, accuracy and currency.

Charlie nodded. 'Did it while you were on holiday. If I hear anything-' He stopped to check the number on the approaching bus. '-I'll let you know. Got to go.'

Piper watched as a sprinting Charlie only just reached the bus before it pulled away again.

Chapter 8

Driving north on the A1(M) wasn't exactly fun, but it was getting Piper there. He reached Newcastle a quarter past ten that evening after a busy day in the station. Foregoing food in favour of collapsing on the bed and getting some sleep, he lay back at tried to calm his whirling mind. The new info on Scott Cassidy, Giles Smith and Vince Talbot wouldn't let him go and it all mashed together in a bad dream.

Up at stupid o'clock, he showered, shaved and read the Hall file as he waited for breakfast to start serving.

Frankie Hall. Went missing when he was eight. He'd be twenty-seven now. If he was still alive. Of the three cases that Piper had reopened, Frankie's was the most similar to Terry Whittaker. They were closest in age and physicality, lithe and fit with blue eyes and shaggy blond hair. They had lived on opposite sides of town, but both had last been seen in playing fields. The big difference was the timing - Frankie in early February, Terry in mid-May.

After a light breakfast (muesli wasn't fun, but it was good for the digestion) Piper was standing at the Halls' front door, about to knock when the green wood opened and he found himself face to face with a young man, maybe nineteen, yet he looked just as Piper would have expected Frankie to look now. There was nothing in the file about a younger brother, but this boy had to be related.

'Gar!' A woman's voice hollered from the house. 'Get back here!'

The boy sneered at Piper and pushed past, from threshold to street in one simple step.

'Gar!'

The woman appeared and stopped to stare at Piper. He moved aside to point Mrs Hall in the direction Gar had gone. Mrs Hall came to the step and looked. Piper looked too, at Mrs Hall, at the lank hair, the poor posture, the feet in Crocs. From there up it didn't get much better. Black overstretched leggings that accentuated the fat under a baggy jumper that had seen far too many days. The arms were stretched, one more than the other. There were scratch marks along her neck, like she'd been worrying at the obvious boil there.

'Lil' shite won't be back for hours now. He knaas I need his help.' She looked him up and down. 'What you, then? Social?'

'Sorry no, Mrs Hall.' Piper showed his warrant card and introduced himself.

'Well I divvent knaa what youse want with us. I heven't done nowt.'

Apparently, she'd been drinking already, he could smell it on her breath. Judging by the thin lips and the lines around them, she was a heavy smoker too.

'I wanted to talk to you about Frankie.'

Mrs Hall reared and walked back into the house. Since she left the front door open, Piper decided to take it as an invitation. He stepped in.

Sour.

Everything was sour, stale. The cigarette smoke, yellowing the walls and ceiling. The lack of fresh air, the windows covered with nets like spider webs. The place hadn't seen a vacuum in so long the carpet was almost like lino, sticky and solid. Dirt tracked so firmly through, there was no getting rid of it. There were grease marks down the walls at hip to shoulder height, Mrs Halls height. It was a traditional miner's cottage, two up two down, poky. There was a short hall then an opening. The door, off its hinges, rested against the wall, before the downward slope to a truncated door that was obviously an under stairs cupboard. Inside the back room, Mrs Hall stood opposite the staircase, by the fireplace. The fire was an ugly gas thing, but the mantel was still the beige glazed bricks that would have been installed when the house was built. The kind of original feature the yuppies would go mad for. The left corner had been chipped, as had the red terracotta tiles of the hearth, but the raised edging was missing two pieces. Someone had had to work hard to damage that.

Mrs Hall's hands were shaking as she tried to light a cigarette. There was an open half bottle of vodka on the tiles, next to a brown plastic bottle of prescription drugs. He didn't know, couldn't read what they were from where he was, but he'd guess antidepressants.

She was already crying when she turned to him. 'Have you found him?' Everything about her was shacking, quivering. The left arm of her jumper, the longer one, was brought over her hand and used as a tissue to wipe away snot and tears. 'Have you found my bairn?'

'I'm sorry, no.'

'Then what fuckin' use are you?' she screamed at the top of her lungs. It forced her into a hacking cough.

'I'm looking into the case, to see if anything new can be —'

Getting a torrent of abuse was hardly a new experience for Piper. He let it wash over him. When finally she stopped, he could speak again.

'Gar? Is he your son?'

'Gareth. It's his fault. I was pregnant wi' him when I lost me Frankie.'

As he listened to her, Piper started to understand. Frankie had got out on his own because Mrs Hall had been busy throwing up in her first trimester with the second boy. Mrs Hall had blamed herself but taken it out on Gareth. That was why the pills and the drink, the mess and the lack of manners. Poor Gareth, the kid never stood a chance. Piper tried asking Mrs Hall about the day Frankie disappeared, but she had nothing to add.

'Do you know where I can find Mr Hall?' His research had confirmed that the Halls were divorced, and traced Mrs Hall here, but he hadn't been able to find Mr Hall.

'Hell.'

Piper blinked.

She huffed and pushed greasy grey hair behind her ear. 'He fucked off. Went with some slapper for a while, but topped himsel' a few years back.'

Piper tried again, but when the abuse restarted, he realised that there was little point, he wasn't going to get anything from the Halls. As he stepped out onto the street and heard the door slam behind him, he took the first deep breath he'd dared to allow himself since arriving. He was in a dirty part of a city he didn't know, there was nothing to recommend the area. Every city had streets like this one, where the lowest in society congregated because they couldn't go anywhere else. What had happened to Mrs Hall was terrible, but what she'd done to herself and her family afterwards, that was her choice. That was worse.

Piper moved to his car, was about to get in when he saw Gareth sitting on the curb about twenty yards down the road. He was close to a corner so if his mother appeared, he'd be able to scarper quick. The boy looked up at him, features so used to resentment and spite that they nearly masked the desperation and need of that immature heart. Locking the car again, Piper strolled slowly towards the boy, half expecting a scrambling and a scarper, but the kid just sat there.

Gareth didn't move or say anything, so Piper stepped next to him and carefully lowered himself to the curb at the boy's side.

'Rough day?' he asked after a few heartbeats.

'Normal.'

That wasn't encouraging, but much as Piper might have expected if he had expected anything.

'You a pig?'

Piper chuckled, taking no offence, it was just what the boy was used to.

'Try not to be, but yes, I'm a police officer.'

'I didn't do nowt.'

Piper could imagine Sheila cringing at that double negative. 'I never said you did.'

'Why youse sniffing round then?'

'I wanted to speak to your parents.'

The boy huffed. 'I divvent.'

'Gathered that.'

'Youse not from round here, are yer?'

Given the accent, that was hardly a leap. 'Nope.'

'This about little saintly Frankie then?' The bitterness in the tone was palpable.

'Actually, yes, it is.'

'She telt youse how it's all m' fault.'

'I don't believe that.'

'So she did.'

Piper couldn't deny it. 'She's a lost woman, Gareth. More pain than she knows how to cope with. I doubt she has any idea what she's done to you most of the time, and when she realises, she'll reach for the next prop to numb that pain too.'

'Numbs something.'

'What happened to Frankie was not your fault.'

The boy turned and looked away. Piper heard sniffing and a gulp. Surely this couldn't be the first time in his life the boy had been told that?

'I just heard about your dad. Sorry about that too.' Maybe if the dad had been stronger neither the wife nor the son would be so damaged now. It was an unwelcome and judgemental thought, but Piper thought it. Of course, he knew nothing about Mr Hall, so he wasn't in a place to judge.

'Yeah, Mam blames him a lot too. Nan says weren't his fault.'

That pricked Piper's ears up. 'You know your nan? I got the impression from what your mum said that it was just you and her.'

Gareth shrugged. 'She divvent talk to Nan. Dad's mam, not hers.' Gareth looked Piper up and down.

Piper realised he was being sized up.

'I'll tek yer to her if youse drive us in that fancy car o' yours.'

It wasn't that fancy. A three-year-old Audi he'd bought when it was six months old. He wasn't planning on heading back south today and there wasn't anything more he could learn from Mrs Hall, so he might as well. 'Okay.' He stood. Gareth stood too.

They went back to the car and Piper unlocked it remotely. Once they were both in, Piper started the engine. When he didn't move, didn't even put the car in gear, Gareth turned to look at him.

'Left down t'road.'

'Seatbelt.'

Gareth rolled his eyes and yanked the belt. Then had to release and pull it more slowly. Only once he heard the satisfying click did Piper select a gear and pull gently into the quiet road. He moved the car slowly, it was a 20 MPH zone. He took the left turn.

'Go to the end and turn right.'

The zone moved to 30 MPH, Piper moved too, following Gareth's directions.

'You missed the turn.'

Piper shrugged. 'You should have mentioned it before I passed.'

'Now you're going to get stuck in the one-way system.'

He did. As he drove, Gareth started looking through the glove box, pressing buttons. Thankfully, Piper had steering wheel control and could switch down or off the radio when Gareth fiddled with it. Fifteen minutes later, he followed another of Gareth's less than brilliant directions and smiled.

'Does it feel good?'

Gareth froze with his hand part way to another button. 'Wot?'

'Getting the dumb copper to drive you around town just because you were bored. We're heading back to your street, aren't we?'

Gareth's hand dropped back to his lap. 'Yeah.'

It didn't sound like he felt good, but Piper took the last turn undirected and parked back exactly where he'd been before. He killed the engine. 'Where's your nan live?'

Gareth pointed to the house Piper was in front of. Three doors down from his mum.

'Cheers.'

With a shrug the boy got out of the car and slouched down the road. Piper took a breath and got out of the car, looking up and down the street. A few moochers, one man walking a pitbull and some kids mucking around truanting. He knocked on the door, white PVC with a small arched window at the top. It took a while and when the door opened, he was looking down at a short woman made shorter as the weight of the years curled her over her Zimmer frame.

'Mrs Hall?'

'What's that scallywag done this time?'

Piper frowned. 'Gareth?'

'Well, wot's he bin up t'?'

'Nothing as far as I know. I actually came to speak to you about your son.'

The old woman had thin white hair and washed-out rheumy eyes. Her thin skin went as white as her hair. 'My Gregg is dead.'

Piper nodded. 'I appreciate that, Mrs Hall. This really won't take long.' He showed his warrant card and introduced himself properly. Mrs Hall let him in and he followed, closing the door carefully as she instructed. He followed her into the back parlour, where she was lowering herself to a hard-looking chair beside the small Formica table. He hadn't seen anything like that in thirty years. There again, he doubted this house had seen redecorating in more years than that.

She didn't invite him to sit down, so he remained standing as he explained why he was there.

'Have you found Frankie?'

'We're not entirely sure.' Piper advised. 'Some new evidence has come to light, but Frankie is only one possibility, we've reopened three cases already and may be looking at more.'

The old woman nodded then seemed to drift away, her eyes wandering to the 1940s sideboards to his right. When she didn't say anything for what felt like a very long time, Piper began to worry what he'd got himself into.

'Mrs Hall?'

Her hand was shaking, he could see the gnarling of arthritic fingers. She pointed to the sideboard. 'Left drawer.'

Without a clue what he was looking for, Piper moved across and slid out the drawer. Inside was an old style biscuit tin. Roughly eight inches square, traditional Fox's box. 'The biscuit tin?'

Mrs Hall nodded and Piper brought it out. It wasn't heavy, and he felt a few things rattling around. He put the tin on the table in front of his hostess. For a minute, she just put her hands on it, taking deep breaths and clearly thinking deeply.

'My son wasn't the strongest of men. Got in with the wrong people. And when little Frankie went missing, Gregg crumbled. But the people didn't. Gregg tried, but...'

Mrs Hall was shaking her head as she pulled the lid from the box. She took a small brown-covered, rather battered notebook from the box and held it out to Piper.

'He was weak, but he wasn't stupid.'

Chapter 9

The offshore breeze was surprisingly bitter given how warm the day had been. Leaning heavily on her crutch, the woman near the shore looked longingly over the wooden rail at the wide beach she didn't dare go walk on. She loved beach walks, but with an open-toed cast on her left leg, she couldn't risk sand getting in there. As it was, she'd had to tie a plastic bag around the foot to minimise wind-blown grain incursion. The cast was itchy enough without any added irritant.

She'd come up here to be alone, to think. But she'd thought too much and felt too alone.

The car murmured to a standstill a few metres behind her. It would have parked directly in front of the house she was staying in. Cars, well, people did that. It was convenient for the beach. The visitor wasn't here to see her, so she didn't bother turning, kept staring ahead over the rolling sea, wishing that like the Little Mermaid at the end of the original story, she could dissolve into its foam and be no more.

The car door closed gently and she head foot falls, they crossed the tarmac, crunched on the narrow strip of gravel and were almost lost in the short dune grass that lead to the railings against which she stood.

A figure appeared at her side. She turned her eyes, her head slightly, but didn't need to fully look at the man to recognise him. She had some idea what he was doing here, but she wasn't ready to pick that particular scab just yet. She looked back to the large clumps of seaweed on the sand.

'They look like washed-up bodies, don't they?' she said slowly. 'Shipwreck victims tossed back to the land. Sometimes I think the seaweed looks like bandage strips, like they were all mummified and now they're going to get up and walk around like zombies until they get their revenge on the men who pressed them to sail.'

The mixed palate of orange and pink sky was too gentle to reflect the horror of the vision.

'Not shipwrecked zombies, just uprooted sea plants. Some sort of kelp,' he said, considering the scene. 'Though I think I like your story more, it's interesting.'

'Imagine how many bodies you could hide in weed like that.'

'Well let's not go look, eh?'

'The casual passer-by would never notice because the seaweed stinks so much the decomposition would be covered by that smell.'

She could see the man had turned to look at her, could feel the concern of his expression even if she wouldn't look to see it.

'Teddington, I think you've been out here too long.'

She forced a smile and finally turned to look up at him properly. He wasn't a bad looking man, quite distinguished in his own way. But he wore the cares of the world and he looked concerned for her now.

'We've never met under good circumstances, Detective Chief Inspector Piper, and given the telephone conversation I had with my mother earlier this week, I know this isn't going to be pleasant either. Oh and please, call me Ari, Ariadne if you absolutely must.'

He frowned slightly. 'Telephone conversation with your mother? I've never been able to get a call through to you.'

'You wouldn't; there's no mobile signal here. There is, however, a phone box down the road. I make sure I call Mum a couple of times a week. She worries.'

'Understandable.'

Ariadne nodded. 'True. I think she worries anyway. Fancy a cuppa?' Adjusting the crutch and with awkward movements, she led the way across the road to the bungalow, opening the door with the key from her shorts pocket.

The door led to a small porch area, where Ariadne leaned against the wall in the struggle to remove the plastic bag, then she kicked off her one flat shoe. She turned to Piper.

'You don't have to take your shoes off to come in, but I'd appreciate it if you did. Less sand on the floor means less hoovering, which frankly isn't easy on a crutch.'

She moved through the lounge area, into the kitchen, though she didn't have to duck, her hair touched the lintel. Would Piper notice and duck or like a few she'd laughed at, would he smack his head too? It was Piper, he'd duck. She switched the kettle on and was back in the doorway to see Piper close the porch door. He was wearing black socks to match the black suit he wore. He didn't offer a smile when he turned to her.

'You any good at setting things alight?'

Her question obviously surprised him.

'The fire's only embers, it'll get cold in here if it's not built up again soon.' She looked to the big hearth and the wood burner there.

Leaving him to decide what to do, she moved back into the kitchen and brought out mugs and tea bags, milk and sugar together. Making tea really didn't take that long but delivering it was going to be interesting given that she was something of a hop-along now.

'Let me.'

Piper appeared in the kitchen, there hadn't been a thunk, so he had ducked. He took the two mugs so she could go hobbling back to the sofa and virtually fall into it. Her mother would complain that she flopped onto furniture, but at this point, she didn't have a lot of choice, with her leg stuck out in front of her, her arm in plaster and most of her body still sore, even if the bruises had faded; she just wasn't capable of more control yet. There was an occasional table at the side of the sofa, and Piper put both the mugs on it, then took over helping her cover her legs with the throw she'd left on the sofa.

'Thank you.'

His laugh was small and low, but full of understanding. 'You hate anyone doing anything for you, don't you?'

'No.' She looked away. 'Well, okay, yeah, a little bit. Mostly I hate that I *have* to rely on others. That I can't just do it myself.'

'We all need help sometimes.' Piper lowered himself on the overstuffed chair to the side. The fire was going strong and already starting to heat the room.

'I love the smell of an open fire. Don't you? So restful.'

His murmur was agreement.

She looked at the mantel clock: already ten to nine. 'Where are you staying tonight?'

'I believe there's a pub in the next town that does rooms. As long as I'm there before half ten, I should be okay.'

'You really think we'll be done in an hour?'

'I can come back tomorrow.'

'You can stay tonight.'

'Ah.' Piper wasn't really sure how to put it.

'Look, this place has three bedrooms, they're all made up and I'm only using one. The room at the back is closest to the bathroom, and I've got an *en suite*, so it's not like we'll disturb one another. Do you need to get permission from the boss?'

'Probably.'

She smiled. 'Wife or Broughton?'

That made Piper chuckle. 'Probably both.' Which was probably the truth, but it would be difficult to get hold of either of them in the absence of a mobile signal. Besides, he was a grown man and was fairly sure he was safe from any accusation from Ariadne. 'I'll be fine without though. If you're sure?'

'Of course. Actually, I'd appreciate the company. It's been great here, but rather lonely at times. Do you want to go get your bag from the car?'

'Are you trying to put off the conversation we have to have?'

She nodded and offered a bitter smile. 'Yep. Till never would be good.' Good but impossible. Even as he stood and went to fetch his bag, she knew, they both knew, that the conversation was going to happen.

The only sounds as Piper came back into the room and sat down were the crackling of the fire and an occasional gust of wind outside.

Ariadne couldn't even look at him, so she stared into the fire instead. 'Why are you opening old wounds?'

'Don't you want to know what happened to your brother?'

'Of course I do. Terry's like a missing part of me. The little brother I never got to see grow into a man. The pain in the butt I never got to tell how much I love-' She had to stop to swallow the tears. 'For Mum it's like the pain and the panic never lessened from the first moment we realised Terry was gone. It's raw and it hurts like hell. When you lose a child it's like nothing else exists but that hurt. When I lost Sasha...' She had to control her throat again. Bile rose in her throat and she had to control her reactions to the memory. Finding her baby daughter cold and limp one morning, taken by SIDS it crushed – *Stop.* Six years hadn't lessened the pain but had taught her how to control it. 'When I lost Sasha, my whole world fell apart, but I got to say goodbye to her, made sure she had a good send off. There's no continually hoping that one day she's just going to come back knocking on my door. Mum never had that with Terry and it hurts her every single day. I just wish you'd come to me first, that's all. Which is probably what you were doing, now I come to think about it.' Until he reached their home, there was no way he could have known she wasn't there.

'Yes, it was. Thank you. I didn't know you'd come so far to recuperate.'

'This place belongs to my ex-in-laws. They like to come up whenever they can to get out of Leeds. I mean, Leeds is great, but not much in the way of seascapes around.'

Piper smiled. 'No.'

'When they heard about the accident, Jeff, my father-in-law was actually the first to call Mum and ask about me. Though to be fair, Ward was overseas.'

'Ward?'

'Edward. Teddington. My ex-husband.'

'You still get on then?'

'In small doses.' She sipped her tea, then turned to look at Piper. 'When are you heading back home?'

'Tomorrow.'

'Can I be a pain in the butt, then? Could I cadge a lift with you? Ward was going to come up at the weekend to take me home, but with all this coming up again, I think I should get back to Mum as soon as I can.'

Piper was nodding. 'Sure.'

Ariadne stared into the flames, seeing not the orange flickering, but the light brown of her brother's floppy hair as he ran around the empty field chasing a ball he really wasn't that expert at controlling. She could feel the rawness growing in her throat, the burning behind her eyes that warned of tears to come. 'Why have you reopened the case, Piper? Have you found something? Him? His body?' When he didn't immediately answer, she turned to look at him. He was looking right back. 'Piper?'

'Did you ever meet Superintendent Broughton?'

Ariadne gave a small headshake. 'But I know who he is. His name was in the paper, on the news stations.'

Piper nodded. 'I pissed him off.'

'How?'

'I allowed a civilian to risk her life and crash a car instead of ordering armed support to shoot.'

That moment was clear in her memories; it crept behind her eyelids in unguarded moments. And the guarded ones - after all the evidence was plastered all over her. 'If they'd shot Blue, he would have shot me. Two deaths for the price of one. It was my idea, my choice. You did nothing wrong.'

His smile was rueful.

'Guess it doesn't work that way, huh?'

He shrugged. 'Large hierarchical structures can be like that. Besides, revisiting cold cases is always part of the job. I visited your mother after you were taken hostage, she told me about Terrence -'

'Terry. He hated being called Terrence. Being called Terrence was a sure sign Mum was annoyed with us.'

'Him, surely?'

Ariadne smiled. 'Nope. Us. Terry did no wrong in Mum's eyes unless it was the two of us together, then we'd find ways to wind one another up, have arguments, fight. He was a right little sod, was Terry.' The memories were fine, even the memories of the bruises, he might have been smaller and a couple of years younger than her, but he couldn't half pack a wallop. 'Nah, never heard Mum or Dad call Terry Terrence unless the pair of us were in trouble together.' It was that closeness that she missed the most. There was no way of knowing if they would have stayed as close as they got older, but she hoped they would have. She wished he was still there to fight with, laugh with. Pushing down the memories with the tears, she blinked and focused again on Piper. 'That still doesn't explain why you reopened this case.'

He was direct, even as she could see that he didn't really have a reason.

'After your help solving Walker's murder and all you did to minimise damage in the bank robbery, getting taken hostage...' he shrugged. 'Kinda feel I owe you.'

'You don't. I get it and I'm grateful, I would like to know. But you don't owe me anything.' She frowned at him. 'Don't you have to have reasons for opening old cases?'

'Yes and no. Cold case reviews are part of our duties, but given that I'm already in Broughton's bad books, I've got my justifications ready.'

She waited a moment. 'Should I take it from the fact that you stopped there that you aren't going to share those justifications with me?'

He offered a small smile. 'On a personal level, I would. However, you are a family member of a victim, so I can't. Unfortunately, as with a lot of investigations, we're not at liberty to share all facts as those cases unfold.'

She nodded. 'So, what did you want from me now? As I remember, I gave quite a detailed statement at the time.'

'You did,' Piper acknowledged. 'And I've read it several times.'

'Then you already know all there is to know.'

'I still need you to go over it all one more time.'

The air in her lungs was stale, but for a moment, Ariadne had no way to replace it. Go over it all one more time. One more time? She'd been over it more times than she could possibly number. But talking about it had never mellowed, never got easy.

Still, she knew she needed to, even as she looked into the dregs of her tea and swirled them around.

'Terry was bored. It was a Saturday. Mum and Dad were busy. Dad was finishing his shed in the back garden. Mum was baking and washing and generally doing stuff around the house. I was reading. *Goodnight Mister Tom.* It was for school. Terry was full of energy, and getting under everyone's feet, so Mum told me to take him down the park. I took the book too. I can't say I found it all that gripping and was really struggling with it, but I had to finish it for the Monday and was well behind. He took his football, so while he had a kick about on the field, I sat on the swings to read. Unusually for a Saturday, there weren't many people around. There was some big game on. They must have been off to that.'

'It was the FA cup final, and several local pubs were opening up with big screen Sky Sports projections.' Those were the days before having Sky at home was just the norm. He had been on call as part of the general reinforcements, just in case there was trouble. He never got called in thankfully.

She shrugged. 'If you say so. Terry wasn't great with a football, a bit like me and dancing - enjoy it, but totally rubbish. So he didn't get picked for teams and often, if there were other kids on the field, Terry would be excluded and have to have a kick about on his own anyway. The only real difference that day was that he had the whole field to himself, there was no one to get in his way or bully him about having no skill. Which was great for me, meant I didn't have to worry about looking out for him like usual, didn't have to take on any of the bigger boys for laughing at him. Anyway, he was having a great time, running around like a loon, ball going off in any direction but the one he wanted it to. He smacked me with it twice. I couldn't take offence because I know he was just that bad that he couldn't hit the broadside of a barn if he tried, let alone one girl on a swing.'

The one that hit her in the face had resulted in a torrent of abuse, and had hurt like hell, but hadn't even left her with so much as a bruise after.

'We were down there ages, at least a couple of hours. Terry got bored and said he wanted to go home. I had a paragraph of a chapter to go, so I said I'd be along in a minute.' Worst choice of her life. 'I-'

She stopped and tried to breathe. It wasn't easy, there was a vice around her lungs, something strangling her throat. 'I should have just gone with him. It only a couple of seconds, I swear, but...' Another breath needed.

'I stood up and saw Terry through the gap in the bushes that let the path through. I headed after him, but there were two men in the way.' She saw Piper move that fraction of an inch closer, paying attention now. 'I say men, they were probably only boys really. Maybe 18, 19. 20 at most. Couldn't have been much older, but I was 11 so they seemed much older to me. I tried to walk around them, but they- I -' She closed her eyes and pushed that memory away. 'Anyway, I dodged and run. Terry was already out of sight, but there was only the one logical way home, so I took it. Ran it. Figured I'd catch up with Terry on the way. Only I, I didn't. The last thing I ever said to my little brother-' Her voice was shaking and the tears falling. '- was "Go home than brat, stop annoying me."'

She put the mug on the table and covered her face with both hands. 'I should have just gone with him. If I'd gone with him, he'd still be here. It's all my fault.'

Chapter 10

Pain echoed in everything about Teddington as Piper sat and watched her, listened to her. He had heard this pain so many times. Survivor guilt. It happened time and time again, especially for those who suffered the trauma as a child. But today this struck a chord in him he hadn't felt before. Watching a strong woman virtually collapse in front of him made him sick with grief. As she cried into her own hands, he did the only thing he could, he moved over and pulled her against him, hugged her close. This was way outside of procedure, the kind of action that could add to the growing army of black marks against him, but this was personal now and he had to do it.

'What happened to Terry was not your fault.'

That he was echoing exactly what he had said to Gareth Hall several hours earlier was not lost on him. They were both collateral damage to the bastards who had stolen their brothers away.

'Ari, you mentioned men in your way.' That hadn't been in her statement. 'What happened?'

He felt her tension, her breath catching. 'Doesn't matter.'

Clearly it did. 'I have to know,' he said gently. 'It may impact on the case.'

'How?' Her question was muffled, but belligerent.

'I can't tell you that, can't even be sure it will until I've heard what happened.'

He heard her swallow.

He felt her wipe her eyes.

'Well, they, er. They got in my way. I tried to dodge around, but they wouldn't let me. One of them grabbed the book, held it up out of my reach. I jumped to try and get it and he grabbed me while I was off my feet. It er, it delayed me.'

There was more to it, but Piper knew he'd have to let her tell this at her own pace.

'Then the other one...'

Her tears were running off her cheek, soaking hot and wet through his shirt.

'Back then I would have just called it a groping. Now I guess it's sexual assault.'

It would have been classed that way twenty years ago too. 'Did they hurt you?'

She shook her head. 'Squeezed my breast, my arse. Thrust towards me. One tried to kiss me, but I nutted him, he dropped me in surprise and I managed to run. It only lasted a few seconds.'

And every second since, Piper guessed. 'How old were they?' She had said, but he had to question everything, check every detail.

'Old-er. That is, they were older than me. They seemed like grown men, but looking back now, I guess they were late teens, early twenties maybe.'

Now for the really unpleasant question. 'Why didn't you report it at the time?'

'Too embarrassed. As I ran, they called me a baby, and I wasn't the baby of the family, Terry was. And he was missing. More important. Finding him mattered, the fact that I wanted to tear off my own skin where they'd touched me didn't.'

That was typical of the Teddington he had come to know. Putting everyone and everything before her own emotional wellbeing. 'It mattered. You matter.' He squeezed her tight and let her cry.

Her words a few minutes later were muffled against his chest.

'I'm sorry.'

'I'm sorry I have to put you through this again.'

She was still leaning on him, and her breath was juddery, but he felt her nodding and then she shifted to sit up again. He let her go but didn't move away.

'If it helps find out what happened to Terry, I'll go through it a million more times. But don't make my mother answer too many more questions. And don't tell her what I just told you. I'm not sure she could take it. When I spoke to her, she said she couldn't stop crying after you left. Said if it weren't for Luke, she wasn't sure she would have made it though.'

Clearly she was trying to get back to some semblance of normality, some level field that made sense. 'Luke? The new lodger?'

Ariadne nodded.

'Nice guy?'

She shrugged. 'Haven't met him. He contacted Mum a couple of days after the accident, popped over to see the room while I was in hospital. He was nice, had the deposit and everything, was happy with the rental agreement papers she gave him, but he had to give notice where he was, so he moved in a week or so after, by which time I was up here. Apparently, he's been great. Even did the decorating I was supposed to be doing.'

There was a certain amount of resentment in that tone that made Piper smile.

'Mum says he did a cracking job.'

Piper nodded. 'Place looked good when I walked in.'

Ariadne smiled at last. 'Did she put Terry's picture back up in the alcove?'

'Actually, no. She hasn't put any of the family photos back out. Said she was keeping them in her room until you get back. Keeping the family together.'

A watery smile and a small nod responded. 'Sounds like Mum.' Then she looked up at Piper. 'Did you meet him? Luke?'

He shook his head. 'I think he was at work when I was there.'

She looked across at her tea. 'I think I need something a bit stronger than that.' She turned back to him. 'Fancy a beer?'

'I could nip out and get some.'

Her smile was more her now. 'You only have to nip as far as the kitchen. The fridge is well stocked. I'll have one of the ciders in there, if you don't mind fetching them.'

When he came back with two full pint glasses, she looked more under control. Her tears were wiped, but her eyes were still red and a little puffy. She thanked him as he passed the cider and sat beside her again. They faced the fire and sipped in silence. Piper mulled over what she'd said, added what he had learned from the notebook Mrs Hall senior had given him. It put everything in a very different light. He wasn't sure it would help though.

'Have-' Teddington had to take another sip before she could finish the question. 'Have you seen Charlie of late?'

Given that the last time they had talked of Charlie Bell, Teddington was clear on the fact that she wanted nothing more to do with him, Piper wasn't sure how much to reveal.

'I saw him a couple of days ago.'

'He okay?'

This time he covered his pause with a sip, thinking about what to say. He could brush her off with a simple yes. But that would be lying. She deserved better than that. 'He's struggling.'

'Job and money?'

'No, actually. He's got a job, making ends meet, though I'm guessing barely. He moved recently, though I haven't found out where to. No, he's struggling with the whole...' Now Piper was trying to put it into words. 'Meaning of life, I guess. He's kind of lost everything he ever wanted. Right now I get the impression that I'm pretty much the only friend he has left.'

'Well, you're a good friend to have.'

There was more emotion in the tone than the words. 'I've got his phone number if you want to talk to him.'

'I'm not sure that would do either of us any good.'

Piper kept his disagreement to himself.

'But leave the number anyway.'

Chapter 11

Piper pulled up the handbrake and switched off the engine. They hadn't moved for five minutes, five vehicles representing ambulance, fire and police services had screamed down the hard shoulder in the last ten minutes, so it seemed unlikely that the motorway traffic was going to go anywhere for a while.

Last night had been surprisingly relaxing after their chat. He figured Teddington had found it somewhat cathartic too. They hadn't been that late to bed, and he for one had slept like a log, then woken refreshed to be greeted with the aroma of cooking bacon. Ariadne had been struggling with two frying pans, a toaster, and the kettle boiling as he stepped into the kitchen. Bacon and egg toasties had been a hell of a way to start the day. Sheila would be upset with him, but then Sheila would never know. He glanced across at Teddington. 'You're very quiet.'

She turned to face him. 'Sorry. Thinking. Didn't mean to block you out.'

'It's fine. Just wanted to know that you're okay.'

She nodded. 'I'm okay. Do you really think that you can find out what happened to Terry? When the guys looking into the case couldn't when it happened.'

'I'm certainly going to try.'

'You said last night that there were things you couldn't tell me, because I'm a family member. Well I've told you everything I possibly can, can we get over that now, so you can tell me?'

'Nice try, but it doesn't quite work that way. There is something more I may need to ask you though.'

A frown creased her brow. 'Go on.'

'What do you think happened to your brother after he went missing?'

She shuddered at the thought. 'I don't know, but I'm guessing it wouldn't be good. You see, I know what Terry was like. I know the last

48

thing I did was call him a brat, but we called each other names all the time, it wouldn't have been enough to make him run away. Which means he was taken. And people who take kids out of nowhere like that aren't doing it out of the goodness of their hearts. So, I guess I've always figured that he was taken, hurt and probably killed. I don't say that to Mum, and I'd rather you didn't either. But it's what I think.'

Piper nodded. 'Unfortunately, in this case, that is the most likely scenario. Wish I could tell you differently, but I have to face facts.'

She agreed. 'So?'

'So you may remember a couple of years ago, some human bones were discovered in a field a few miles from town.'

'The Joskins Field find? Yeah, I remember that hitting the papers. I jumped every time the phone rang for weeks after, wondering if we were going to get a call to tell us DNA proved one of the victims was Terry. But it never happened.'

'Because the DNA sample we had on record for Terry was purged from the system.'

She was frowning at him. 'You purged a victim's records? Well not you personally, obviously, I hope, but you know what I mean.'

'I do and normally we wouldn't, but it seems a number of samples from around that time all went missing.'

He could almost see how she was thinking.

'Is that why you wanted to go through Terry's stuff at home? Looking for something that might still give you another DNA record to match?'

Piper nodded. 'We have something, but it's not good. That's what I need to ask you. Would you be prepared to give a sample to see if we can match it?'

'Would I be a close enough match?'

'That's what I'm told. Something about the mitochondria holding a replica of the mother's DNA in all her children. Don't ask for more details, I really don't get the science bit of it.'

'Wouldn't Mum still be the better match?'

'Do you want me to ask her for a sample?'

'No. Yeah, of course I'll give a sample if it helps.'

The outside lane had started moving, and the middle lane was inching forward, so Piper started the engine again.

'Perhaps I can do it when I get the cast off.'

'When's that?'

'Not sure. The hospital was supposed to send through an appointment letter to let me know, but Mum hasn't said anything's arrived yet.'

The truck in front pulled forward and Piper shifted with it. They didn't go far or fast, but they were starting to move. It took another forty-five minutes to get past the obstruction, a caravan that had pulled the car towing it off the road. It must have collided with at least one other car, and it looked like that had hit others. There were tire tracks in all directions, sweep marks suggested bits cleared up, there were chippings from the central reservation, which itself was looking in need of care. Little wonder all three lanes had been closed.

'Some people are having a really bad day.'

'Hmm,' Teddington agreed. 'Let's hope it's not *that* bad a day though.'

It was another two hours before they reached Teddington's home. Parking was an issue, as it usually was. Victorian terraces hadn't been designed for modern car proliferation. Teddington's own car was in the garage at the back of the house, reached from a lane between the two sets of houses. Piper was four houses down before he found a gap to manoeuvre the Audi into.

Getting out of the car with a full cast was awkward, ending in a fit of giggles and a painful jolt, but at least it wasn't entirely undignified. Piper sent her on ahead of him as he reached into the boot for her suitcases.

Catching her up in the street was easy, since she was rather slow moving. He went ahead a little to knock on the door, stepping back to let Ariadne be the one who greeted her mother. The happy reunion nearly knocked Ariadne off her feet, but they were soon bundled inside. Piper put the suitcases to one side of the hall before he closed the front door behind him.

'Oh I'm so glad you're back,' Mrs Whittaker smiled at her daughter. 'Come on in, you can meet Luke at last.' Mrs Whittaker headed into the sitting room. 'Luke, my Addy's home.'

Teddington beamed as she turned to Piper. 'So you want to meet this fabled new lodger or what?'

'How could I refuse?' He followed her towards the sitting room, watching her closely because of the crutch, which was just as well when she stopped short a step inside the sitting room, half turned to see the other occupant. He saw her jaw was loose, her eyes wide and her face pale. When he looked past her, he understood completely.

'Charlie!'

He and Teddington said it at the same time.

'No,' Mrs Whittaker said. 'This is Luke.'

'Luke?' Teddington repeated, incredulous. 'As in Lucas?' Her mother nodded. 'As in Lucas Charles Bell! This is Charlie Bell, Mum.' Ariadne leaned against the wall, like she needed more support than the crutch could offer. 'Charlie Bloody Bell.'

'What the hell were you thinking?' Piper demanded of the other man.

'That monster?' Mrs Whittaker was aghast.

'I needed somewhere to live, how was I to know a Mrs Whittaker was the mother of a woman named Teddington?'

'How about the papers?' Piper pointed out. It was in them.

'Details I didn't read.'

'You have to get out,' demanded Mrs Whittaker.

'Details are our job.'

'You have to go.'

'Not mine!'

'You can't stay here.'

'Stop!'

Teddington's scream stopped them all. The sudden quiet felt like an intrusion. Piper looked at the young woman; he wasn't sure what he read in her clouded eyes.

'Okay,' she said very calmly. 'Let's be logical here.' She pushed herself away from the wall and leaned on her crutch.

'He has to go.'

'Mum, it's not that simple.'

Mrs Whittaker drew herself to her full height, which in this room left her at least four inches shorter than the next person. 'Yes, it is. He's a monster.'

'No, he's not. You know that, you know how he's been since he moved in. Right up until this moment, you've not had a bad word to say about him.'

'But he kidnapped you.'

'I keep telling you, it wasn't like that.'

'You've got the bullet scar to prove it.'

'Yes, because Charlie saved my life! If he hadn't got me out of that firefight, if he hadn't got me to doctor who pulled the bullet out and sewed me up, I wouldn't have a bullet scar, there'd be a bullet hole in a rotting corpse!'

Mrs Whittaker gasped and put her hands over her mouth, sinking to the nearest chair.

'Oh my God, Mum. I'm sorry. I shouldn't have said that.' Teddington tried to reach out, but it was virtually impossible with the plaster cast.

She moved closer to her mother's chair and used it for support, so she could take her unplastered arm from the crutch. Her mother gripped her offered hand in a way that looked bone-crushing.

'I can't have him here now.'

Piper thought that was a bit rich.

'Tough, because we don't have a choice.'

Three faces turned in surprise to Teddington at that, but she was looking only at her mother.

'When you told me about Luke, I asked you about the rental agreement, and you were quite clear that you'd got him to sign it.'

'That was what you told me I had to do.'

'I know, you did, and it was a good move. But I wrote that agreement, I know what was in it; including a minimum six-month tie-in. Unless strict rules are broken, then the contract can't be broken.'

'But he -'

'Hasn't broken the contract.'

'He lied to me.'

Ariadne frowned. 'About what?'

'His name.'

'No, he didn't. Lucas is his name. Charlie is his middle name, but if I'd just come out of jail, I'd be looking to start over, and a new name is as good a way of doing that as any.' She paused for breath. 'If we chuck him out, we're breaking the contract and we'd have to pay any addition rent he was forced to take on elsewhere for the remainder of the six-month term.'

'Fine.'

Teddington's intake of breath was audible. 'We can't afford that. If we could, we wouldn't have taken on another lodger, would we?'

Piper could see that Ariadne was struggling with the situation and struggling to keep her struggle under control. Her stance was tense, and he'd noticed that she wasn't even looking anywhere near Charlie. Her breathing was just a little too controlled.

'Look, if there is anyone in this room that has the right to object to Charlie being here, it's me. And I don't. So, we are going to stick to the agreement.'

Mrs Whittaker's lips compressed, her chin pushed forward. Very much the look of belligerence Piper had seen on Teddington's face. The older woman stood and faced Charlie. Teddington readjusted her stance with the crutch, she still wasn't looking at Charlie. 'Well I suppose I have to put up with you for the time being.'

'Mum.'

'No. He hurt you.'

'I hurt me!' Ariadne snapped. 'He took care of me when I was in trouble. He saved my life - twice. Possibly three times. He's been nothing but nice to you since he got here. No!'

Again the three were surprised by the power in Teddington's voice when her mother moved to argue. The younger woman was actually crying.

'Just no. With him asking about Terry again,' she said, pointing to Piper, 'and a fair chance that I'm about to lose my job, I really can't take any more stresses right now. And we can't afford to lose another source of income. So we are going to honour our agreement. Charlie is going to stay.' She turned to glare at Charlie. 'Though he's got a hell of a lot of explaining to do.' Then she turned back to her mother. 'I'm sorry I've upset you, I didn't mean to. But there is absolutely no reason for you to take against Luke just because you've found out he's Charlie.' She shook her head then looked to the sky. 'I can't believe I just said that.'

Mrs Whittaker sniffed, then looked at Charlie. 'Well I suppose I can try.' Then she stepped over to hug her daughter. Words were exchanged that Piper couldn't make out. Then Mrs Whittaker moved back, offering tea.

Teddington looked small and tired as she wiped her eyes and sniffed. She was struggling and there was little Piper could do to help her with that. He turned to Charlie.

'We will talk about this tomorrow.'

Only when Charlie nodded did Piper look at Teddington.

'And if he gives you any trouble, remember I can still arrest him.'

At least he had the pleasure of seeing her smile at that.

Chapter 12

It was ten to four when Piper put the key in his front door and walked into his home. He wasn't in the least surprised to see Sheila sitting at her desk in front of a monitor displaying a script covered in blue edits and side comments.

'Not great, that one then?'

She turned in her office chair and smiled over her glasses at him. 'Good idea, appalling grammar.' She stood up and moved to him, kissing his cheek. 'Missed you the last two nights.'

'Me, you, too.' As she tried to move away, he pulled her back and kissed her properly.

Giggling, she moved away. 'I'm still on duty, Chief Inspector.'

He let her go. 'I'll make tea then.'

'New York Breakfast, please.'

She was already back at her desk as Piper headed for the kitchen. He had just put the glass cup and saucer beside Sheila when there was a knock at the door. Her look up was a little accusatory. He shrugged.

'Sir!'

Whatever Piper had expected when he opened the door, it wasn't to see Broughton on his porch, especially not in worn brown corduroy trousers and a dark green Arran knit sweater.

'Let me in then, man.'

Shaking off the funk of surprise, Piper stepped back. The man mountain stepped inside, filling the hall. Piper pointed to the kitchen and the big man headed through, nodding in acknowledgement to Sheila as he passed. Once Broughton had gone through, Sheila sent her husband another questioning look. All he could do was shrug again.

Broughton was looking curiously into the glass teapot. 'Smells like liquorish.'

54

'New York Breakfast tea,' Piper supplied. 'Sheila loves it. Would you like to try some?'

'What I'd like,' said Broughton, pinning Piper with a look, 'is to know what you are playing at.'

Piper swallowed. 'I'm not sure what you mean, sir.' He knew exactly what Broughton was getting at. He got the kind of hard stare that reminded Piper of reading Paddington to his children.

'Why are you bothering Kyle Wilson?'

Piper reached for his own tea. 'He's an ex-colleague I hadn't seen for a while. I just thought I'd drop by and see him.'

'He said you'd just dropped by as ask him about Joskins Field.'

'Did he?'

'Don't go and open old wounds.'

'Don't intend to.'

'Don't go there again.'

'Don't plan to.'

Piper considered Broughton. Considered and worried. Was Broughton in on it? Did the DCS know more about what was going on than he should? 'You sure you don't want a drink?'

'I'm not staying,' Broughton announced. 'Why the Terrence Whittaker case?'

'You told me to work cold cases.'

'I didn't tell you to lengthen your association with Mrs Teddington.' Broughton sighed. 'Look, Matthew...'

Piper knew he was in trouble now.

'...Whatever else has happened, I don't want you heading down a dead end chasing a spectre that doesn't exist.'

'Don't exist *anymore*,' Piper pointed out. 'Because of Charlie.'

'Screw Charlie, he's beyond my help. You're not.'

Piper stood back and blinked.

'Yes, well.' Broughton rolled his shoulder and stretched his neck. 'While you were away, I got permission for an extra DC in the team. Had a couple of applicants. I appointed, starts tomorrow. I expect you to work closely with the new recruit, no more skulking around with Uniforms. Clear?'

Piper took a breath, the liquorish filling his nostrils. Well it saved him from the sour flavour of his thoughts. 'Yes, sir.'

Suddenly Broughton was smiling, then he moved to leave. 'You're not sucking lemons, Matthew, stop looking like it.'

* * *

Ariadne was exhausted. She wanted to go to bed, but the idea of facing those stairs was just too much. She reached for her wine glass and took another sip.

'Should you actually be drinking?'

She looked up at her mother and bit back the sharp retort. 'I'm not on painkillers anymore.'

They were both surprised by the knock at the living room door. Even more surprised when Charlie asked if he could come in before opening it. It was her mother who gave permission. Ari heard the door open, but didn't have the courage to look up, so she drank again.

'You didn't have to knock.'

'Thank you, Mrs W.'

Ari moved her eyes to look at her mother. Her mother looked back and for a moment bit her lip, then she looked back at Charlie.

'Addy and I have spoken.'

Ari control her smile. That was putting it mildly.

'We're not about to ask you to leave.'

'I hope not, Mrs W. I've loved being here.'

Her mother nodded. 'Well, I can't say I'm as comfortable around you as I was, but Addy says I'll get over that.'

'Hope so.'

'Which leaves only one question. Do you want us to call you Luke or Charlie?'

For a moment, Charlie seemed flummoxed. 'I'd really like Luke. If that's okay?'

The older woman nodded and stood. 'All right, Luke. I assume the two of you need to talk more now. I'll see you in the morning.'

Ari accepted and returned her mother's goodnight kiss, something that wasn't a ritual between them, but it had been a tough day. When she was gone and the door was closed, Ari saw Charlie move to stand in front of her. She looked up.

'Luke.' She frowned. 'Lucas?' She pursed her lips and tapped her nail on the foot of the wine glass. 'Luke.' She frowned up at him. 'I guess I can get used to that.'

'You don't have to.' He offered a small smile. 'I can answer to both names.'

'Which would confuse both me and Mum.' Looking up at him was too far. She pointed to the wine in the cooler on the coffee table. 'Top me up and if you want a glass, they're in the sideboard there.'

First, he picked up the bottle and topped the glass she held out to him. It was a generous measure, but he put the bottle straight back.

'May I?'

He indicated the empty seat next to her on the sofa. She nodded and drank.

'Are you really likely to lose your job?'

Nodding was all she could manage at first. A big breath helped steady her. 'The doctors say I did so much damage to my leg that it's likely I'm going to need some support to walk with for a long time. Months at least. The Prison Service won't wait that long, and I can't walk the wing with a gammy leg.'

'Sorry.'

She turned to him at last. 'Me too. I liked that job.' Her face broke into a smirk. 'Well, some of it. Could have lived without the physical attacks and the riot.'

He offered a smile and his hands reached up.

'I saw you shot dead.'

The hand moved forward. She moved back.

'I'm not dead.'

'I didn't know that then. It hurt so much.' Suddenly her sight was blurry. 'Oh, sod it.' This time she pushed forward and pressed her lips against his. His hand went to her head, cradling her and deepening the kiss. With a shift or two his arm went around her shoulders and pulled her close. Finally she had to break the kiss and drag in a breath. But she placed her forehead on his. 'Next time you hurt me, I'm going to prison.'

She felt his frown against her forehead before he pulled back.

'What? Why would you?'

She smiled. 'Because I'll kill you.'

He laughed.

'I'm not joking.'

'I know.' He smiled and stroked her cheek. 'I'm happy because it means you care. I haven't had that before.'

She kissed him. 'I have.' She moved back. 'It didn't work out well.' The wine was still cool and it slipped down easily. 'And I think you and I, well you, are, is… Oh God I've been drinking too much to even get the grammar right. You're dangerous. You're dangerous to my equilibrium. If you're still informing for Piper, still investigating, I know you and I know you won't let anything go. That makes you *more* dangerous. I worry about the lengths you might go to.'

He was nodding, but he looked serious. 'I would never go to the lengths I did before.'

Contemplating him, searching his eyes for the truth, she was satisfied he wouldn't kill again, but that wasn't the only danger.

'You can't guarantee you won't put yourself in the line of fire again though, can you?'

He shrugged. 'You can't guarantee that some dick behind the wheel of a car won't smash int-' His words snapped off as his eyes dropped down to the various plaster casts she was still wearing.

'No. I can't guarantee that I wouldn't smash another car to stop a killer either. Which is part of what worries me about any potential relationship between us.'

'Potential relationship?' he asked. 'Are you saying we aren't already in the middle of one?'

She took a deep breath. 'I hate that you make me challenge everything about myself. I didn't want to see you after the accident because I thought that that was what I needed. But seeing you again, everything feels...' She huffed. Took another deep drink. 'I have no idea what I'm feeling.' She turned to him. 'Except tired. Thanks for taking my bags up earlier.'

'You're welcome. You want help getting upstairs?'

She laughed. 'I'll need help just standing right now.' As he stood, she finished the wine and moved forward on the sofa. She was expecting him to help her up, not *pick* her up. Throwing her good arm around his neck, she shifted her plastered arm from being squeezed and held him tight as he carefully manoeuvred her to the door.

'You'll have to scoot down a bit so I can reach the handle.'

He did and for a moment she had to let go of him, but she got the door open. It was undignified and difficult, but they got out with only a slight bump of her plastered leg on the door frame.

'Charlie?' she blew in his ear as he carried her carefully up the stairs. Another awkward affair since he had to walk sideways to accommodate for the unbending leg.

'Yes, Ari?'

'First door on the left.' It was probably the drink, but she leaned up and ran her tongue along his earlobe. His chuckle rumbled through her and she felt it in all the places she was supposed to. He stopped and stooped so she could open the door. He took her inside. The idea of him laying her down on the double bed and stretching out beside her was tempting, but not practical. He was leaning down over the bed. Lowering her to the duvet. She pulled his head to her, kissing him deeply before she moved along his chin to his ear again, having to ignore the shivers and quakes being set off as his hands moved over her. She sucked his lobe in and whispered, 'You can't stay.'

'Spoilsport.'

Chapter 13

DI Langdon surprised Piper before the morning briefing by asking his advice on how to continue the morning briefings he had taken on in Piper's absence.

'Any reason why you can't carry on the way you did it yesterday, the day before and in fact the whole of last week?'

'Well no, sir. I just thought you might want to take it back.'

Piper offered the younger man a reassuring smile. 'If I thought for one second that you couldn't handle it, I'd offer to lead; but you can handle it. To be fair, the only thing of any real interest is that spate of burglaries on the Eastwold and you're SIO on that anyway.' Besides, Broughton had praised the man to the hilt for his briefings. And in fairness praised, just, Piper for giving the younger man the opportunity to develop.

Langdon looked surprisingly nervous as he moved to the front of the briefing room. A few people were still filing in, and Piper took the end seat on a middle row that had already mostly filled up. He leaned forward to pass a greeting to the DS in front of him, so he didn't see who was last in, but he saw Langdon's eyes momentarily widen, so he glanced to his left.

Broughton.

Broughton nodded to Langdon and after a momentary stuttering start, Langdon launched into the briefing. Piper was ashamed to say he didn't hear most of it, he was too concerned about what the DCS was doing in here. This wasn't at all usual. He was so concerned that he nearly missed it when Langdon asked him to stand and update the crowd on the missing children cases he had opened.

Piper rose from his chair and moved to the front, where the board was still up from his briefing a few days ago.

'I've re-interviewed the remaining families, I have one interesting new fact and one odd post-facto connection. The DNA records of all three victims are missing. I want to do a check on some of the other missing kids from that time and see if this is just a coincidence or if it's symptomatic of something else.'

'You think someone maliciously removed the records?'

Piper turned to the man who had asked, DS Covington. Fifty-six years old, tenacious and bitter, now just working towards his retirement, a gold watch and a crappy pension. Not that gold watches were likely in these days of austerity. Covington had worked with just about everyone over the years.

'I didn't say it was malicious.'

''Spose you've got someone in mind for this *maliciousness*?'

Piper held himself back from the sigh. 'It could just be a clerical error or a computer glitch. It may just have been a mistake that affected a few cases, or it might be something wider. I don't know why it happened, just that it did. The concern now is that if it *is* wider than these three cases, then we might have missed something else.'

'Like what?' Covington demanded.

Piper dragged in a breath and tried to make it look like he hadn't been worrying about that for the last week. 'Like the seven unidentified body parts from Joskins Field. We have those DNA records because the find is only three years old, but we don't have any matches. It's not beyond the realms of possibility that that or something else could be links that we've missed in losing records from the database. I don't know what the link could be or if any link actually exists, but the possibility is there and it has to be checked out.'

'What about DNA from remaining family members?' Broughton asked.

Piper nodded. 'I've got agreement from the Butler and Whittaker families, and I'm going to ask our colleagues in Yorkshire to see if they can get a sample from the Hall family.'

'What was the extra fact?' Broughton asked.

Piper had to be careful how he phrased all this. 'Terrence "Terry" Whittaker was last seen in the playing fields at the end of Woodlands Walk. It was the FA Cup final and not many people were around, he was there with only his sister. She now says that when she went to follow Terry from the park, there were two men that got in her way. It's possible that those two men were working with whoever took the boy.'

'Why didn't she mention it before?'

'She was too embarrassed. Worried that her parents would think she was making it up to get attention.'

'Is that possible?'

Piper looked up at Broughton's question and considered it. 'Not from what I saw when she was telling me.' He shook his head. 'No. We get lied to all the time, she was telling me the truth. Besides, she's simply not the kind to crave attention of that nature.'

'IDs?'

Apparently Broughton wasn't going to give Covington's grumble of disagreement any more dignity than Piper was trying to.

'None yet,' Piper admitted. 'But I've got descriptions and I'm looking for help to put together some mug shots from around that time and see if we can get anywhere.'

'Hang on,' Covington put in, 'isn't Terrence Whittaker the older brother of Ariadne Teddington?'

There was a general murmur that rippled through the room at that name and didn't seem as happy as it might.

'No,' Piper said evenly. The ripple had a smirk or two in it now. 'He was her *younger* brother.'

The murmur was distinct dissention-in-the-ranks now.

'You have a problem with Ariadne Teddington?'

'She didn't exactly do us any favours. You said she wasn't the kind to seek attention, but she's been a right attention-grabber every time she's been here.'

Piper sighed. That attention had never been her choice. 'Ariadne Teddington is a prison officer who put her life on the line to expose a conspiracy in HMP Blackmarch, then she was instrumental in stopping a bunch of armed bank robbers, and she put her life on the line doing that too,' Piper threw back. 'What exactly is your issue with her?'

'DS Carlisle nearly died to save her.'

'The point -'

Piper was surprised Broughton responded.

'- is that that is Carlisle's job, to protect the citizens of this county. It is not Teddington's job, but she did it all the same, and at great personal cost. And while we're on the topic of Carlisle, I know he's popped in a few times in the last week or so. While I am happy for all of you to welcome him - he is still a serving, if not an active officer - may I remind you that not only are we a working station, he's still in recovery after his injuries, major injuries, and he needs to rest. Encourage him to rest at home so that he can recover in peace and be back on active duty sooner.'

That calmed most of the crowd. Covington grumbled under his breath.

'Teddington is why you opened the case though, isn't she?'

Apparently, Covington wasn't going to be diverted. The urge to cross his arms was strong, but Piper wasn't going on the defensive, he shouldn't need to. 'I can't say it didn't figure in my thinking, but the fact that this and these other cases haven't been reviewed in nearly twenty years is a huge failing on the part of this police force and don't think-' He pinned Covington with a look, the man had definitely been working here twenty years ago. '-I won't be looking into why that is.'

The weight of the air seemed to bear down on him as Piper meet Covington's challenging look. He was sure the older man might have said more had Broughton not been in the room.

'Sounds like a lot of grunt work,' Broughton said from his position by the door.

Now Piper looked up at him. 'Yes, sir.'

'Best get the new kid on it then,' Broughton suggested.

Piper turned to look where Broughton indicated and felt the ability to speak dessert him.

'DCI Piper, this is Detective Constable Siddig, she started with us yesterday. I'm sure she won't mind digging through the archives for you.'

Chapter 14

Piper sat at his desk frowning over a battered notebook. He was doing that more and more these days. Frowning. Linda Small stood in the doorway and looked at him.

For more than twenty years she'd been following him up through the ranks; though they hadn't worked directly together it was impossible for them not to know one another. "Friends" was probably an overstatement but "colleagues" wasn't enough. She was worried about him. Since that prison murder last year, he had been different; since the Invicta Bank job, he'd carried tension around like a cloak, an expression like he was staring defeat in the teeth. The last few weeks she'd seen him frowning, teeth gritted, rubbing his stomach like he was in pain, she'd seen enough ulcers around here to suspect that was the problem. Thankfully, none of it seemed to have affected his performance on the job. Whatever he was going through, she was sure he'd get through it.

The brown leather book looked well used, there were lose pages and additions. She could see handwriting, but couldn't read it from this distance.

'Can I come in?'

Piper looked up, surprised again. Closing the notepad, he left it on the desk in front of him.

'Linda, come in.'

She closed the door behind her as she did.

'Should I be worried about two visits in three days?'

'Why not? I am,' she said as she sat opposite him. 'Anything interesting?'

He followed her point to look at the notebook, the pause and deep breath suggested he was thinking about something. He seemed to make up his mind, pulled a loose sheet from the book and placed it on the table in front of her. 'What does that tell you?'

The last thing she was expecting to see was a photograph of a man performing fellatio, being watched by a group of other men. She was only familiar with the man being treated, though his look was more of triumph than excitement. 'That Phillip Mansel-Jones really needed to get a life. It's not a great shot, looks like it was taken from a concealed camera given the bad framing and off-level angles.'

'That was my thought too.' He took the photo back and slipped it into the closed notebook but kept looking at is.

'Whose notebook?'

'Greg Hall. Father of one of the kids in the cold cases I'm looking into.'

'He gave you that?'

'He's dead.' He lifted the notebook. 'His mother gave me this, I just hope she didn't give it to me too late.'

'What's in there?'

'A collection of reports and incidences and perpetrators, all pointing to the fact that Phillip Mansel-Jones was kidnapping and abusing children. The man took risks just to gather this. Shame.'

She frowned, that was exactly what he'd been wanting for years. 'Shame?'

Finally, he looked up at her. If there was emotion in him, he hid it well. He took a deep steadying breath. 'It's insufficient evidence for a conviction, but with all the names in here, if we'd have this before Phillip Mansel-Jones died, we'd have had the right foundation to build an unstoppable case.'

Then it was too late to do any real good. 'Aren't the cases you're looking at twenty years old? Will it not help close them?'

His expression expressed a reluctant agreement. 'Possibly.'

Yet he wasn't hopeful. Suddenly she understood his fascination with the surface of his desk; she could only look that way too. What was there to say?

'Linda?'

'The worst thing about my job is that if I don't bring them back within 48 hours, I don't usually bring them back alive.'

'Good thing you have a pretty good clearup rate, then.'

She smiled at the compliment. Good to know that her colleagues had faith in her. 'I came to give you a quick update. We followed the route most likely to be taken away from Harriot Gardens and managed to identify the Mondeo. Followed its path for a while, then lost it as it headed out of town. We got enough to get the reg number though. That particular blue Mondeo is registered to a Toby Jacobson. Who matches the description of the man seen with Madeline, in as much as he's within a couple of inches of the estimates, male and has short mid brown hair.'

'That's good news.'

If only. 'Not really. Tony Jacobson is a 34-year-old geography teacher.'

Piper's lip curled. 'Not a great image, and a bit of a cliché, but it happens.'

At first glance. 'He lives in Bolton, Lancashire.'

His brow drew together, as if he wasn't ready to accept what she had to. 'It's rather a long way to come to pick up kids, but not impossible.'

'He was in Bolton, in a Parent Teacher Association meeting, his car parked right in front of the school, on their CCTV and all, at the time that Madeline Stolz was going missing from Harriot Gardens.'

Piper didn't look surprised. 'Ahh. A cloned plate.'

'Yep. And to make things even better, we found it. The car.' Which should also be good news, but wasn't. 'Burned out and dumped, and to really add insult to injury, is the fact that it was burning was called in by one of your favourite people.'

She could see the dread in his eyes.

'Who?'

Exactly who she didn't want to have to talk about. 'Rhys Mansel-Jones.' Everything about that slimeball left her cold. She had dealt with enough perverts to see his lack of empathy in his reactions, he had learned the right kinds of things to say, but some tones couldn't be faked. Though there was nothing to suggest he was a paedophile himself, but she wouldn't trust him to keep a goldfish alive. She certainly wouldn't leave him alone with a kid. 'The bloody car had been dumped in a small industrial park beside some fields he owns and he didn't want the fire risking his grass land. Thankfully the Fire Service responded quickly and put out the fire, so while there's no hope of getting any DNA from the vehicle, we did get a VIN of the car, it's an insurance write-off that was supposed to have been destroyed in 2016. We're following that trail, just to see if it turns anything else up.'

'Thorough as ever, good to see.'

Thankfully, she didn't detect a hint of patronising. Though she didn't need his compliments, it was always good to know she had the respect of her colleagues.

'I take it that the parents haven't heard anything else? No ransom demands?'

She shook her head. 'Neither family would really be in a position to pay one. The Pearsons are struggling to make ends meet at it is. The Stolzes are comfortable, but not rich. They could probably get hold of a fair whack of cash if they had to, but they'd be in hock for the rest of their lives if it was enough to make kidnap worth the effort. No, whatever Stephen and Madeline were taken for, it wasn't for a ransom.'

This was bad news. Very bad news. The most difficult thing of all. It told her that the perpetrators had plans for those kids, and that they didn't expect to hand either one of them back. Ever.

'The parents must be distraught?'

They were, naturally. What was interesting was how he had phrased the question, with all the understanding of being a father himself. She'd found that those who didn't have children were always more distant in their questioning than those that did. It was one of the reasons she had chosen not to have children herself. 'Distraught and desperate. You saw the two appeals?' Both sets of parents had separately been on national television praying, begging, for the return of their children. It was gut-wrenching.

Piper nodded. 'Mr Pearson didn't seem exactly upset at the time. Do you think that could be another parental-led case?'

It wasn't unheard of for desperate parents to fake a kidnapping just to get the attention. Thankfully, Linda had never had to deal with such a case. 'No, I don't. If I'm any judge, and I flatter myself that I am, Mr Pearson is actually more affected by the boy's loss than Mrs Pearson, he just doesn't know how to deal with that emotional loss. He's the old school stiff-upper-lip type. I think he's closed himself down to be able to cope.'

'How long's Stephen been gone?'

'Nearly four weeks.'

'And Madeline, a week?'

Linda nodded. The chances of getting either kid back alive were so slim as to be non-existent now. 'I've been wondering if you had any evidence of longer-term storage of victims?' Something to give her just that little bit more hope.

He looked at the notebook again; she itched to reach out and read it.

'Piper?' She asked when he didn't answer. 'Matthew?'

'This –' He placed his hand over the notebook. 'was written twenty-one to sixteen years ago. I'm not sure how relevant it is, but...'

It was a long time ago, but that was no guarantee that whatever he was referring to had been stopped. She found herself leaning forward, intent on what he had to say. Piper wouldn't be this uncomfortable if it wasn't something to worry about.

'It mentions holding cells, and transporting. A staging post.'

'That's not an instant turnaround.' Her heart was pounding. That meant storage. Kids kept and stored. This was the hope she so desperately needed.

Chapter 15

Piper tried to organise everything in his head. It wasn't especially helping.

His own cases were going nowhere, Small's cases were am extra worry, he couldn't concentrate on the information in Hall's notebook. And he couldn't stop worrying about what had happened during this morning's briefings. What was Broughton was playing at? Was he being played for a fool? It was starting to feel like…

Actually he wasn't sure what it was starting to feel like. Broughton didn't want him going anywhere near Wilson, yet he'd brought Siddig into CID. Had Broughton known Siddig was already helping him? Siddig said she'd been given the nod to apply for a position that was very short notice in coming up. Yet here she was, well, she was downstairs looking for old mugshot folders. And what was with Covington? He was used to the man being obnoxious, but the earlier standoff had felt more personal.

'Maybe I'm just getting paranoid.'

'Hardly surprising in your job.'

Piper looked up, surprised to see Ariadne Teddington at the door. She was still leaning on a crutch, but the casts on her arm and leg were gone.

'Sorry to barge in. One of your colleagues told me to come straight through and pointed out your door.'

That was hardly standard practice. 'Did you get a name?'

'Nah.' She smiled as she limped into the room and sat carefully on the chair in front of his desk. 'Just a lousy attitude and some insulting remarks.'

Covington probably. 'Sorry.'

She shrugged. 'I've worked in a men's prison for five years, trust me, he wasn't quite so cocky when we parted company.'

'Good.' He looked her over. The casts were gone, but she wasn't completely healed yet. 'How are you doing?'

'I'm okay.'

'Are you?'

She frowned at him. 'What's that supposed to mean?'

'Well you're hardly looking like yourself anymore.'

'I was in a major car crash; a few scars are inevitable.'

'I'm not talking about the scars.'

She frowned, looked down at herself, and took a deep breath. 'Oh, the clothes? I see your point. Dungarees and a jumbo-jumper, not exactly my usual style. But at the moment, my choices are based on what I can get into without a fight. It's not some deep insight into my state of mind, I haven't sworn off corsets and leggings forever, I've literally just come from the hospital after having the casts removed and I needed clothes that were capable of going over them as well as me. My hair is down because it's virtually impossible to do anything with it one-handed. I probably won't be wearing my leggings *that* much in the future though. Some of the scars on my legs are deep and would give a very odd profile under close-fitting garments.'

'Well I'll look forward to the return of the corsets then.'

This time she looked at him and laughed. 'Only a happily married man could get away with saying something like that.'

Piper smiled. 'Shall we get back to a more official conversation then? What can I do for you, Mrs Teddington?'

'What happened to calling me Ariadne? Official is one thing, no need to be officious.'

'Sorry. What can I do for you, Ariadne?'

'I believe that you wanted a DNA sample and I believe you can do the swabs for that here.'

'We can.' Piper nodded. There were other things he wanted to discuss with her first, but he saw movement at the open door and was surprised to see Carlisle back again.

Piccadilly Circus here today.

'Ariadne.'

Piper watched her surprise as she looked up. She didn't look as pleased to see Carlisle as she might, then she forced a smile. Piper slipped the notebook into his top drawer, closing it softly.

'Carlisle. It's good to see you out and about. When I was wheeled down to see you in hospital, I got the impression you'd take longer to recover than I would.'

Of course they had both been in hospital at the same time, the shooting and the car crash being related to the same incident. He hadn't realised that Ariadne had gone to see Carlisle while they were both in hospital though.

'You know what they say.' Carlisle smiled as he wandered in. 'You can't keep a good man down. So, what are you doing here?'

She shrugged as she sat back to look up at Carlisle. 'You know, just… helping the police with their enquiries.'

Carlisle looked quizzical. 'The missing items after the bank robbery?'

Now Ariadne looked confused and turned to Piper. 'Missing items? Didn't you recover all five bags?'

'We did, but-'

'But a few items were still missing.'

As Ariadne's attention turned back to Carlisle, Piper schooled himself to stay calm, impassive. Carlisle shouldn't even be here.

'Did you see them take anything from the bags?'

Teddington was shaking her head, but her eyes were forward and slightly unfocused. 'I was pushed onto a sofa. I faced forward, shocked by watching them kill a man and throw that poor little girl from the van.' She blinked and seemed to come to her senses. 'Lucy, the little girl, is she all right now?'

Piper nodded. 'Bounced back better than her mother.'

Teddington smiled. She had very straight teeth, not brilliant artificial white, but the lightest touch of yellow to indicate they were natural and well looked-after. 'Kids can do that. I'm glad she's-'

'The bags?'

Ariadne shot Carlisle a vicious look, but then Ariadne shifted again, she looked at the wall, but neither man, her eyes unfocused as she went inside herself, Piper assumed she was trying to remember. 'I was on the sofa, the table was to my left and slightly back, only just on the periphery of my vision.' Her left hand raised, fingers wide, giving a clear indication of where the table had been in relation to her. Piper saw the accuracy, having been in the room during the initial forensic sweep. 'I didn't really see anything much, wasn't looking, just kind of waiting for them to get bored and shoot me. Guess they must have opened the bags though, because the woman definitely said something like "I want this" over a piece of jewellery.'

Her eyes narrowed as if she was thinking hard again. Then she shrugged, blinked and looked back at Piper. 'Is that any help?'

'Not really.'

Now Teddington openly glared at Carlisle. 'Well I am sorry.'

She sounded anything but.

'Calm down.'

That was a guaranteed red rag to a bull.

'Calm down!'

'Mrs Teddington,' Piper interjected before this could escalate. She looked to him was narrow eyed and tight lipped. 'He was simply responding to your question, however lousy the tone.' Something that had happened a fair few times in the past when Carlisle was interviewing.

'Are you sure that's all you can remember?' Carlisle pushed. 'Not covering for-'

'Yes, that's all I remember.'

Piper was neither surprised by the snap nor impressed with either of them right now. They glared at each other like pugilists preparing punches.

'Just so happens I was concussed at the time. I do apologise, but you, Detective Sergeant Carlisle, do not get to speak to me like that.' This time she turned on Piper. 'I still owe him a slap, would now be appropriate?'

'Hardly. Carlisle here may not be on active duty, but he is still a serving police officer.'

'If he's not on active duty, why is he in the office?'

Teddington's light tone was as forced as her smile. 'Good question.' Then he turned to Carlisle. 'Why *are* you here?'

'Can't a man visit friends?'

'At a police station?'

It was Carlisle's turn to glare at Teddington.

'Don't you visit the prison?'

'No.'

'Not even to see Charlie Bell?'

'Wouldn't be much point, would there?'

'Charlie served his time,' Piper reminded Carlisle. 'He's out. Free. As are you. Free to go, that is. I have work to do.'

Thankfully, Carlisle had worked with Piper long enough to know that this was a moment when he wasn't to be pushed. The younger man visibly controlled his face and brought out a smile that looked thoroughly genuine, even though Piper didn't trust it for a second.

'I'll be off then.' Carlisle moved towards the still open door. 'But I'll be back.'

'Not till you're well enough to work, I hope,' Piper called out.

'And shut the door on your way out.'

Piper was a little surprised by the command in Teddington's tone, and more surprised that Carlisle obeyed. For a moment, there was silence. Then he heard Teddington take a deep breath.

'I don't like that man.'

Piper smiled again. 'I couldn't tell.'

Her laugh was short and light. 'So, what's in the notebook you didn't want him to see?'

Piper looked at her, deadly serious. 'You really don't want to know.' He wished he didn't.

* * *

Piper checked his watch. There was time. He could…

He could, but he shouldn't. He'd told Broughton he wouldn't.

Sod that.

He had time and he had to know, besides Sheila was used to him being back late. Piper parked outside of Wilson's house again. Something was going on. The front door wasn't the same as it had been the last time he'd visited. Home improvements?

His gut said not. Still wondering, he reached for his beeping phone.

Go home. I've enough trouble. Don't give me more.

From Wilson. That was a surprise, he hadn't given Wilson his card. There again, it was his police phone and that number hadn't changed in years. It was not beyond the realms of possibility that Wilson just remembered what it was. No clearer as to what was going on, Piper started the car and pulled away.

Chapter 16

Perhaps it was a sign of the times that Piper, an older man, alone and wearing a suit, when choosing to sit on a bench in the park, was glared at by all the young mothers, and a fair few of the fathers with their kids. He wondered how any of them would feel if they knew that in the past thirty years, this was the last place six boys had been seen. Or if they understood that most abusers were actually family and family friends. As a father, he shuddered at the thought

Piper saw the blond man jogging as soon as he entered the park. He was soaked with sweat, the straps of the pack over his shoulders edged the dark lines on the light blue t-shirt he wore. Clearly, he was jogging home from work. Piper checked his watch. 17:16. This was hardly the usual time for him to be returning from work.

'How come you're so late?' Piper asked as Charlie virtually collapsed on the bench next to him.

'Meeting at... work till... half four.' The words were forced out between heavy breaths. 'Sorry for the... short notice.'

They had been meant to meet at three, all logged with CHIS, but Charlie had called to change the arrangements at 14:10. Piper shrugged.

'Happens. I need to go over what happened at Phillip Mansel-Jones' house.'

Piper heard Charlie swear as he hung his head and looked away.

'I killed a man, what more do you want to know?'

'Not that time.' Piper sighed. 'I want to know about the time before, when you led the search team through Mansel-Jones' place.'

He waited as Charlie grabbed a few deep breaths, took off the pack and slumped against the back of the bench.

'Would have thought that was all in the records too.'

'It is. I want you to tell me what didn't make it to the records.'

'Not a lot,' Charlie said.

74

The sharper tone suggested that Piper had hurt his feelings somehow. Piper realised he might well have done. Charlie had been a good officer, meticulous in his reporting. The fact remained though, not every nuance made it to the reports.

'We took that place apart and found nothing. Phillip let us in because of the paperwork, but he was there during the day when we weren't expecting him to be. Like he was waiting for us. He-'

'Waiting for you?'

Charlie had been looking out over the field. Now he looked back at Piper. A frown marred his forehead as he considered the point. Slowly, he started to nod.

'Yeah. He was waiting. He was ready.' One hand came up and scraped back his sweaty hair. 'Hadn't thought of it that way before, but yes. He was waiting. He knew we were coming.'

'How?'

As he studied Charlie, Charlie studied him back, looking for an answer.

'We only knew we had the warrant an hour before we got there, and we hadn't told anyone we were going for it. We gathered the search team without telling them what the target was. Briefing was 45 minutes before we struck. There wasn't time for anyone outside the team to find out what we were up to. The only people outside the station who knew were the judge and the clerk. You think one of them was in Mansel-Jones' pocket?'

'No, I don't.'

Charlie's frown deepened. 'You really can't think someone in the team did it.'

'You said you'd heard of the Don. What did you hear?'

'Whispers, but that was all. And only in the last year or so that I was working.'

'Well, the whispers didn't go away, and the Don appears still to be operating. Who could have known?'

'Well, you and I secured the warrant. We called Carlisle and he prepared the team. We walked straight into the briefing, Carlisle was leading it. But we told the team where we were going and why. Once the briefing was done, we got straight into the van and left. No one made any calls. Or as far as I know, sent any texts. I know I didn't tip off Mansel-Jones, and neither did you. So, who's left?'

Piper didn't want to think about it. But Charlie wasn't a fool.

'Carlisle?' His head was shaking. 'No.'

'He was more able than the rest of us to make that call. Don't forget, we phoned him before we went back to the station. We don't know what he did in that quarter of an hour.'

Charlie looked away. Piper had known him long enough to know that he was thinking everything through. He watched as Charlie tried several times to formulate a question without coming up with anything coherent enough to voice. Finally, he sat up and turned more completely to face Piper.

'If this is possible, which I can't rule out, nothing of it showed while we were looking into what happened to Tommy Walters in Blackmarch, and that was connected to the Mansel-Joneses.'

'Only peripherally. Besides, he wasn't exactly ready to accept that you were innocent, kept pointing out that the CPS would happily have taken the evidence we had and prosecuted you. And Teddington.'

'He was still angry at me for what I di-'

Piper raised his hand. 'Yeah, that's what I kept telling myself. Carlisle hasn't done anything I can pin on him, he just didn't move things forward in the way I would have liked. The way you would have done in his position.'

'We were always very different in how we operated. But the point is, if Carlisle was working for Mansel-Jones, he'd have stopped us getting to the bottom of what was really happening.'

'Not necessarily. Peter Jones is a distant cousin, who was actively disassociating himself from the Mansel-Joneses, he couldn't run for office and be seen cosying up to them.'

'Didn't hurt Sheldrake any.'

Police and Crime Commissioner Paula Sheldrake had been photographed with Rhys Mansel-Jones, even on the front pages of the *Chronicle*. 'That's only a public face as far as I can tell. Mansel-Jones does still qualify as a legitimate businessman - even if it is just a front.' Piper sighed. At least with Charlie he could be honest. 'Thing is, we were gathering enough dirt to stop Peter Jones eventually anyway, Carlisle would have seen that, and there's no reason why Mansel-Jones wouldn't have decided to cut the man loose. Jones would have been useful in office, but without it, he was just another worthless relative. Besides, that's not actually the part of the Tommy Walters' murder investigation that's causing problems at the station.'

'Then what is?'

'I am. When I arrested Teddington and you on suspicion of murder, I knew it was a set up. And you know that had anything had to go further,

I'd made sure you both got off on technicalities anyway because the arrests weren't properly enacted.'

'I thought Broughton sanctioned that.'

'Sort of. Verbally, but you know what things were like when you were there - any excuse to put someone on a disciplinary, get rid of officers to make the cuts, well not much has changed. Besides, Broughton has his own career to worry about, he's not about to throw himself under the bus for me. The fact that I put you both in the same cell for the night has got more than him fired up. I keep expecting the Professional Standards Department to come knocking with a yellow slip.'

'Well I hope they don't. You deserve better than that. Just so you know, I'm not about to forget what you did for us. I'm not sure how Ari would have coped locked up on her own.'

'She's a strong woman,' Piper assured him. 'She'd have coped.'

'Probably, but like the rest of us, it's hard coating, vulnerable on the inside. She is more resilient then most though. I'm glad I was there for her.'

'And now?' He looked for signs of joy but didn't see much in the other man's face. 'Are you there for her now?'

'Always will be, but it's a tricky situation and I don't want to screw it up. So I'm taking it slow.'

'Understandable.'

'Frustrating.'

Piper smiled. 'Oh, there's nothing better than a good woman to drive a man mad. But we're veering off topic again. Do you recall Covington being at the briefing?'

Charlie frowned, Piper waited while the other man searched his memory. 'Covington wasn't on the raid.'

'No, but do you remember him being at the briefing?' It was an idea that had been bugging Piper ever since it inveigled itself into his head earlier that day. He held his silence while Charlie considered the point.

'I don't think he was there.' Uncertainty marked the tone. 'There are a few faces that were there who are blurry to be me now, so I can't be absolutely sure, but no, I don't think he was there. Why?'

Piper shook his head.

'Don't give me that, you must have a reason for asking.'

He did. Covington's involvement, all be it peripheral with several of the cases he was looking into. It was peripheral, but a lot less peripheral than Carlisle's. DS Covington was actually a very good sergeant, he administered an incident room as well as any, and that was the place where information could really be controlled. Add in all the years of service, the resentful attitude and just how many people he knew, how much he knew about them, then he was a distinct person of interest. 'Yes, I have my reasons, but I don't want to share or prejudice. Okay, let's say that someone in the department is a traitor, who would you think of?'

Charlie puffed out a breath. 'That's unpleasant enough as a concept, not sure I want to actually name names.'

Piper look at his hard. He wasn't going to let this go.

'Okay, then I'm not sure I would pick Covington. His personality often separates him from the crowd, Carlisle has the same issue to a lesser extent. I'd probably start looking at someone who fit in with everyone.' He named a couple of individuals, but even before he got the last name out, he was shaking his head. 'No, that just feels mean.' Again, he scrapped his hair back. 'Nah, sorry, but I can't see it.'

'Can't or won't?'

'Both.'

That was a fair enough answer to what had been an unfair question. 'Going back to the night of the official raid, had Phillip Mansel-Jones been tipped off or not?'

'Yeah, he was waiting.' Charlie's features reflected his certainly. 'Definitely. There was no surprise when he answered the door. Not much delay either and that's a big house. If I had to swear on it, that's what I'd say, but I can't give you any actual proof.'

'The night of your unofficial visit. Where did you find the girl?'

'Back bedroom, second from the right as you look at the front of the house, it was the one that connects to the master suite.'

'Where was she?'

Charlie's eyes drifted down. His thumbnail pressed into the grain of the aging wood on which they were sitting. Whatever he was remembering, it wasn't good. 'She was in the bed.' He swallowed. 'I didn't notice at first, was about to give up and try another room, but something drew my attention back to the bed. Don't ask me what, because I don't know. I don't know if it was a sound or a movement, or just instinct, but as I looked at that bed, I knew something was wrong, so I picked up the duvet. It was a thick thing, but lightweight, and there in the middle of the bed was this tiny little girl. Half starved, she looked. She was just lying there, staring at me. Terrified, but too scared to scream or move. Even when I picked her up, she didn't make a sound. The only time she did whimper was when I told her I was going to get her back to her parents.'

The idea that any child, let alone one so young, could be put in a position made Piper sick. There was also that smell, the smell that had hit him as Charlie appeared over the wall, that was stronger on the girl when he carried her away. 'At what point did she pee?'

'At the back door. I was about to run across the lawn to the back wall to get away, the lights came on and we both heard Phillip Mansel-Jones' voice. She instantly started shaking and she wet herself with fear.'

'All over you.'

He shrugged. 'Small price. A moment later I ran across the grass. Got to the wall. Couldn't have been more relieved when I saw you on the other side, so you could take her home.'

Piper considered it. There was a question nagging in his head that had bothered him for years. It was time to ask it. 'What if I hadn't been there?'

Now Charlie looked up, his face marked with confusion. 'But you were.'

'What if I hadn't been? What if you had grabbed the girl and just left. Just got her to safety and never gone back in. Never shot Mansel-Jones?'

He shrugged. 'Then I would probably have found some other way of screwing my life up to stop that bastard. What happened, happened. And it happened by my choice, not your fault. We can't rewrite history on what-ifs. We shouldn't even try. The guilt is mine, and mine alone.'

He should have guessed Charlie would view it that way, and it did help, but it didn't remove the question, just gave him a better reason to ignore that question. The field had bunches of kids around; girls sitting in circles on the grass, fair too many phones on display; boys played football – no wait a couple of girls were in that mix too; there were three dogwalkers; several parents with children of all age; a Frisbee thrower; joggers coming and going; two fishermen down on the bank. And a big gap in the privet fence that let people flow in and out from the street. No one was really watching anyone that closely. How easy would it be to take someone from here and not be seen?

'Piper?'

He looked back to Charlie.

'You drifted away. What's going on?'

The breath wanted out more than he wanted to sigh. 'Another kid went missing.' Charlie made a sound of disgust. 'From here, again, a boy named Stephen Pearson. He even matches the general description of Terrence Whittaker.'

'When?'

'Nearly a month ago.'

'Jesus.'

Piper had to agree. 'I was just thinking that no one here's really watching. Anyone could get away with anything as long as the kid didn't protest, and not necessarily then. I mean I got some weird looks when I walked in on my own, but no one tried to stop or question my right to be here.'

'They could watch.' Charlie nodded towards the other side of the park.

Piper looked but saw no one of any note. 'Who?'

'The residents.'

Behind the high hedge were the back of a row of seventies semi-detached houses. Bodine Street. The big plate windows in the upper bedrooms looked black in the daylight now, and Charlie might have a point, standing in there, one might have a good view over the park and be able to watch the kids playing. He hadn't thought of that. Had Small? He'd have to have a word.

'Ari said that when she went to see you, Carlisle popped in. Said that you instantly hid a notebook.'

Typical Charlie, give him just enough time to formulate an idea, then twist him onto something else. That was why he'd been so good in interviews, always knew with to change direction. He smiled. 'Smart woman, that one. Observant. Good instincts. Never liked Carlisle and she tore a strip off Covington this afternoon too.'

'She did?'

Piper nodded. 'He was complaining about her; about how rude she was. I had to point out that maybe he shouldn't have started from a point of being rude to her.'

Turning his head, Piper looked over at Charlie. 'Ask her about what happened when Terry went missing. She's only just started talking about it now, which means she's going to have to deal with something she's been burying for twenty years. I doubt she'll talk about it to her mother and you're the next best candidate.'

'You avoided my question.'

'Yes, I did.'

'She said you said she wouldn't want to know.'

'She wouldn't.'

'I do.'

Piper looked away. 'It's not pleasant. But then things in our - *my* job rarely are.' Facing Charlie again, he considered the man. 'What's in there will disgust and upset you. It's the kind of evidence we wanted six years ago, stuff that actually could have stopped Mansel-Jones in his tracks. It explains a lot.'

Charlie was frowning again. 'Will? You said will, not would.'

Elbows on knees, Piper leaned forward and dropped his face into his hands.

'Matt?'

Tipping his head up for a moment Piper looked at Charlie, his hands still over his face. Could he do this?

'I'm good at my job.'

Frowning, Charlie nodded. 'You are. That's one of the things I've always admired about you.'

'I've never broken the rules before.' His mouth was dry, had to swallow the lump that had appeared in his throat. 'Bent a few. Stretched them as far as I had to. But I've never actually broken them before.'

'Don't do what you're not comfortable with.'

Not comfortable? Not comfortable was going to the station every day and feeling he couldn't trust the people around him. But he still trusted Charlie.

Piper picked the notebook out of his pocket and passed it across. 'Anyone finds out I gave this to you, I lose my job.'

Chapter 17

'Say something.'

Ariadne sat and stared at Nigel Turner. She'd known him for five years and considered him a friend, even though for the last eight months he'd also been her boss: Governor Turner of HMP Blackmarsh. She blinked. 'Training?'

The big man shifted, uncomfortable with the situation, rather than his seat in Ariadne's sitting room.

She ran the possibility through her mind. Would it work? Go back to working IT? Training? It wasn't her preference, but she couldn't go back to working the wing for a few months, possibly ever, with the way her leg was, SSP was a pittance, and not what she'd want to live on. And of course, her qualifications all fit with the job being offered. 'Train others as the Prism system gets rolled out?' It was the new prison records system that had been trialled at Blackmarch. She'd been trained in its use and she's got on okay with the trainer, who, if she took the position, would become her line manager. It would mean travelling during the week once the roll out started, but she wouldn't be gone for a whole week at a time and maybe they could look at pulling staff more locally for training rather than her having to go remote all the time. She'd have to look into that. 'Ok, sounds like a reasonable prospect. I guess that means you need me to resign.'

'Actually, no. I've also spoken to HR and we can put you on a twelve-month secondment at the end of your full pay sick leave or immediately if you feel ready after talking to Tony. While on secondment, the service will add a secondment supplement to your pay, and you'd be able to claim expenses for travel and such. Then at the end of the year, we can see how you are physically, what the situation is with the prisoners and how you want to go forward with your career.'

The prisoners. Those bastards who'd held her and others at gun point all for the sake of money they didn't get away with. They were on remand in Blackmarch, which meant that as their victim and witness for the prosecution, she wouldn't be allowed to work there during their incarceration. If she were still fully able bodied, she could transfer to another prison, but that would mean moving and she knew Mum wasn't in a fit state to do that with all that was going on. No, the secondment was not only the only option, it was a good one too.

Nodding Ariadne offered Turner a smile. 'Okay, I can see you really went into bat for me and came up with a workable plan.' The truth was, he hadn't had to do any of it. He could have just written her off and let her get on with life unemployed. Thankfully he was a better boss and friend than that. 'Thank you.'

'Glad you like it.' He returned her smile.

'I appreciate it too.' And in the same spirit, she owed him some honesty in return. 'There's something you're not going to appreciate though.'

His smile became a frown. 'Oh aye, what's that then?'

'Well, you know my mother decided to take in another lodger?'

'Yeah, Sanchez said she had and it's working out fine, though he hadn't met the lodger before he went on holiday.'

'No, and I'm dreading what will happen when he does.'

'You don't like the lodger?'

'Oh, I more than like him.'

Turner laughed, 'And you're worried Sanchez will be jealous?'

'I'm worried he'll be furious. Not entirely sure how you're going to take it either.'

'Okay.' It was carefully said. 'Now I'm worried. Who is the lodger?'

She opened her mouth but the name refused to go. When forced, then it came out in something of a rush. 'Lucas Charles Bell.'

Everything stopped. Ariadne didn't dare breathe, nor even blink. Turner stared at her.

'You and he are… together?'

'No. Yes. Sort of,' Ari admitted. 'Taking it slow.'

'So slow you're living together?'

'No, he's lodging here. Made all the arrangements while I was laid up. In fairness, he wasn't to know that a Mrs Whitaker would be anything to do with me.'

'I guess. Did any of this go on while he was under our care?'

'No.'

'Look, this is off the record. It's not like I don't know some of the things we don't talk about go on.'

She smiled. 'I appreciate that, Guv, but nothing happened. Not even while we were together after his son's funeral. Well there was a kiss or two, but that's all. We didn't... still haven't. So no, no physical stuff. But obviously we met in Whitewalk, so that must be where the attraction started, where the emotions grew. But I never stepped over the line or broke professional boundaries.'

'Good. And are you happy with him?'

Was she? Judging by the smile that spread over her face just thinking about him... 'Yes.'

'Good. He's a good kind of bloke.'

That surprised her. 'For a murderer?'

'For a man who got pushed to the limit. I knew the guy he killed. Unfortunately. And trust me, the world's a better place without him. No, I think Bell's an okay sort. If you're happy with him, I'm happy.'

'Thank you.'

'Well, I guess that's it then,' Turner said. 'I'll get Tony to call you and we'll sort the rest out from there.'

'Great. Don't tell Enzo about Charlie before I can though, please.'

'I won't tell anyone.'

'Thanks.'

They both shifted to stand.

'Don't get up,' Turner instructed. 'I'll see myself out.'

He leaned down to kiss her cheek. 'You take good care of yourself. Make sure he takes care of you too.'

She thanked him and stayed put. She could already hear the key in the door so he'd pass her mother and that was one conversation she didn't want to get caught in.

* * *

The notebook added little weight to the rucksack, but Charlie could feel it weighing on him even as he slowed the jog and got to the front door. Slipping the sack off his back, he found the key. The door opened a lot easier now he had planed down the sticking side. He automatically stepped into the house and stopped short, coming face to face with Senior Pri - no - Prison *Governor* Turner. Somehow, Turner didn't look as surprised as Charlie felt to see him.

The older man nodded once. 'Bell.'

'Turner.' Unsure what else to do, Charlie stepped aside to let Turner leave.

One step forward and Turner stopped, perpendicular to Charlie. He turned only his head, and the fact that he had to look up several inches didn't lessen the steel in his eyes.

'You hurt her and I'll beat you into next week.'

Then he stepped away.

'Turner?' Charlie spoke softly as Turner had. Turner stopped, but didn't look around. 'I don't doubt you, but I won't hurt her either.'

The man nodded and left.

After closing the door, Charlie turned to see Ariadne in the doorway to the lounge.

'Do I want to know?'

As ever, Charlie couldn't stop himself from smiling when he saw her, but he just shook his head as he stepped up to kiss her and say hello.

'Hello.' She smiled back. 'Now go shower.'

Since he could taste the salt of his own sweat, he turned.

'Dinner'll be ready in about twenty minutes.'

Her voice followed him up the stairs as he heard the front door open. He paused to say hello to Mrs W and felt an overwhelming flood of homeliness. For a second it weakened his knees, but he forced himself to keep stepping up. He'd not had a home or a sense of belonging in so long, he wasn't sure how to deal with it. The idea that he was in the right place was so new he didn't know what to do with it even as he scrubbed the dirt of the day away.

Could he do this? Manual work all day, come home to a family at night? Just be normal?

He smiled as he towelled himself dry. Ariadne would be waiting for him. *Yeah, I can do this.*

Dry and dressed, he grabbed his pack, wanting to get his clothes hung up so the creases would fall out. What fell out was the notebook.

Frozen, he stared at it. Was it a trap?

Turning away, he found the hangers he'd taken the shirt and trousers off that morning and hung them back up. As the second hanger came to rest, his eyes rested on the watch he'd been sent.

Oh yeah, I fucked up big time.

* * *

'Do you want another beer?'

85

Piper turned his head to Sheila and tried to work out what she'd asked. Then he glanced at the pint glass balanced on the arm of the chair. He'd only taken a sip. 'Got one.'

'Yeah, it's the one you've had for the last hour while you've been not-watching this documentary.'

'What makes you think I wasn't watching?'

'Because it's about fictional detectives and you haven't complained once about the lack of proper procedures.'

He sighed. 'What would you say if a fictional detective was pointed in the direction of three cold cases and within days the person who pointed him that way had a new front door?'

'Depends.' She shrugged. 'Does he also have any extraneous bruising and when did it appear?'

Now Piper frowned. 'What difference does that make?'

'It would indicate whether the pointing was done voluntarily or under duress. If he was bruised before, that's an incentive and the names were given under duress. Therefore, the cases are a distraction. If there's no bruising and the door was from money paid as a reward, the cases are just a distraction. If the bruising was post-pointing, that was a punishment and the cases could well be the key to something important that the real villain doesn't want you knowing about.'

Logical reasoning. It was one of the many things he loved about Sheila. And it was likely that last; Wilson had been in good health when he'd visited the first time.

'Of course, new front doors, especially the security types, tend to be made to order and fittings have to be booked weeks in advance, so it could just be a home improvement coincidence.'

Piper couldn't help the chuckle as he leaned over and kissed his wife.

* * *

Charlie was pretty sure he'd fucked up again as he sat in his room reading the notebook and wishing he hadn't. The dread of what he'd find in its covers had dragged him down over dinner, and he'd quickly made his apologies, well aware that Ari and her mother were looking at him oddly. What he read was worse than he'd expected. He felt sick.

'Charlie?'

Only when she popped her head around the door and called his name did Charlie register that there had been a light knock at his bedroom door. Sitting on the sofa in the middle of the room, back to the foot of the double bed, he just put the book aside and held out his arms to her. The frown suggested worry, but she came straight to him anyway, sitting sideways on his lap, arms around his shoulders as he pulled her tight against him.

'What's wrong?'

'Nothing.' He smiled, but it wasn't a real smile and it earned him a light slap on the back of the head.

'Do you think I'm an idiot?'

He couldn't completely focus on her eyes, being long-sighted, but he saw enough. 'Of course not.'

'Good. So what's in that notebook really isn't something I want to know then?'

This time the smile was more genuine, if bitter. 'No. Wishing I didn't know it either. And it's all made worse by knowing that if I'd had that book six years ago, I would have had Mansel-Jones banged to rights.' The implications that had on how his life would have turned out churned his stomach. The way she squeezed him, placed a quick kiss on his cheek then really hugged herself to him suggested she was thinking similar things. He held her tight and concentrated on the feel of her, how good that was.

'I told Turner about us when he came over.'

'I guessed.'

'He said you were a good sort of bloke.'

A small huff of a laugh escaped Charlie as he stroked her hair. It was so soft and smelt of apples. In a soft voice, she told him what had happened with Turner, it was like she understood that he needed something normal, yet she wasn't expecting him to respond.

'Think I'm getting paranoid as well.'

'Why?'

'I went down to the shops earlier and it felt like I was being watched the whole way.'

'Probably because you know the area so well you feel out of place when you have to use a crutch for longer walks.'

'Yeah,' she laughed lightly. 'That's probably it. Well that and the fact that the walk just takes so much longer now.'

'That will improve with time. You'll be fine once you can manage completely without the crutch.'

'Yeah.'

She didn't sound entirely convinced, as she rested her head on his shoulder, apparently having run out of things to say. The day was running out of light too.

Pretty soon she would head for her own bedroom.

'I don't want to spend another night without you.'

Her head came up and she looked at him, clear and direct. 'Then don't.'

* * *

Charlie lay back and looked up through the skylight. There was a curtain, but he never closed it. After so long of not seeing sky, he welcomed the sight. Night had fallen, but the window allowed a little light to fall over the bed and though he was tired after their exertions, he was too happy to sleep. The way Ari was breathing as she lay with her head on his shoulder, he knew she was awake too. Her fingers idly circled his navel; it was a little ticklish but he couldn't complain.

'What you thinking about?'

'Nothing much. Ouch!' He couldn't believe she'd grabbed a handful of his chest hair and pulled. 'What was that for?'

'Prevarication.' Now she shifted up to lean on her elbow and looked down at him. 'I know enough to know there are plenty of times when men really are thinking of nothing, especially after sex. But I also know you well enough to know that this ain't one of those times. So... what are you thinking about?'

'I was thinking how different tonight is from all the other nights before.'

She frowned. 'If you're going to say something sickening like because it was with me –'

'No.' He laughed. 'Well, yes, there is some of that, but mostly, I've never had a woman in my own bed before.'

She frowned as she looked at him. 'Okay, I get that for the last four or five years but what did you do before that?'

He shrugged. 'Went to hotels or their place.'

'Why?'

'Didn't want anyone intruding in my life that way.'

'What changed your mind? Assuming you *have* changed your mind.'

Reaching up, he pushed a strand of her hair behind her ear. 'Yes, I've changed my mind, and you are why.' He pushed up to kiss her then lay straight back down. 'That a problem?'

'Nope.'

'Hey, where you going?' he asked as she turned away and got out of bed.

'Loo.' She threw the word over her shoulder as she headed to the other end of the room. 'I'll be back.'

Charlie lay back. *Steady job. Nice home. Normal life? Yeah.* He smiled. *I can do this.*

The moon had disappeared behind a bank of cloud and the room was darker now. He heard Ari return before he saw her and then it was only as a shadow within the shadows. The thump was loud, followed by some solid swearing and another lighter thump.

'You okay?'

'Stubbed my toe.' She sounded in pain.

He reached over and switched the light on. He turned back to find her grabbing the throw their earlier activity had tossed on the floor. She covered herself with it, which made no sense given that they'd just spent over an hour exploring one another's bodies.

'Ari, what's wrong?'

'I don't want you seeing my scars.'

'Like I care about those.' He moved to sit up. When he looked back she was white as a sheet, eyes wide, features showing nothing but shock.

'Ari? Ari, what is it?'

When she couldn't answer, he shifted across the bed, bounding up, guiding her to sit on the edge of the bed. She was trembling from more than just the cold, the whole time her eyes were fixed on one point. A quick check past her showed him the second thud must have been Hall's notebook. As it fell it had spewed forth the various loose pages and bits that had been in it. Including a photograph, and it was the photograph she was fixed on.

'What is it?'

She pointed. He reached over and picked the picture up. Of the four men in the skewed picture she indicated the middle out of the three on the right-hand side.

'He was one.'

'One of what?'

She closed her eyes. When she opened them she wouldn't look at him or the picture. Then she told him what had happened the last time she saw Terry. This had to be what Piper was talking about. As she spoke, he pulled her to him, holding her, supporting her. As she came to the end, he looked at the picture over her shoulder. The man she had pointed to was

Dion Searlotti, general creep and sex offender. Charlie's big worry was the man on the left.

Phillip Mansel-Jones.

Chapter 18

Piper sat behind his desk hating Monday mornings and almost wished he was still a DI, even a DS. *Anything not to be stuck behind a desk.* The amount of admin on everyone was high, but now he felt paperwork was all he was getting to do. Rereading statement after statement wasn't helping. Even though they were different cases, the recurrence of statements from Ariadne Teddington bothered him. The woman seemed to attract *colour. Which probably explains her and Charlie.*

The thought was unkind and Piper mentally slapped himself, sat straight and concentrated on her additional report. If they could identify who those two blokes were, they might have a way in.

His thoughts were interrupted by a knock at the open office door. A quick eye shift showed him Siddig. As a plain clothes officer she might as well still be in uniform; white blouse, black trousers and black combat boots. There was probably a black jacket on the coat stand in the open office. There was another anonymous file in her hand.

'Come in and close the door.'

The young woman did, but only sat when Piper actively indicated the chair.

'How's it going with the ID photos?'

'Not easy. Records tend not to keep photos that old, they've kind of been archived from the archive. I've got a few possibles though.' She passed over the file.

Piper flipped through them. He recognised a couple, known associates of Phillip Mansel-Jones, one who still worked for Rhys. They were as good a guess as any.

'While I was in there, I looked into those other cases, found two of the three. One's from the year before Terrence Whitaker disappeared, and one two months after. Both boys, both match the same general description of Terry. Scott Cassidy and Vince Talbot.'

Piper nodded and looked up at her. 'Let me see the files.'

Two more buff files were handed over. Worryingly thin buff files. Piper put them on his desk. Siddig didn't look as comfortable as usual. He couldn't put his finger of why, just a vibe she was giving off. 'What is it, Siddig?'

'Sir, I'm more worried about some of the other stuff I found.'

'Such as?'

She shifted in the seat and pulled a few folded sheets from her back pocket, placed them on his desk. Regulation notebook size. His handwriting, neater all those years ago than now. The name that jumped out was, not surprisingly, Phillip Mansel-Jones. He read the first page and turned to the last. He remembered the incident. He also remembered the notes went on for more pages than this and the last couple didn't make him look like a completely biased arsehole.

'Where did you find these?'

'In the wrong place.'

Even when she gave a fuller answer, it didn't make sense to Piper.

'Did you find the rest of the notebook?'

'No, sir.'

'Have you reported this to anyone else?'

'No, sir.'

Of course he was tempted to just bin the pages. *Another form of cover up.* 'How do you feel about talking to the super?'

'Broughton?' Unbelievably, she paled. 'Okay I guess, he's been good to me of late.'

'Hmm.' Piper pushed the loose sheets to her again. 'Take these to him and let him decide what he wants you to do.'

'What do I tell him?'

'The truth.' His phone started ringing. 'Surprisingly enough, it really is the best defence. When you're done with Broughton, look for the Smith connection.' It was the one name Wilson had given him that she hadn't come up with. He answered the phone as Siddig stood and took what she'd brought off his desk.

'Siddig.' He stopped her at the door. 'Put her in an interview room, I'll be right down.' Now he stood. 'I'm going to need that file.'

* * *

'So I'm not allowed in your office today?'

Teddington smiled, and there was a laugh in her tone as Piper pushed open the door of Interview Room 2, but the tone was brittle and so much of her seemed fragile. At least she was dressed more like herself, in a long flowing shirt and though she wasn't in a corset yet, the blouse was fitted and feminine without fuss. She was definitely on the road to recovery.

'Sorry.' He put both files on the table and sat opposite Teddington. 'I figured we wouldn't be interrupted here. Even Carlisle wouldn't barge into an interview room.'

'Maybe he's just clinging on while he can.'

'That's possible.' Piper looked at the files in front of him and wished that was all there was to it.

'But you don't think so.'

The insight was uncomfortable.

'I guess that's something you can't talk to me about.' She sighed. 'Still, I came here to talk to you about the men that… you know. When… you know. Oh God.'

Her voice was muffled when she put her head in her hands, but more so by the obvious pain she had in the knowledge.

'There's no need to worry, Ariadne, I understand this isn't easy for you. But we've got plenty of time to sort through this.'

'Yeah.' She still didn't move. 'Because I'm doing this way too late.' She huffed and sat up. 'Sorry. I just don't know where to start.'

He offered a small smile, and flipped open the file Siddig had put together. 'This might help.'

Her eyes switched to the file, he was about to place the photos out –

'Not as much as this will.'

A new photo was placed in front of him. Actually, it was an old photo, battered, folded, edges frayed. It was the photo from Hall's notebook. A handkerchief wrapped bundle followed it, Teddington flicked open the cotton. Hall's notebook.

'If anyone asks, I'll say you showed me the picture and I have no idea where it came from.'

She was so the right woman for Charlie.

She pointed to the man in the middle of the group. 'He was one of the two.'

'You're absolutely sure?'

'Hundred percent.'

Piper picked up the photo and looked at it. 'How did you get this?'

'Luke had put the notebook on the arm of the sofa. It fell off, that fell out and I saw it.'

Now he looked up at her. 'Luke?'

'Yeah.' She shrugged. 'He wants to make a new start, use his real name. I keep having to remind myself not to call him Charlie, but it's what he wants and I'm okay with that.'

'Have you told him that you love him yet?'

'God no, I don't want to frighten him off!'

Piper had to laugh at that. 'Probably a wise move.' He held the photo up for a second. 'Has he told you anything about this picture?'

'No. Should he have?'

'He shouldn't have even let you see it.' He turned to the file again. Carefully, he placed out the eight photographs. 'Do you recognise any of these men?'

Sitting straight, she looked carefully at each of the faces. Frowning, she picked one up, squinting at the image. 'Is this a very young looking Hodson?'

'Yep. Was he...?'

'No, or else I'd have recognised him when I booked him in.'

'But you didn't?'

'No, I just recognised him now from Whitewalk.'

Whitewalk. The native's name for HMP Blackmarch. Her recognition would mean they could exclude any suspect who had spent any significant time in that facility in the last five years.

'What's the other file?'

Piper looked at the file. 'Terry's missing person's case.'

'Got a photo of him in there?'

He nodded.

'May I?'

Though it was well within her reach, she held out her hand, respecting the sensitivity of the material.

Piper opened it carefully, removed the photo, an 8' x 10' colour school photo. It was the same one he'd seen in Mrs Whittaker's living room.

Ariadne took the photo in both hands, focused on the old image. 'That was his rebellion, you know. That pendant.'

Piper knew from looking at the incident board that the boy wore a pendant over the top of his school tie.

'School rules only allowed studs in the ear and necklaces of religious significance. Crosses, crucifixes, St Christophers. But Terry wore a St Jude. It was right there in front of them, breaking the rules.' Though she smiled, her voice cracked a little and she stopped, studying the picture.

Piper quietly gave her all the time she needed.

'I know the probability of Terry being alive is practically zero. But I hate to think of him being dead. I imagine what he'd be like now. I reckon he'd be tall, maybe even six foot like Dad. I think of him married and having kids. Being happy.'

She swallowed, blinking away tears, stroking the image as if it really were her brother.

'Do you have brothers or sisters, Piper?'

Family wasn't something he talked about in work. Especially not with civilians caught up in cases. Only Teddington was more than that. If for no more reason than as she and Charlie – he'd never get used to *Luke* now – were a couple, Ari would segue into becoming an actual friend.

'I have two sisters. One older, one younger.'

'Does your older sister still treat you like you're the kid brother?'

Thinking about how Tracy treated him, Piper had to smile. 'It's something she reminds me of constantly.'

Eyes still on the photo, Ariadne was smiling now. 'And every time she reminds you, she's telling you she loves you. Bet you anything you like she actually really admires you, looks up to you.' She swallowed and unsuccessfully blinked tears away. 'Probably worries like hell about you.' Passing him back the picture, she wiped her eyes. 'Sorry, tend to get a bit maudlin when I think about Terry.'

Offering a weak smile, he slipped the photo back into the folder. 'Don't apologise, it's natural.'

'Even after twenty years?'

'Yes. Especially where there's been no resolution. And that's something I should apologise for.'

'You weren't on the original case, but at least you're on it now.' She looked away, seemed to steel herself. When she looked back, she was clearly in search of the truth. 'If I'd come forward and identified that guy then, would it have saved Terry? Would it have saved Charlie having to kill that man?'

Probably. And apparently she couldn't get used to calling him *Luke* either. 'You can't allow yourself to think like that.'

His words wouldn't stop her. She wiped the heavy tears that fell from her eyes. He couldn't wipe away her guilt, because in this case, there probably was some. It was unlikely she could have saved Terry, but she might have stopped Phillip Mansel-Jones. She took a deep breath and reached for calm, though he could still hear the tension in her voice.

'Is there something else, Ariadne?'

She nodded. 'I was thinking about what Carlisle said the other day, about items missing after that bank raid.'

Now Piper was interested. 'What about it?'

'Well in my defence, I actually *was* concussed so a lot of what happened is fuzzy, but after what he said, I vaguely – and I do mean vaguely – remember that Mr White – I think you called him Lincoln?'

Piper nodded, made an affirmative noise.

'Well he did leave the room for a while. Don't think he was very long, but he went out carrying something, came back empty-handed.'

'Do you know what he took?'

She shook her head slowly. 'Not really. I think I remember it was flat and red, foolscap sort of size, so I'd guess either some kind of ledger or possibly a box-file.' She sighed and slumped back. 'Or it could just be my imagination. She shrugged. 'I'm sorry, I just really don't know for sure.'

'That's okay.' And it was, but it also needed to be investigated. He concentrated on her, judged her willingness to help. 'Do you remember any other details?'

As she had when Carlisle had asked her about the incident, she unfocused on the here and now to try to get into the memory, and she gave him vague directional pointers.

Chapter 19

Piper was just finishing a text when he stepped into the open office of the CID. The four officers were in various stages of fatigue; DC Penn seemed to have been on shift forever and needed props to keep his eyes open; DC Long was yawning, he had a four month-old daughter, and reported that he hadn't had a full night's sleep since she came home; DS Covington was worn down after too many years on the Force and his failure to get above DS despite a solid conviction that he was DCS material; and then there was Siddig. She was the only one looking even vaguely awake. Bored, but awake. The joy of paperwork again.

Stepping up to Siddig's desk, he barely had time to open his mouth when Covington did.

'Showing favouritism already?'

Piper turned to the older man. 'She's the closest to the door, but a volunteer is worth ten pressed men, so you can have the task instead. Get in touch with Northumbrian Police, see if you can get them to request a DNA sample from Mrs Hall or Gareth Hall. I'd like to check against the DNA for the bones found in Joskins Field.'

Covington's face grew tighter as Piper spoke. Piper had the excuse of his mobile beeping to look away and turn.

'Oh, and I want a response within the hour,' he threw over his shoulder, reading his text messages as he went down the corridor.

From Hayley, his younger sister. *Love you too. You okay?*

Then one from Tracy; *Oh, you're a such a sop, kid brother.*

* * *

The frustrating thing about working missing persons when the missing person was a kid was the knowledge of the fragility of childhood. Not just the fragility of a child's body under attack, but the fragility of childhood itself. She's found too many and brought them back to the fold with a haunted look in their eyes, that sense that they'd seen a part of life they just weren't ready for.

Small wasn't ready for Piper to just step out of his incident room without looking and straight into her. The phone he'd been looking at beeped even as it went skidding across the floor.

'Ahh, the curse of modern life.' She smiled as he apologised and retrieved his phone. 'Too engrossed in your phone to look where you were going. Good thing you were walking across a corridor and not a road.'

Was that a blush on the older man's face?

'Worst thing is, last night, I had to tell my boy off for doing the exact same thing but in the face of an oncoming car.'

She smiled at the scene. 'Scared a neighbour, did he?'

'Scared me! I'm the one he stepped in front of...'

Piper's voice trailed off as he read the text, it brought a small smile to his lips.

'Good news?'

'My sister, calling me a sop.'

That didn't seem like something to smile about, but Piper took on a serious look and moved her to the side of the corridor, out of the way anyone passing.

'I've been thinking about Woodlands Walk Park, its rather overlooked by Bodine Street, have you done a house to house up there?'

'Of course, didn't really turn much up. Well, anything in fact.'

Piper's eye slid away as he mulled that fact over. Had she missed something?

'Piper?'

'Come with me.'

Too curious to do anything else, she followed him into the incident room. There were other bodies in the room who showed a certain interest, but were largely getting on with their jobs. The smell of cold coffee and warm bodies wasn't overly appealing but it was hardly unusual either. He led her up to a board covering the cold cases he was working on.

'This was Terry Whittaker.'

He pointed to a young face, smiling in school uniform. The air froze in her lungs. He was the spitting image of Stephen Pearson. She swallowed. 'How long did you say he's been missing?'

'Twenty years.'

Dead then. Only that wasn't the kind of thought one shared readily. Made her wonder what the relevance was, then she saw the writing on the board. He was also taken from Woodlands Walk Park. And Piper was asking about Bodine Street. Piper's phone beeped again. Another smile, broader and genuine.

'Your sister again?'

He nodded. 'Just reminding me I know where she lives if I need to chat.'

Seemed like an odd thing to text, but if she could see he was having a tough time of late, it was bound to affect those who actually cared about him on a personal level. 'You think there's a spotter in one of those houses?'

'It's a nice area, people do tend to live there a for a long time.'

It was certainly a thought. 'I'll double check the reports from the house to house, speak to the people who visited, see if anything comes up. Thanks.'

Turning around she left the room, the idea that they might have stumbled over a paedophile ring successful enough to have lasted twenty years without detection was sickening.

* * *

Wanting to get home quickly didn't stop Charlie making a detour to the florist on the hill. The only time he'd ever brought flowers for a woman was for his mother on her birthday and that was years ago. Today, he wanted to take something home for Ariadne, and flowers seemed appropriate. She hadn't been right since she'd seen that photograph. She was going to see Piper this morning, so today wouldn't be easy for her either. One bunch of flowers wouldn't make everything right, but they would show her that he cared.

The over-sweet smell of fresh flowers was something of an assault on his senses. The price tags were more of an assault on the wallet.

Not a dozen red roses, then.

Ten minutes later he left with a small mixed bunch and a lighter wallet. Four steps down the road, he stopped short. Frank was leaning against the Jaguar clearly waiting for him.

'Ahh, flowers, you shouldn't have.'

Charlie's mood plummeted. 'What do you want?'

'Me, Killer?' Frank played nonchalant well. 'Nah, I don't want nuffin', not me.' He had however, pressed something on his phone and it was at his ear. 'Sir, I've found him.'

Clearly he was talking to the phone and it didn't take a genius to work out who was. Frank held out the phone to Charlie. He took it with as much joy as he'd have grabbing an angry rattlesnake.

'Hello, Rhys.'

'It's *sir* to you.'

Charlie passed the phone back to Frank and stepped away. Frank took the phone, talking frantically. Charlie was several steps away when Frank grabbed the back of his shirt and stopped him.

A glare didn't work, Frank wasn't the problem. Charlie took the phone and put it to his ear.

'Rhys.'

'I admire a man with balls, but that wasn't a wise move.'

Charlie could tell he had pissed Rhys off. Which improved his mood no end. On the other hand, Rhys was unpredictable and prone to violence; he had to play the game carefully.

'What have I got to lose?'

'Whoever the flowers are for.'

'My landlady.' It wasn't exactly a lie. 'How desperate would you need to get for her to be a target? Look, Rhys, let's not waste each other's time. What do you want?'

'Thought you might be interested in a little extra work.'

Charlie swallowed. Glanced at the flowers in his hand. There was a chance he would make a life with Ari. There was a chance he could work his way into the Mansel-Jones organisation and bring it down. Settle down with Ari. Bring down Mansel-Jones. Hell, Ari had already called it; he was never going to stop. Besides, Piper managed the job and a family, Charlie could do it too.

'What's the job?' He'd hardly even hesitated.

Charlie was whistling when he walked into the house. The sitting room door was open and he could hear voices, he just didn't think about them as he went in.

'Piper!' His face fell to see the DCI there.

'Bell.' Piper was way too comfortable and Ari was sitting with her legs curled under her, looking surprisingly relaxed. They each had mugs of tea and the biscuit barrel was open on the occasional table between them.

'Am I interrupting?'

'No, we were waiting for you,' Piper said.

'Oh do come in properly,' Ari said. 'Nice flowers, they'll brighten up your room a treat.'

'They're for you.'

'Well, isn't that nice?'

Charlie looked at Mrs W as she stepped through the wide arch from the adjoining kitchen. She swapped the bunch of flowers in his hand for the mug of tea in hers.

'Here, I heard you come in. You sit down and chat; I'll put these in water.'

Since he didn't seem to have a choice, he stepped inside, decided to sit on the other end of the sofa from Ari, facing Piper.

'What's going on?'

'We've pretty much established that I really am getting paranoid, but other -'

'What do you mean?'

She rolled her eyes. 'Still got that whole being watched feeling. And I'm pretty sure I saw Carlisle twice today. Once when I went to station to give Piper that photo.'

'He hangs around more than he should,' Piper advised. 'So it wouldn't be a surprise if he was there.'

'And my thinking I saw him at the library is probably just an overactive imagination - paranoia.'

'You did say you felt like the freak on the street.' Charlie took her hand and squeezed it. 'Which you shouldn't, because you're not. You're just in recovery and you hate that you're not as physically able as you were. But you'll get there.' This time he picked up her hand and kissed it, smiling at her. Rewarded by her smile.

'Nothing worse than an understanding man.' She turned to Piper. 'So, now he's here, what did you come round for?'

Piper took a steady breath and focused on Ari. 'I'd like you to come with me to Penruddock House.'

Ari went white.

'Penruddock House?' Charlie asked.

'The place I was taken after the bank raid.'

The place she thought she was going to die, the place she was having nightmares about. He reached out and she grabbed the offer of support with an unsteady hand, gripping him tightly, drawing him down to the sofa, closer to her than he had been before.

'I was hoping being there might help you remember what you saw, might help us find those missing items.'

A weak smile was offered, but she turned back to Piper. 'Can he come with me?'

Piper frowned at Charlie; he recognised that look. The DCI was envisaging problems.

'I don't think that Piper thinks that's a good idea,' said Charlie carefully. 'And he's usually right about such things, but what's this all about?'

He watched Ari swallow. She dragged in a breath that seemed to steady her some. When she smiled it wasn't brilliant, but it was understanding. Perhaps even courageous. Much more the Ariadne he expected.

'It's okay. Piper wants me to go back to the house where I was held. To walk him through everything that happened. I may have seen more than I thought I did. You know, the concussion and all.'

Given the nightmares he now knew she was having about the incident, no wonder she wanted someone to go with her. And since Piper couldn't go alone, he'd need support from SOCOs at least, uniform too probably. Many of whom would react badly to Charlie's presence. Little wonder Piper was reluctant to agree to his being there.

'It's possible,' Charlie agreed.

'I know. But I don't want to go there. Don't want to think about that place being local. Wherever it is, I want to be able to make myself believe that it's a million miles away and not a danger closer to home.'

'Unfortunately, danger is always closer than you think.'

Ari looked to Piper. 'Why do you think I've never been back to the Woodlands Walk park? I just -' she stopped and looked at Charlie. 'Why wouldn't it be a good idea for you to come with me?'

'I'm kinda *persona non-grata* with anyone else from the station. Best I keep away.'

She squeezed his hand. 'I s'pose. And I very much need to learn to stand on my own two feet again. Physically and mentally. There's a risk if I lean on others that I'll become too dependent.'

He didn't want her pulling away now. 'You can depend on me.'

This time her smile was much warmer. 'I know I can, but I need to prove to myself I can still depend on me too. Wanting you with me was a knee-jerk reaction and rather unfair of me. Selfish too.'

'On the other hand-' Piper put in '-if you do want him with you, the rest of the station will just have to put up and shut up. Under my say so if necessary.'

'It won't be necessary.' However much he wanted to support Ari, she was right that she needed to know she could be self-reliant. That independence was a part of what he loved about her. It was part of what made him want to be better, to be worthy of her. 'When is this likely to happen?'

'Early next week probably, but that doesn't change the fact that there might be a need for me to put the order out.' Piper switched his attention back to Ari. 'I'm also going to need you to come back down to the station for an identity parade as well.'

'What for? You got the surviving gang members from the armed robbery.'

It was clear to Charlie that that wasn't the problem.

'The man you identified from that photograph. Do you think you'd know him if you saw him again today?'

Charlie watched Ari pale as she watched Piper.

'I'm not sure.' She took a deep breath. 'I mean, it's been twenty years. We've all aged. I might recognise him, but I can't guarantee it.'

'Are you willing to try?'

She swallowed. 'I'm willing to try, but you should be aware that I'm back working now. I can be flexible, but can't guarantee constant availability.'

Piper nodded. 'Fair enough.' He turned and looked to Charlie. 'What is it you have to say?'

Of course. Knowing someone didn't go away just because they did. And Piper had always been able to read him like a book. Charlie swallowed.

'Rhys Mansel-Jones offered me a job.'

'What?'

'Why?'

Charlie wasn't sure which question was more shocked or which to answer, especially since he didn't really want to answer either. Taking a steadying breath, he said 'It's a one-night, one-off sort of thing. A driving job. He'll lend me a car and a phone, tell me on the night who I'm to pick up from where and where I'm to take them.'

'What about the return journey?'

'Someone else's task.'

He could see Piper was thinking, calculating. A glance at Ari showed she was worrying.

'Do you have to do it?'

'Saying no to RMJ is not exactly good for your health.' He wasn't going to worry her with the implication it could have for her or her mother either. He was worrying enough for all three of them.

'Far as I can tell, saying yes isn't either.'

Anger coloured her cheeks as she stood, the gritted teeth a sign that she wasn't fully recovered yet. Proof positive that he couldn't risk giving Rhys Mansel-Jones a reason to come after her. Her hand scraped through her hair as she reached for the crutch she still needed, then she turned back to him.

'For God's sake, you've just got off one stretch, do you want to go in for another?'

Her frown, the sudden anger, the things he saw in her eyes, things he didn't want to define, left him mute.

She shook her head and turned away. 'Unbelievable.'

Calling after her wouldn't do any good, all he could do was look dumbly at the self-closing door.

'I thought she'd be okay with it. She said she was.'

'I think she's just starting to understand what *it* is.'

Chapter 20

It was tight, but Charlie made it to the rendezvous just in time. Frank looked him over.

'Starting sweaty's unusual.'

The outfit was as light as he could make it and he'd used a sports deodorant, so he knew he didn't smell. The redness he could feel in cheeks would soon pass once he was behind the wheel and it was never said that he had to be a uniformed chauffeur. 'Frank.'

With a shrug, Frank tossed Charlie the car keys. 'There's a phone on the dash. They'll call you with instructions. Take the phone with you when you're done. Just keep your sweaty mitts off the merch.'

Not knowing who or what the merchandise was, Charlie was pretty sure that keeping his hands off wouldn't be a problem.

At least sitting in the driver's seat allowed the lactic acid to dissipate and with it went the tic that had developed in his left thigh. The promised phone was sitting on clear view. He barely had time to breathe when the thing rang.

Here we go.

'Hello.'

'The Marriott car park. She'll come to you. Marina.'

The phone went dead. It hadn't been Rhys either. One deep breath, one slow release. The memory of Ari telling him she didn't want him doing this, but she understood why he wanted to and wouldn't stop him. It was quite the worst thing she could possibly have said to him. Now he knew he'd royally fucked up. He should never have got involved.

* * *

Ariadne went up to her room, her head aching after the all the thinking and extra hours. Having been out of the IT world for five, nearly six years, she was finding getting back into that kind of thinking was a brain-frazzler. Mum was watching some drivel on TV she just couldn't face. She had got into the habit of going up to the old attic to spend time with Charlie. Though she managed to call him Luke most of the time, she still thought to him as Charlie. And she was lonely without him. Today he was on shift, and had something to do after, so he'd be home later than usual. Tony had started her working on Prism, so she'd spent the day studying the system, but now she was really missing the distraction of being with Charlie. She could manage the stairs now, though preferred when Charlie carried her. Warmth spread through her.

Charlie. Lucas.

It really didn't matter what name he used, she was stupidly in love with -

Her phone trilled, and the warmth notched up. Charlie could be calling while on break. It didn't happen often, but it happened. Allowing herself a wide smile, she grabbed her phone and bounced down on the bed to speak with him. She flipped the case open and swiped the screen to unlock it. A message.

Not from Charlie.

Frowning now, because the number was withheld, her finger paused over the open icon. Did she want to know? Oh, it would only bug her if she didn't. Besides, when that scrote Rogers had found her personal number after getting out and started sending her pictures of his junk, she'd reported it to the police and a routine *word* turned into an arrest for attempted rape. His bound victim had been very grateful.

She hoped it wasn't another knob picture, it generally wasn't an attractive part of the anatomy. Even an erection couldn't guarantee that. Taking a deep breath, she pressed the icon. There was the inevitable buffering moment.

Her world went cold.

Not a knob. Her hand on a knob. The knob of the front door. Wearing the outfit she still had on.

She sprung up and started to pace. She wasn't paranoid. Someone really was watching her. This was bad.

Two circuits of the room and she walked out and into her mother's room. The immaculate show-house neatness gave her the shivers, so different from her own casually haphazard room. She went to the front windows and looked out. The evening was still light enough to see, the streetlights still orange, they hadn't fully warmed up yet. Perhaps only just come on at all. There were people in the street. She recognised some of the neighbours. She saw a couple she didn't know. But no one seemed to be watching her or the house. Her eyes shifted down the street. Opposite but two doors down.

That was where Enzo lived. He was her oldest and closest friend. The man who had seen her through thick and thin. Enzo Sanchez knew the best and the worst of her. But she hadn't seen him in weeks. She knew that he'd been visiting his parents in Italy, thought he was due back tomorrow. He knew everything about her, but he didn't know about Charlie. He couldn't. If he'd seen Charlie here while she was away recuperating, Mum would have known who he was. But she hadn't, which meant Enzo didn't know either.

It was one surprise that she didn't want coming to her door. She'd have to give him a call. One more look up and down the street did nothing to ease her mind but-

A light came on in Enzo's front room.

Frowning, she tried to see into the house, but of course she couldn't. Rushing - well hobbling - she went back to her room, grabbed her crutch and phone, then hobbled down to the living room. She'd timed it just right; the soap was on a break and her mum muted it to talk to her.

'You alright, love?'

'Fine,' she said, still in the door. 'When's Enzo due back?'

'Tomorrow. The nineteenth.'

Ari smiled, the tension easing. 'Today's the nineteenth. I'm going to pop over, just to see if he's back already.' She didn't mention that she'd seen the light because the only bedroom that was visible from was her mother's and somehow admitting she had been in there felt like admitting a home invasion.

'Okay love. If he is back, don't be all night.'

Standing by the front door, Ari's stomach flipped. Someone out there was watching her. Did she want to show them more of her?

No, but she did want to see her friend.

She looked down at the crutch. If someone did come for her, she couldn't exactly run far or fast. She could and would smack them one in the chops with the crutch though. She grabbed her keys from the narrow console table and put the ends between her fingers like a knuckle duster and hoped she didn't need it.

Soon she was knocking on another door.

The door was flung open.

'Ari!'

She was enveloped in warm suntanned arms and swung into the house. He kicked the door closed as her crutch clattered to the floor. Laughing, she hugged him back and he started towards his sitting room.

'You can put me down.'

'Will do eventually, you're a bit of weight.'

'Ow!' She slapped his shoulder, knowing full well that she'd lost a stone while in hospital and hadn't regained it all yet. He put her down in the very masculine-toned front room. Once free, she moved to his big leather sofa and eased herself down into the brown. He jumped to the other end, lounging back, arms stretched along the back and the arm.

'Still struggling?'

He has no idea.

'Well I did drop the crutch in your hallway. Anyway, you look great. Have a good break?'

She let him talk about the break and his holiday and she was happy to hear all the good news, but everything else was nagging in her mind.

'Go on then, what's going on?'

She took a deep breath, and tried for an unconcerned tone. 'You know how my mum took in a new lodger?'

'Yeah, some bloke called Luke.' Enzo nodded. 'I tried to check on him, but never seemed to catch him home.'

'Which is just as well, really.'

He frowned. 'Why?'

'Promise me you won't freak out.'

His arms drew in and crossed. 'Tell me.'

'His name isn't Luke, it's Lucas.' Ariadne felt every muscle clench. 'Lucas Charles Bell.'

Enzo went pale, then red with anger. He looked like he was trying to say something, and then he shot to his feet, paced around the room.

'Enzo?'

His back was to her, one hand on his forehead, the other at his waist.

'She didn't know who he was. And she got him to sign that rental contract, so we're as tied in he is.'

'Charlie Bell?'

'Yeah, look-'

'Charlie fucking Bell!'

The anger in his face was so deadly, she found herself sinking back into the sofa. Her heart was speeding, but her brain wasn't functioning. She needed a friend; had she turned him into an enemy? Teeth bared like a feral animal were slowly covered by relaxing lips as he looked down at her wide eyes.

'I'm sorry.' He stood straight and moved away again. 'I didn't mean to scare you.'

It took her a moment to respond, to get the shivers under control. 'You didn't.' She forced the whisper out. Swallowed her fear and looked back at him. 'Enzo, please. I really need a friend right now. Please. Come and sit with me and let me tell you what's going on.'

'Do I need a drink to get through this?'

'Dunno, but I bloody do.'

He disappeared into the kitchen and came back with two open bottles of beer. She accepted one and he sat carefully beside her. They sipped and she explained her reaction to finding Charlie in her house. She told Enzo about the secondment. She even told him that Piper was looking into Terry's disappearance.

'So,' he asked as she finally stopped to drink again. 'Are you and him…'

'I have no idea what we are.'

Enzo turned to her, his eyes narrowed and hard. 'Are you in love with a murderer?'

'Yes.'

His head snapped away.

'It hasn't changed how I feel about you. You're still the best friend I have. As soon as I knew you were home, I knew I had to come see you. Please don't turn your back on me. I need to tell you something that I never told you before. Something kind of terrible.'

'What's he done?'

'Nothing. It's something I did. Well, didn't do. I told Piper and he says it didn't make a difference, but I think he just says that to make me feel better about it all.' Shaking, she told him about the men who had stopped her going after Terry.

Chapter 21

'Hello!'

Ari recognised Enzo's voice as he called through.

'Has he got a key?' Charlie whispered as they stood in the kitchen making lunch.

'Yeah.' Ariadne whispered back as she fried the chicken for hot chicken salad. 'Has had for years. He checks on the place if we go away. I've got a key to his too, to reciprocate.'

Charlie wasn't entirely sure how he felt about that. 'You're just friends, right?'

He watched the smile spread across her face. 'Yes.' She looked through the arch to where Enzo now came into view. 'Hiya, you staying for lunch?'

His smile was broad until he looked at Charlie, when it dimmed and his eyes narrowed. There was a moment of calculation, then he smiled again. The smile was a little twisted. 'Sure, love to.'

As Enzo sat down and started chatting about his break with Mrs W, Charlie wondered just how far Enzo had his feet under the table. Ari reached for the currently unused breast of chicken she had planned to put in the freezer.

'You and he ever?'

As she started slicing the meat, she glanced up at Charlie, her eyes laughing at him. 'Kissed him a couple of times, but that's all.'

'When you were teenagers?'

This time her chuckle was low. 'Last year.' She looked up at him, but kept her voice low so it wouldn't carry. 'After I kissed you, actually.' She stretched up and planted a light kiss on his lips. 'Guess who I chose?'

That felt good.

'Now do you want to stop peeling that carrot while there's still some carrot left to grate?'

Ten minutes later, the four of them were sitting around the table, eating. Charlie sat opposite Enzo and it was clear that the other man was much more familiar and comfortable with the family than he was. He glanced at Ari. *She chose me.* It was the thing he had to keep hold of.

'So,' Enzo said after regaling them with too many stories of sun, sea, sand and his own family. 'You said the police have reopened Terry's case. Have they got anywhere yet?'

'Not really.'

Ari reached out and covered her mother's hand with hers.

'When I last spoke with Piper, he had done a cross-reference for the St Jude necklace Terry always wore, but nothing had come up.' Ari swallowed. 'I, erm... I'm going to work with him again, see if I can identify some men who were in the park when we were last there, but I'm not sure what will come of that.'

Charlie floundered for a way to show his support, then Enzo covered the joined hands.

'Whatever happens, you know I'm here for you. Both of you.'

'Thank you.' Mrs W pulled back and sniffed, pretending she wasn't upset.

Ari smiled at him. 'Yeah. Thanks. But I also know you have to start your shift soon.' She switched her attention to Charlie. 'As do you. Do you think you can drop me at the supermarket on your way through?'

Charlie nodded. It was a little out of the way, but it wasn't a problem.

'You've got your own car already?' Enzo asked.

'No, Ari put me on her insurance.'

'It's not like I can drive at the moment.' Ari shrugged. 'And I don't want the car just sitting there seizing up.'

* * *

Another picture.

Ariadne looked at it. Thankfully she had the supermarket trolley to lean on for support. And quickly not, as it started to roll away from her. Looking around, she moved to the side of the isle to be out of the way. The picture was of her in the fresh vegetable aisle. The first section through the doors, where her trolley was empty. It was full now, and her hand was shaking more than she wanted to admit.

Returning the phone to her shoulder bag, she pulled her quaking nerves together. If they, whoever they were, wanted to scare her, they were going to have to try a damn sight harder than that. Just because

Charlie - she would have to try harder to think of him as Luke - was working this afternoon, didn't mean she was vulnerable. She had survived being shot. She had survived being in a car crash. She had survived telling Enzo something she knew would hurt him. She could damn well survive doing the shopping and a receiving a couple of photos. Besides, it might just be a shy admirer.

Yeah right, who do you think you're kidding?

A movement caught her eye - Carlisle?

Stop it! Carlisle wasn't around every corner, it was just some other guy who her fevered imagination had made her think was Carlisle. With a huff she moved on, checked her list and headed towards the wine aisle. The additional yellow label announced a new discount. Working from home on a laptop meant she could get up at a relaxing eight rather than the old five am. *Two bottles tonight, then.*

Taking her time, telling herself everything was just normal, she paced through the last items on the list and headed for the checkout.

Stacking items on the conveyer belt, Ari felt her hairs stand on end, the weight of being watched slumping her shoulders. She looked up and around. The guy in the line three checkouts down was watching her. He winked. Blew a kiss. She shuddered.

'Do you want me to pack?'

She turned to the guy behind the counter. A spotty youth who was probably working his way through uni. There was a surprisingly large gap between where she was and the last of the items she'd placed on the conveyer.

'Please.'

For once not caring that she never liked the way other people packed the bags, she passed the for-life bags over, and went to pulling items out of the trolley.

* * *

Piper was reading through Charlie's report on the taxi job. There wasn't a lot to it. Pick up at the Marriott, drop at the Marina. No speaking in between. He concentrated on the passenger. 25 to 35 years old. Stand out feature was a small round mole on her upper right lip - very Madonna. Her hair was up in a bun, so of indeterminate length. She wore a tailored grey suit, black tights and sensible black shoes. Carried a slim black briefcase.

There were a million women like that all over the country. Could be an accountant, a lawyer or even a dominatrix.

Piper sighed. Even the fact that Charlie had seen her go down the alley from the Marina that went behind the Den of Angels didn't prove anything. Problem was that that was also the most direct route to the pedestrianised area of town; one full of boutique stores and fancy restaurants. He pushed the report aside and stood.

Time for tea.

The phone rang.

Of course.

He sat back down.

'Piper.'

'Mayhill,' the senior SOCO identified himself. 'About that Penruddock House check you mentioned. I've got a team set up for tomorrow. That okay for you?'

'That's fantastic, thanks.' He had no idea what Teddington's plans were, but he'd make sure she was there. They agreed the details. There wouldn't be as many people as he'd expected and it seemed unlikely that he'd need uniforms at all. Thanking Mayhill again, he ended the call, taking the phone up to make another. Five rings and then an answer.

'Ariadne, it's Piper.' He gave her the arrangements. 'That okay with you.'

'Erm, yeah. Sure.'

She didn't sound sure. She sounded nervous.

'Ariadne?' All that came back was the sound of... was that a car horn? 'Ariadne?'

'Sorry.' The level of background noise fell, there was a clunk. 'I'm at the supermarket.'

'You're driving again?'

'Yeah - no. I erm...'

Piper frowned over the pause.

'Just got in a taxi, hold on.'

He heard her give the driver her address.

'Sorry. Yeah, fine. I'll erm, I'll come to the station.'

'I can have you picked up -'

'No!'

That was a little too quick.

'Sorry. No. I'll erm... I'll meet you at the station.'

She clicked off the phone call. Was the prospect of visiting that house again really so frightening to her?

Locked Down

Chapter 22

Piper was pulling on his jacket as Covington slouched into the room, papers in hand. The Chief Inspector watched that the yellow globule of yoke from the bacon and egg bap the man was also carrying didn't drop on the reports, since Covington was showing no interest. Thankfully it looked like the egg had congealed, though the waft of now forbidden bacon was calling to Piper's own appetite.

'Sir.' Covington talking around the masticated remains of his last bite killed off Piper's aroma-induced hunger. 'That lot from up north said that the Halls refused to help with a DNA sample, but turns out the little bleeder Gareth got arrested seven months ago so his DNA sample is still on file anyhow.'

That was somewhat short of the one-hour response he'd asked for and had never reasonably expected to get, but several days was pushing it. For a moment Piper wondered if there was any part of Covington's life that the man didn't take a lackadaisical attitude to. 'Thanks for letting me know. Did it match with any of the Joskins Field results?'

'Dunno, sir. Haven't checked.'

He just about controlled the sigh, more because he saw Siddig in the corridor waiting for him than out of any consideration of Covington's feelings. 'Then please make that your next priority.' He looked behind Covington, effectively dismissing the man. 'Yes, Siddig, what is it?'

She waited for the older man to schlep past her before she spoke. 'Just had word from Mayhill, he and the SOCOs will be on site in about ten minutes. He wants to mark out the walkway as before where he can.' Detective Sergeant Alan Mayhill was one of the most efficient Crime Scene Managers Piper had worked with. He knew today would be as good as any for evidence collection should there be any to be collected. He nodded. 'That's great. Why don't you go ahead and shadow Mayhill, learn some of the technicalities?' Though all staff were given some training in crime scene protocols, it never hurt to learn more and if Siddig was, as she claimed, a career copper, she needed to have her eyes open to all potential career routes. She left with a nod, and a quicker, eager step.

* * *

The drive into Penruddock House seemed much longer now than the day Piper had arranged it be blocked to trap a bunch of bank robbers. He parked behind the SOCO van and switched off the engine. He wondered if the foam of the passenger seat would spring back or would be forever crushed by the vicelike grip in which Teddington had its edge.

'You okay?'

She nodded. 'It's just seeing that wall.'

The battered and fallen wall she had smashed a car into, seriously injuring herself and killing the man who had a gun to her head at the time.

'Didn't realised I'd made as much of a mess of it as I did of me.'

'You survived, and it's just a wall.'

He watched her tight, frightened features split into a wide grin. 'You have a very interesting take on life, Piper. Thank you, I need that right now.'

But she wasn't moving, and there was strain in every fibre of her being.

'Are you sure you're alright about doing this?'

Her swallow was hard. For a moment she sucked in her lips before she nodded and turned to look at him. 'Life's just gone a bit crappy at the moment. Enzo's back from holidays and it's great to see him again, but he keeps coming over, which is fine. Well, usually it's fine. But I'm pretty sure he's just doing it to piss Charlie off. And even if he's not, it's pissing Charlie off. They're basically just being arseholes to each other, I mean it's nothing overt, but it's arseholery all the same.'

Piper smiled. 'If that's your biggest worry, you're okay. It's just typical male behaviour. Each wants to be alpha dog in your eyes.'

'If only it were my biggest worry.' It seemed to be a struggle, but she released her grip and stretched out her finders. 'Right,' she said. 'If we're going to do this, let's do it before I decide running away is the only option.'

'There's no rush,' he said, though the tension thrumming off her was palpable. Running however seemed unlikely given the walking stick on the back seat. 'We'll go at your pace.'

She looked at him. There was worry in her eyes, but part of the smile remained.

'What and waste the time of all these good people?' She nodded to the team of four SOCOs and Siddig waiting for them. 'Besides, I want to get this over and done with, so there's no point in delaying.'

Teddington had the passenger door open before Piper could get to that side of the car, but she was struggling to get her leg up over the sill of the car. He considered offering to help, but suspected that was the last thing she would want. Instead, he moved to retrieve the walking stick. Her expression was grim as she used both hands to lift her leg out, pain etching lines that she didn't deserve.

Getting out of the car was a lopsided affair; clearly the damaged leg wasn't strong enough to take its share of her weight in such range of movement yet. He offered her the stick and waited as she adjusted herself to move with the support. The scent of apples wafted over him as he reached behind her to close the car door.

Even the air was holding its breath as Teddington hobbled forward towards the waiting van.

Five faces turned towards them.

Piper adjusted his pace to match Teddington's. Thankfully it wasn't much of an adjustment. They joined the group and Piper introduced Mayhill and Siddig, allowing Mayhill to introduce his own team, then led the way to the house.

He heard more than saw Teddington's overly controlled intake of breath as they followed the squat officer towards the garage door, the front door having been long since boarded over. The shadow of the house loomed over them as the afternoon turned cold, a chill made more of horror films than temperature.

Inside the garage was empty, the marked route took them around the edge of the cavernous space, just as it had on his previous visit. Teddington stepped in and followed without hesitation. Walking behind, Piper watched her; her head position indicated she was looking at the doorway into the main house, but with her hair loose, he couldn't be entirely sure.

They reached the door. Mayhill had clearly propped it open on his run through, and set up the standing light so they could see. Without that harsh illumination to send the stones into stark relief, the corridor would be dark, dank, forbidding. It wasn't entirely welcoming now, but they could see where they were going at least. He couldn't imagine that this would ever have been a nice place to be. Pulling up short, he just about managed not to walk into Teddington, who had stopped about two yards into the corridor, looking at one of the closed doors. He knew from his previous visits there was a wet room behind that door. One Teddington had used only under unwelcome supervision.

'Problem?'

Her head turned, he could just about see the tip of her nose beyond the flow of her hair.

'Just memories.'

Memories were good and bad. It was good she was remembering, he needed her to do that, for all that he knew the memories would be bad for her. Like seeing that wall. As she moved confidently forward, he still worried. That sight had affected her, what they were doing here was going to affect her more. Was she going to cope? He looked her over. Jeans and thick plaid shirt over a baggy vest t-shirt. It was within the bounds of current fashion, but it wasn't the way she had dressed before. She wasn't going to snap straight back to being her old self, and part of her never would. The scars were more than physical, but she was getting back to some form of equilibrium. He hoped today wouldn't set her back.

Inside the main room, she stopped two steps in.

Piper had read the statements. He'd listened to her recounting the experience of being held here at gunpoint by men who had told her they were going to kill her. He'd seen the body of Simon Lincoln on the floor, right in front of where she had said she and the sofa had been when his fellow bank robbers shot him.

The sound of air being dragged into her lungs stuttered with the trembling of fear. Otherwise still, she was trying to control the reaction as she looked around.

'The table is gone.'

There was an empty space where the large piece had been. Who had moved it, where to or when, he had no idea. Or interest. 'Yeah.'

'That's not quite where it was when I was brought in here either.'

Heedless of Mayhill's warning to stop her treading where he didn't want her to go, she moved toward the sofa. Regency styled though much younger, fabric hung off the back of the seat, exposing pine that was now rotting, splitting, the foam a ghastly yellow going black with mould. The smell of damp so prevalent in the garage and corridor was partnered here with stale air and mildew. The elegance that had once graced this house had disappeared with its owners. The proportions, like a good bone structure, would never change, but now the flesh was corpulent and corrupt. No amount of remodelling would restore this beauty. Piper refocused on Teddington and tried not to see the reflection.

There was little room between the sofa and the wall by the huge hearth. Teddington moved herself between the two and plonked the walking stick on the piece before she grabbed the nearest arm, braced and pushed. Her teeth gritted, clearly the exertion hadn't been easy. She looked it over, measuring the distances, the index finger of her right-hand dancing as she played back the memories.

'Yes. It was here.' Limping on her bad leg, she moved to the other end of the sofa, lowered herself carefully to the seat. He wasn't sure if that was consideration of the sofa or her injuries. Now she was sitting, she looked around again. 'Definitely.'

This was clearly to herself. Then she turned.

'He went through there.'

Her hand was steady as she pointed to the door at the far end of the room, virtually opposite where he and Mayhill were standing. Mayhill moved, but Piper stopped him, one hand on his forearm. This was his investigation, he'd go first.

Carefully, no rushing, he stepped passed the SOCO. His footfalls on the bare floorboards were dead empty thuds, as though the noise didn't dare disturb the decay. The doorway was wide enough for two doors. Though it didn't have a door now, torn wood that had once been neatly chiselled to take hinges spoke of a time when it did, but that was some time ago. Beyond was another big festering room. There was-

'Wait!'

Still in the doorway, he stopped and looked back. Teddington was looking up at him. The frown was slight, but her eyes were direct and clear. Whatever she had to say, she knew it clearly.

'It wasn't White.'

Frowning himself, Piper turned back. 'What wasn't?'

'I thought it was Mr White who took the stuff out. It wasn't. It was Mr Blue. Andy.'

Andy. Andrew Beamish. The man who had been in the car with her when she crashed it. The man she had killed.

'Ok. But he definitely came through here?'

'Yes. Don't move yet.'

He froze mid-turn, looked back. Her lip was between her teeth, her hands moving as she mentally walked through what happened. 'I think he was further towards the left edge. He'd moved from the back of the table so he was more that way.'

Piper took half a step to his left. 'Better?'

'Think so.'

This room was square, there was another door immediately to his right, the windows were boarded. The floor was thick with dust, but also with disturbance; the SOCO team had been through all this once, it would be difficult to find anything new.

'Having doubts?'

Piper turned his head to find Mayhill at his shoulder.

'I told you my men went over every inch of this place. You won't find anything new here.'

That was all too likely the truth, but those things were missing, and if he was right about Carlisle, and Carlisle was still asking about the missing items, then they had to be retrieved and he wanted to be the one to find them. He took a step towards the door.

'No.'

Her voice wasn't very loud, but it stopped him. He stepped back and turned to Teddington.

'He was in sight for longer. He walked off at a different angle.'

Piper looked back into the room. If he took a different angle, the one place he couldn't have gone was through that door. 'How long was he gone for?'

There was a pause, she must have been trying to think about it.

'I don't know. Not with any certainty. But not long.'

'Long enough to go into another room?'

'Possibly.'

He looked up. The door did open, but he remembered it stuck badly. Made a noise. 'Did you hear anything? A door being opened?'

Another pause. More thinking.

'Don't remember, but I can't rule it out.'

He remembered the noise of that door, so he was fairly sure that if it had opened, Teddington would have heard it and she would remember it. So Beamish only came in here. That had to mean that whatever was taken, it was in here. Still, he needed to be sure. Twisting the handle, he put a burst of energy into pulling the door open and the nerve rattling squeal it gave yelled again.

'Definitely never heard that!' Tedding confirmed. 'That I'd remember.'

Just as he thought. Piper turned to Mayhill.

'Tear this room apart until you find something.'

Mayhill beckoned his men over and set them working, while Piper looked back into the other room. Teddington was sitting forward, her head in her hands. He moved carefully to her side, pausing as he started to sit. Would it take the weight of two of them?

'You're okay, it's stable enough.'

'Ariadne?'

Her brows rose as she switched her attention to him.

'You okay?'

'Unexpectedly and unreasonably not. Turner was right.'

That was too left field for him. 'Sorry?' He decided to take her word for the stability of the sofa and sat down.

She took a deep breath. 'Turner says I can't go back to work because two of the robbers are on remand. De Silva and … erm…'

'Stubbs.'

'Yeah, that one. And it is because of them I'm realising that I'm not going to be able to go back to working the wings. Ever. If facing one house full of nothing but memories gets me this worried, I'm never going to be able to face a whole prison full of convicted criminals.'

How she felt about going back was her business, but after being a hostage, he wasn't entirely surprised she was questioning her life choices. That was her decision. His choice however, meant she was in a place she had clearly told him she didn't want to go. It was little surprise she was struggling.

He took pity on her. 'I've seen police officers go through trauma, get guns pointed or fired at them. Even if they aren't shot, some never get back to the job, can't face the risk again. And some do. But it takes time, and that's something I'm not sure you're giving yourself.'

Her lips compressed, but she nodded as she took a deep breath and turned to him. 'Thanks. Good to know. I'll be okay. Eventually. I guess.' The smile was weak, but she would be strong. 'I just never thought I'd be back here and even though you gave me time to think about it, I'm still struggling with it.' Next came a big swallow. 'Do I need to stay any longer though?'

He shook his head. Her relief came out with a smile. The stick was behind him and lighter to lift than he'd expected. After giving Teddington a hand up, he allowed her the necessary moment to settle into standing and using the stick, then she led the way out.

From the close confines of the dank corridor, the more open area of the garage felt much fresher. Teddington took another moment to look around. He wondered what she was remembering here. Beamish? The gun he held at her head? He waited at her side.

'At least this time I get to walk out.'

Walking out was much faster than walking in had been, and he couldn't blame her for wanting to get away from here. When they reached his car, he opened the front passenger door and waited, surprised when she stayed standing.

'Enzo.'

She didn't immediately go on, so he waited.

'He's not happy with me.'

'Because of Charlie?' It wasn't a big leap of logic. It was clear that Enzo had feelings for Ariadne, and just as clear that he was resentful of anyone he considered might hurt her.

'Actually because of you.'

Piper reared.

'Because there's something I haven't told you.'

He was about to speak when he heard Siddig calling after him. The van was in the way of his view, so he moved to the front of the car to see Siddig running towards him, a large evidence bag in her hand, and what appeared to be plaster dust in her hair. White teeth shone brightly behind the broad smile.

'We got it!'

Yes!

The bag was held out like the golden prize it was. Instinctively he raised his hand to take what was on offer. He opened the bag like a kid given a bag of sweets. There they were: accounts ledgers. Red accounts ledgers.

'Piper?'

He looked over. Teddington was still standing behind the open door to the car.

'What is that?'

It was, with a bit of luck, everything he and Charlie had been looking for for so many years. He closed the bag and passed it back to Siddig, congratulating the young woman on her find. Once he'd ensured she was comfortable finishing things off here, he moved back towards the car.

'Is that what you were looking for?' Teddington ask as he approached.

He offered her a smile. 'I hope so.' She got into the car and he carefully closed the door before moving to take his own seat behind the wheel.

'You desperate to get a look at it?'

Hell yes.

'They're account books, and they're evidence. They have to be logged. They'll have to be gone over by a forensic accountant. Not a lot that I can do until we get their report.' Irritatingly, that was all true. Procedure had to be followed if they were to get a solid conviction. The hope was that they could pin whatever it was on Rhys and not just on Phillip. The elder brother couldn't be said to have escaped justice, but he was never going to face a court of law. 'Besides, I believe that you've got something to tell me.'

She sighed. 'Wish I hadn't said anything now.'

'Tough. You did. So tell me the rest.'

'Any chance this can stay off the record?'

'Probably not.'

She tutted and rolled her eyes. 'Can you at least not tell Char-Luke?'

It really wasn't easy to change thinking in that way. 'If it's a police matter, I have no reason to tell him. What's going on?'

'You know how I said I thought I was being watched and you and Charlie managed to convince me that I was just being paranoid.'

'Actually, you started that conversation by telling *me* you were being paranoid.' It was a technicality, but it was also true.

'Well I don't think I'm being paranoid anymore.' She reached inside the bag she'd left in the car, and drew out her phone. A simple swipe and she was in.

'You know you should code protect the phone.'

'I put a lock code on this and I'll forget it, unless it's something obvious like my birthday, and we both know how easy that would be to hack, so it doesn't seem worth it. Here.'

She hadn't looked up as she'd spoken and now she was showing him a picture. One of her opening her own front door. She took the phone back, swiped and showed him another. Her getting into a taxi. These were not photographs she could have taken herself.

'That one arrived as I was still in the taxi.'

'When did the first one arrive?'

'Tuesday.' She moved the phone screen again.

Three days ago. The same day Charlie did the taxi job.

Her phone beeped. She tapped the screen, then turned it towards him. Another photograph. Her walking into the station. Three hours ago.

Chapter 23

'Hello.'

Ari looked up from the notes she was making. Her spirit fell on seeing the man taking the seat opposite her at the library table.

'Carlisle.'

She tried to go back to her notes. It was difficult under the weight of his stare. Her pen stopped above the page and she turned her eyes up to the younger man. Her vision didn't quite reach so she faced him, eyebrows raised in question.

'What are you up to?'

'Working on an algorithm that'll unmess a load of messed-up computer records and restore the original data.'

Now he was frowning. 'Can that be done? Lost records restored?'

'Oh yeah. As easy as it is to delete the files from the user access, it's actually quite difficult to remove all trace of them from the original storage system. I'm okay at that, but I know people much better. You probably do too. Police computer forensic teams are experts at this.'

The blood seemed to have drained from his face. 'They are?'

She nodded. 'And they have access to the dark web, which is something I don't ever want to delve into. Makes them even more tricksy at getting that sort of hidden stuff.'

Somehow his features looked tighter than they had before. Was she upsetting him? She hoped so.

'Yeah. Do any business on that and the police will find it on your hard drive.' She smiled. He didn't. 'But you'd know that better than I would.'

Turning back to her notes, she re-read the last couple of lines and tried to remember what she'd been doing. She sighed in relief when Carlisle simply got up and walked away.

* * *

Charlie was walking home. It wasn't that far and it was good exercise. What was less enjoyable was realising that the phone he carried was ringing.

He pulled it from his pocket and looked at it. No caller ID, but it was only going to be from one person.

'You did well last week.'

Rhys Mansel-Jones. Hardly a surprise.

'Thanks.'

'Same this Saturday.'

The line went dead. Not sure it was okay, Charlie took the phone from his ear and returned the lead weight to his pocket.

Chapter 24

The corridor to Broughton's office was neither long nor imposing; it certainly wasn't on an incline. So Piper had no idea why it felt like he was slogging up a mountain to get there. It was probably the way he'd been told that Broughton wanted to see him. It hadn't felt like a welcome invite.

His hand ran down his chest, ensuring his tie was straight. A steadying breath and he knocked.

'Come in.'

The door hardly muffled Broughton's response, and Piper followed the direction. Broughton was at his desk reading a file. It could be important, or it could be for show, Piper wouldn't know unless the Superintendent told him. He moved up to stand in front of the desk and await Broughton's attention. Piper tried to calm down his heartbeat as he watched Broughton sign a document; the dot he ended with was a flourish for appearances' sake, then the folder was closed, the pen placed carefully down and the DCS turned to look at him.

'Piper, sit down.'

The tone was less convivial than the words, but it would be foolish to refuse. With a small thank you, he complied.

'What can I do for you?'

A small frown bobbed and disappeared from Piper's brow. 'I had a message that you wanted to see me.'

Broughton's regard was steady, it told him nothing. The man was a good politician. 'What do you think I might want to see you about?'

Dread to think. 'I'm not sure, sir. An update on the cold cases, perhaps?' It was the least innocuous thing he could think of.

'We can start there. Go on.'

Start there? Just what kind of trouble am I in? 'Well, we have new evidence in the Terrence Whittaker case. His elder sister has —'

126

'You mean Ariadne Teddington?'

'Yes, sir.'

'Then why not just use her name?'

Because when that name appears in this station, trouble isn't far behind. 'As you know, Ariadne Teddington has added detail to her testimony that wasn't revealed before and it indicates that there may have been two other men involved in the disappearance, if only as a diversion.'

'Why didn't she mention it before?'

'She didn't think it was relevant, and remember at the time she was just a scared kid herself.'

'What use is it now?'

'Actually, sir, it may be quite a lot of use. She's already identified one of the two men, Dion Searlotti, a known associate of Phillip Mansel-Jones.'

'Have you pulled him in for questioning?'

'Not yet, sir. I'm arranging a line up, see if she can recognise him now.'

'What about the DNA matches?'

'Nothing yet, but we're still waiting on some results.'

'Anything else?'

Piper swallowed. 'We've followed a lead on some items that might have come from the Invicta Bank raid.'

'Lead?'

The temptation to squirm was great; he just about resisted. 'Ariadne Teddington.'

Broughton nodded. 'Ariadne Teddington.' He took a well measured breath. 'I thought it was Bell had a thing for that woman, I'm starting to wonder if maybe you do too.'

'Well you can stop wondering. Sheila is the only woman I *have a thing for.* It just happens that Ariadne Teddington is involved in both a standing investigation and a cold case. It's unusual, but given the large number of investigations that go through the Force, it's bound to happen sometimes.'

'And did anything useful come of this lead?'

'Possibly.' Piper reported the find of the ledgers and that they were with the forensic accountant, from whom he was awaiting a report.

'And if this book does prove fraud, who do you think it will point to?'

'Until the examination is complete, we can't know.'

'You must have a theory.'

'The majority of the items taken from the Invicta were connected to the Mansel-Jones family and businesses.'

This time Broughton crossed his hands on his desk, taking a moment to look at them before concentrating again on Piper. 'Mansel-Jones?'

'Yes, sir.'

'The same Mansel-Jones that Charlie Bell killed?'

'There are two brothers, sir.'

'Yes, there are. But I don't want to get another accusation of harassment, so you had better tread very carefully.'

'I am sir, I won't make a move until I have something rock solid.'

'Good. Anything else?'

'A stalking case has been reported to me.'

Broughton shrugged. 'Move it on.'

'Can't really do that sir.'

The sigh was long suffering. 'Why not?'

'The woman being stalked.'

'Well at least it's not Ariadne Teddington.'

Piper said nothing.

Dark clouds gathered over Broughton's brows and Piper's future.

'Tell me it's not Ariadne Teddington.'

'Really can't do that, sir.'

The boss' sigh seemed to go on forever. 'Pass it off to someone else all the same.'

'I can't do that.'

'Why not?'

'I'm not sure that anyone else would take the matter seriously.'

The way Broughton breathed in was like a bull getting ready to charge. 'Are you calling the professionalism of -'

'No, sir.' Stopping the bull full charge wasn't a great idea, but Piper wanted to head that one off. 'It's more that if I didn't know the full situation, I'm not sure that I'd take the matter all that seriously. I'm in that awful place where because the water isn't boiling, no one thinks there's a problem, but I can tell you that the steam is rising.'

'Your metaphor is faulty. Steam only happens when water is boiling,' Broughton pointed out. 'But I get your meaning. Details.'

Piper gave them.

'Actions?'

'Tracing the messages. Two numbers. Both burner phones, checking for any other activity on those numbers. She's going to keep me updated if she receives anything more.'

'How serious do you think it is?'

'Low level at the moment. I think she's annoyed more than upset, but she's being sent at least one picture a day to show someone is watching her, and they're frequently taken by her home, so it really isn't a comfortable position.'

'Any idea who or why?'

Plenty of ideas, just not a lot of proof at the moment. 'Nothing concrete. She's getting images only, no text so we've no real idea what the sender wants.'

'Other than to scare her?' Broughton looked at him. Piper recognised the thinking time, and experience told him that it was best to let Broughton think at moments like this. 'Okay, you keep that case, but it's not to be your main focus, understand?'

'Yes, sir. The cold cases are higher priority.'

Broughton was nodding. He was also still watching Piper, his lips a tight flat line, eyes slightly pinched. Whatever the boss was after, apparently Piper hadn't provided it, he was simply out of ideas about what the man wanted.

'Anything else to tell me?'

The sinking feeling in the pit of his stomach suggested that there should be. But he couldn't think what. 'No, sir.'

'Wilson?'

Piper fought the urge to frown. 'You told me not to go back.'

'Yes I did.'

Broughton's look was as cold and uncompromising as a cliff edge. The same cliff edge he was probably about to throw himself off.

'And I didn't. Exactly.'

That the DCS wasn't speaking wasn't a good sign.

'I went to his house. I didn't see him, didn't speak to him. Didn't even get out of my car.'

'Don't.' The word was intoned like a death knell. 'Go there. Again.'

Piper nodded. 'But –'

The glacial look stopped him.

'I won't, sir.'

'Good. Now – Siddig?'

He felt his forehead crinkle. 'She's doing fine since she joined us, as far as I'm concerned. Seems to be working well with the others.'

'Since she joined us?'

Piper could see a trap when he was faced with one, but that didn't mean he could avoid it. 'Yes, sir.'

'What about before she joined the department?'

Even his teeth felt dry, never mind his throat. 'Well, she proved very useful during the Invicta Bank raid.'

'And between the two?'

'Sir?'

Broughton sighed. It was a little overly dramatic. 'I'm not an idiot, Matthew, I know you were skulking around with Siddig, looking for something. It's time to tell me what.'

'I haven't turned up much. I need a little more time.'

'Time is one thing you do not have.'

The frown was intentional as he sat forward. 'Sir?'

Again Broughton looked at his hands. 'I'm not telling you this, understand?'

Piper nodded, even as concrete poured into his guts.

'A comment was made and PSD pricked up its ears. They have found some inconsistency in some of your cases. As far as I know, you're not about to get a yellow slip, but you need to watch your step.'

Chapter 25

The beer was cold and refreshing. Not that much was refreshing Piper's mind at the moment. He listened to Charlie's report on the second drive, and the details of the merch. Marie Ann, probably no more than 16, and clothes only just bigger than underwear, which Charlie doubted she'd been wearing.

'Dropping her at the Marina doesn't really tell us anything.'

'The Den of Angels backs into an alley that leads to the Marina.'

'One you can't see from the parking area in the Marina, so you can't even confirm that that was where she went.'

Positivity. Knowing he needed it wasn't the same as finding it. Especially in a crappy pub too many miles from home, the draft chilling his ankles and the company hardly scintillating. *I shouldn't be here. Should be home with Sheila.* In fairness, it wasn't even Charlie's hangdog expression that was affecting Piper. Or the fact that it sounded like the man shouldn't even be in the game anymore. It was-

Snap!

Long fingers snapped in front of his face and he refocused on Charlie, who was looking at him with concern and deep curiosity.

'What?'

'I just asked you the same question three times and you didn't even blink. What's going on?'

What's going on? After 26 years in the service I'm being looked at by the Professional Standards Department because I made the mistake of trusting the appearance of honesty, when what I should have been doing was questioning that honesty. The fine line I've been skating since you decided to kill a man is becoming a tightrope and I'm not sure how much longer I can maintain my balance. That had been his train of thought for the last two days since his talk with Broughton.

'Nothing. I was just thinking.'

Charlie's top lip curled. 'Nothing, my arse. I know you, you don't zone out like that. What's going on?'

Piper sighed. 'I was just thinking. Thinking that maybe you should just walk away from this whole thing.' He shifted in his seat, raising a hand to forestall the impending objection. 'Look, you want to make a life with Ariadne, right?' A small nod agreed. 'And she needs support right now. She's lost enough and she's got a great deal to cope with. You getting involved with RMJ again just puts you in danger and I'm not sure how or even if Ariadne would cope if she lost you now. Why not just step back away and keep clear of it?'

The frown that had developed on Charlie's forehead looked like it was settling in to stay. 'You weren't against it before.'

'You only had yourself to think about before.'

'So only single men should fight for what they believe is right? Is that what you're telling me? What would Sheila say about that?'

The lines were like ingrained furrows now.

'I'm telling you that maybe *you* should get out while you can.'

'It's too late for that now.'

'Not quite. We both know how this works. He'll get you to do something that seems mildly incriminating and use it against you. He'll drag you in slowly but surely. If he can't get you, he'll threaten those around you, Mrs Whittaker, Ariadne, and -'

The way Charlie's eyes dropped told a story of their own. The question was, had Teddington told him her story? 'Has something already happened?'

There were too many heartbeats before a denial, so he knew there was something coming. Had Ariadne told Charlie about the stalking? That would put him, Piper, in a better position, but he still couldn't risk saying anything until he was sure Ariadne already had. Charlie sat back and drained his pint.

'I bought flowers last week for Ari, Frank turned up just after, must have told RMJ, and on the phone RMJ said something vague about having the person I bought them for to lose. I made out they were for my landlady, but ultimately it doesn't make a difference.'

'Exactly. Either way, Ariadne gets hurt. Is that what you want?'

'Of course not. But that man needs to be stopped and if I can do -'

'I think you've done enough.' Again, he had to stop Charlie with a raised hand. 'Has anything else happened to make you think RMJ is going to go after Ariadne?'

'No.'

Sod it. She hasn't told him.

'Look, between the books, and Ariadne's identifying of the man that stopped her, we may well have enough.'

'May well? What happened to wanting to be sure? Besides, there's every chance that what you have there, RMJ can wriggle out of by saying it was his brother, not him.'

Not if we can show that Carlisle is the Don and that he works for RMJ. And therein lay the rub. *IF.*

'We need something definitive on RMJ.'

'No,' Piper was clear. '*I* need something definitive on RMJ. You need to pull yourself together and create a decent life. That's what I want from you now. Leave the detective work to me.'

There wasn't much of a hope in hell that Charlie would listen, but he had to try.

'It won't be that easy. RMJ called. He said I did well, and that if I kept it up, I'd earn a promotion.'

Piper's gut twisted. The vibration in his pocket told him he had a phone call. 'That is not the kind of promotion you want.'

It was automatic to reach for the offending item. *Work.* Just what he didn't need. His desire to forget the bloody job and the sense of duty warred inside him. The battle was undecided when the summons stopped.

'Now I know something's wrong.'

Piper's eyes shifted from the black screen to Charlie's blue eyes. Perceptive friends could be such an irritation. 'I'm sure the Force can survive without me for the evening.' They might have to do without him for a lot longer than that if things really went south. Besides, technically he was working. He'd registered this meeting with CHIS. And he wasn't going to give in to the threatening gloom.

'What's going on, Piper?'

He shook his head. It wasn't for Charlie to know. Aside from anything else, he knew Charlie too. Charlie would feel the need to do something to help and right now the best help was doing nothing. Before he could make up some suitably innocuous lie, his phone rattled again. He glanced at the screen.

'Bugger.' He answered the call. 'Sir?'

He listened to Broughton's bark and paled. It was clear that questions would not be tolerated any more than tardiness ever was. Broughton disconnected.

The tone had barely dissolved before Piper was standing.

'What's going on?'

'Not sure, but you know disobedience is not a good idea when Broughton has to make personal telephone calls.'

Chapter 26

The gathering darkness outside the car matched the darkness crowding in on Piper as he drove towards the capital, a stranger in the passenger seat beside him. He glanced across at his silent companion. Early 30s, cropped hair, in need of a shave, several stone too heavy. Piper figured the man would struggle to get through his next physical.

'Okay,' Piper broke the frosted silence. 'I know where we're going. I know who we're going to see. I know your name, but I have no idea who you are. Care to enlighten me, Detective Constable Grantham?'

'You know what you need to know.' The guy just looked dead ahead, didn't even do him the courtesy of looking at him.

'Well, this is going to be a fun working relationship.'

'If the work gets done right, it shouldn't take long enough to be a relationship, and fun is irrelevant.'

Bet he watches Star Trek.

'Listen Grantham, your inspector might let you get away with this disrespectful shit, but I won't. I so don't give a crap if you don't like me, but you will show respect for my rank. Now, I want details or you will not be sitting in on this interview. Understand?'

'I'm PSD.'

Apparently, that was all Grantham was going to say. It was all he needed to say really. They were heading to Lewisham where the Metropolitan Police were holding Detective Constable Paul Watson, arrested two hours ago. The charge had not been made clear, but Broughton was clear. He was sending Piper because he had never worked directly with Watson and he wanted to be sure he had someone he could trust on the case. He'd also given the warning that Piper better not give him reason to regret the choice, as he'd deny it should he have to.

The remaining journey was taken in silence, except for the double expletive when some young moron sped through a red light and only just missed them. Definitely more luck than judgement, that survival. Frustration tightened Piper's jaw muscles to the point of pain. Nothing about this evening was good news.

There was too long a wait for the gates to be opened, then a right turn into the dedicated multi-storey car park. Thankfully Piper found a space on the ground floor. He felt his knuckles might crack as he pulled them free of the steering wheel at last. Grantham got out without a word.

Recognising that PSD was a tough job at the best of times, Piper tried to make allowances for the younger man. The attempt was hampered by the suspicion that Grantham was here as much for him as for Watson.

The guy on the Lewisham station desk looked knackered - it had clearly been a long shift. The uniformed officer who came to greet them wasn't exactly full of the joys of spring either. He offered tea and a comfort break, both of which were gratefully accepted by both men. As Piper stood by the urinal, he was aware from the sound that Grantham was doing exactly the same in a cubicle. The unavoidable exposure of male toilet habits could make for embarrassing situations and comparisons, but this seemed an unusual and unnecessary action on the DCs behalf. *Perhaps he's just bladder shy.* There was little point in taking offence; Piper really didn't know enough about the man to be a good judge.

Like every other interview room, room 1 in Lewisham was bland and boring. But then the point of interest was always the interview not the decoration. Watson sat in his chair, looking like his body was held together by perished elastic bands. His bones had forgotten how to be hard and his skin was too tired to have colour. Only his eyes were bright. Over bright. Perhaps he'd taken something earlier in the evening. Or maybe it was unshed tears that caught the light. *Or maybe I'm the one who needs the sleep.*

The interview started typically enough, names and ranks and purpose. Of course he couldn't give his real reason for being there, in part because he didn't understand it. Broughton wanted him to investigate Watson's assault, on behalf of the County Constabulary; the PSD was a secondary matter according to the DCS. Nothing felt comfortable. Especially the comment that Piper was one of the few that Watson hadn't worked with.

There was a statement of the offence Watson had committed - common assault - and an admission of guilt that was scraped from the bottom of a soul which had abandoned all hope. Even as he gave the admission, water tension broke and a tear rolled from Watson's right eye.

There was little chance Watson was going to keep his career after this, but he was unlikely to spend any significant time in jail - if any at all.

They dealt quickly with the incident of the evening, but even as they did, Piper's gut told him that there was more to the incident and to Watson. So he kept asking the same question in every way he could thing of - why?

Through most of the interview, Watson stared resolutely at the table top. But as Piper pushed, Watson's colour rose and his temper shortened. The more agitated Watson got, the more Piper knew there was something to find. So, he asked again. And again. The legal aid solicitor didn't say a word. Neither did Grantham. He asked again.

Watson slapped the table and shot to his feet. 'Because the Don told me to!'

Grantham and the solicitor moved back in reaction. Piper didn't shift one inch. This was exactly what he wanted, possibly why Broughton had sent him. Watson was huffing like a bull at the charge. Piper made sure his breathing was slow and controlled. They watched one another. This could go either way and Piper didn't want it to go wrong.

'Please, Paul,' he said quietly. 'Sit down.'

Two more huffs, the shoulders slumped and Watson sat down again. This time he was leaning forward, more engaged in the process.

'So,' Piper said, 'the Don?'

Watson hung his head. 'I shouldn't have said that.'

'But you did say it.'

Watson covered his head with his forearms.

'How do you know the Don?'

Watson said nothing.

'What did the Don tell you to do?'

'Stop asking.'

It was a plea, not a demand. Like a man with a broken leg begging for painkillers.

'What did the Don tell you to do?'

Watson sniffed and sat up. Caged and beaten. 'Nuffin'.' Another big wet sniff. 'I don't know the Don. I don't know what you're talking about.'

Watson knew exactly what he was talking about.

'What does he have on you? Explain to me why you would be willing to throw away your career, your future, everything you have, all on the say-so of someone who's too scared to show himself?'

Watson just looked away.

'If I'm to stop the Don, I need evidence.'

'You'll need a virtual miracle.'

Piper knew he wasn't kidding. 'What did you do to get his attention?' Another non-answer. 'What else have you done for him?'

'I did nothing.'

'You assaulted a suspect without cause,' Grantham finally spoke. 'I don't take that lightly.'

Watson just sneered at him. No one liked the PSD.

'You could spend time in jail for this. Ex-cops don't do well in there.'

Watson returned his attention to Piper. 'Your mate Bell survived.'

'Bell's six four and built like a brick wall. He takes no shit off anyone. You're five six, skinny as a whippet and if the details of today's assault are anything to go by, not much use in a fight. They'll target you because of what you were. Within a week you'll be every hard man's bitch.'

'No one's safe inside, I'll take my chances.'

'Your chances would have been a whole heap better if you hadn't committed assault and had stayed inside the Force.'

Watson huffed. 'Not really. As you'll soon find that out.'

The questioning continued for another hour, but nothing new or worthwhile came out. Piper left the station wanting to break something, to scream at the sky. He'd never expected his job to be easy, but did it have to be this difficult?

Annoyingly, Watson wasn't the only one Piper couldn't make out. Grantham had said little and done less. Except to slurp tea and eat all the biscuits the Met had offered. Now he sat looking resolutely forward as they drove the M25 back. Though late, there was still plenty of traffic around and Piper felt like he was crawling along in the inside lane doing a steady seventy miles an hour while everything else sped past. He wanted to put his foot down and get home to Sheila, only speeding would just give the PSD something to hang their hat on.

'Grantham, was tonight about you watching Watson or me?' At least asking the question took his mind off the idiot driver in front, who had his fog lights on. It was dark, but there was no issue with visibility.

'Have you been served with a Reg 15?'

Reg 15. Notice of alleged breach of the Standards of Professional Behaviour Regulation 15 Police (Conduct) Regulations 2012. The dreaded yellow slip. Not that they were yellow anymore but whitewashing the colour didn't bleach out the dread.

'No.'

'Then why would you think I was investigating you?'

138

'Paranoia, probably.' Thankfully Fog Light Boy wasn't turning off, though Piper did, and the usual relief washed over him at being outside of the M25 enclosure.

'What do you think Watson meant when he said, "You'll soon find out"?'

The curve off the motorway was tight, turning them 270 degrees. Piper didn't answer until he'd negotiated most of it and was straightening up, checking the mirrors for the merge with the next road on the route. 'Maybe my paranoia isn't paranoia.'

'Because it's not paranoia if they really are all out to get you?' Grantham finally looked at him, like he was an actual human being. 'Look, in my position I can't afford to get pally with other police officers, I'm not doing anyone or any investigation any favours if I do that. But I'm curious, why do you think someone would be out to get you?'

'I don't know.' Back in the slow lane and doing seventy, Piper signed. 'I pissed off a lot of people because of my links with Charlie Bell.'

'You certainly did.'

Grantham watched him. It wasn't the most comfortable Piper had ever been, but there wasn't much else to say.

'What do you know about the Don?' Grantham asked at last.

'Not a lot. It's a name you hear whispered occasionally. You?'

'Rumours. Probable lies. Nothing substantial.'

Piper sighed again, maybe he and his ulcer were getting too old for the game. 'Chasing ghosts isn't recommended.'

Grantham shifted in his seat to stare out of the side window this time. *And so concludes our conversation for this evening. Joy.*

Chapter 27

By the light of the dashboard, Piper looked at the note.

It's Sunday, and I need the day of rest.

The note told him a time and place. But little else. It was handwritten in a hand he did not recognise. The paper was torn from an A6 unlined notebook. It was good quality paper. Possibly a sketchbook. He didn't know anyone who carried such a thing. It arrived in a paying-in envelope, the kind used by the Invicta Bank for automated deposits. That intrigued him, given his involvement in the raid there. And it was his bank. But the envelopes were stacked by the cash and deposit machines; anyone could go and get one, so that told him nothing either. The worrying thing was that it had been pushed through the letterbox at home. Sheila had picked it up.

'Should I be worried?' she'd asked when she handed it to him.

It was time to find out.

The night air chilled his lungs as Piper headed towards the Colin Ruck memorial bench. Piper had no idea who Colin Ruck was, but there were many a dedicated bench along this walk and this was the one he was to meet the note sender on. The bench was empty when he arrived. He checked the brass plaque, then checked his watch. One minute to eleven.

Four cold slats supported his weight as he sat. At least they were dry. He stuffed his hands in his pockets and tried to stay warm, but the bench was sucking the heat out of him. There was dense woodland directly behind him and he was looking out over a common where people played. Where kids played.

Where Terry Whittaker had been playing the last time his sister saw him.

It couldn't be a coincidence. This spot had been deliberately selected and Piper needed to know why. Looking to his left he saw another bench - the one where he'd met Charlie. As he sat and waited, his mind swung through all the possibilities. When Sheila saw the note, she'd told him not to go, virtually begged him, which wasn't like her. She worried in case he was literally putting himself into the firing line. He'd calmed her nerves on the point, but right now the point was stretching his nerves to their limit.

He heard a rustling to his right and looked that way. Nothing.

Just the leaves in the breeze. Calm down.

Easier said than done with a heart thundering in his chest like it wanted out. The snuffling to his right caught his attention, and the tick-tick-tick of fixed claws on concrete. A tall mass of dog appeared on the walk, the distinctive racing figure of a Doberman nosing along the path on the scent of something. Him? He'd walked that way. Oh God, was he about to be attacked by a vicious canine? Hands came out of his pockets as he rested one on the bench ready to push himself up. If that thing came for him- A high pitched human whistle rent the air.

'Come on, Dilbert.'

A woman's voice sounded like it was at the edge of the walk. The dog picked up its slim nose and lolloped toward the voice.

'Getting-'

Piper leapt to his feet, swung round to face the deep-voiced male who had appeared out of nowhere. 'Jesus!'

'Sit down, Matthew.'

Broughton was keeping his voice low as he waited for Piper to obey. The way his heart was hammering like a budgie with a cat in his cage, Piper wasn't sure what else he could do if he wasn't to have an actual heart attack. Broughton moved around him to sit on the other end of the bench.

'You should be scared, Matthew.'

'Why? What are you about to do?'

Broughton chuckled lightly and looked at him. 'Oh unclench, Matthew, I'm just here to give you a bit of a history lesson I don't want to be seen or overheard giving you.'

That didn't make sense. 'Your office or mine wouldn't be better for that?'

'No.'

It was unequivocal and that didn't make Piper feel any safer.

'Did you know that my grandfather was a police officer?'

Piper nodded. He'd seen a reference to it in some article about Broughton a few years back. 'I believe he served at our station too.'

'He did. He's the one who put my father off joining the Force. Tried to stop me doing so too.'

Unusual. 'Okay.'

'Although he wasn't happy that I'd gone against his express wishes, I think in the last few years of his life, my being a police officer helped bring us closer together. It certainly gave me a better understanding of him. Anyway, after I started, I was in a few years by then, something happened. Nothing major, but it made me think and it nagged at me. When he came over for Sunday dinner that weekend - back then my mother was insistent that the whole family have a roast together after she'd been to church - he noticed I was distracted. He made sure that he and I were the only ones to wash up that day.'

Somehow the idea of Broughton as a young man being told to do the washing-up jarred with the tough, occasionally foul-mouthed superior he was used to. It was humanising, but Piper still didn't see the point.

'While I washed, he dried, and he asked. And I said. And then he told me.'

The pause was probably more for Broughton to process the memory, but it had a dramatic effect all the same.

'Told you what?'

Broughton took another deep breath, his exhale condensed into a wisp before him. 'He told me about the Don.'

The Don? But -

'You're not chasing a phantom, Matthew. There really is a Don in the station. A back-stabbing bastard who cheats the cause of law the rest of us have signed up to do our part to uphold. The problem is that it's not just one man. I can't even be sure that it's only one man at a time. It's a title that's handed around. Been around for decades. I don't know who it is. I do know that a lot of those who have gone looking have found themselves in hot water I couldn't cool down. I thought when we had that trouble with Charlie that it was him. Everything went quiet for a while. I even thought that might be the actual end of it. Only things started happening, and I knew the Don was back.'

'It was never Charlie.'

Broughton sighed again. 'No, I don't really think it was. He was too good. Too dedicated to what he thought was right. Which was the whole problem from the start. It's why he ended up killing a man he couldn't stop any other way. He couldn't bend, any more than you seem able to right now.' Broughton looked him up and down. 'Is there any particular reason for your especially upright posture?'

There was and given what this meeting had turned out to be, it seemed foolish. Lying wasn't going to do him any favours though. 'Stab vest.'

'Why?'

'Because I don't have a bulletproof one.' That sounded even weaker.

The huff was amused, but uninformative. 'You're right to be afraid. You've started looking for the Don and that is going to get you into trouble. Just like it did Wilson. And I don't want to lose you from the team. So, you have to be bloody careful. Understand?'

A lot more careful. 'Yes sir.'

'You told Sheila about this meeting, didn't you?'

He nodded.

'The vest her idea?'

'Best compromise I could come up with.'

'Well, she's a smart woman, she won't say anything when you get home fit and well. Can I trust you not to mention what happened to her?'

'Of course.' He nodded, but there was something else. 'Why not the office?'

'Walls have ears, Matthew, and I don't know which ones belong to the Don.'

Chapter 28

Piper took the briefing because DI Langdon had been called out in the early hours, and still wasn't back. There wasn't a lot of good news, but they assigned tasks on the various cases, so everyone knew what they were doing. Piper was just about to close the session when a very tired-looking Langdon walked in.

'DI Langdon, do you want to bring us up to speed on your call out?'

Langdon looked too knackered to want to do anything, but he came forward and Piper sat down to listen. It was a position he was glad of as Langdon addressed the group and told all about the body found in an alley. Looked like the girl had been raped first. Possibly last, it was difficult to know at this point, the PM might or might not be able to clarify.

'Our one bit of good news is that we have an ID on her now. Possible ID, anyway. I just walked past the missing person's board and she's on there. Marie Gallo.'

Nausea threatened, and Piper's head pounded.

'She was fifteen, Romanian, been in the country - legally I should add - for four years. Her parents run a general store on Frith Street. They reported her missing yesterday morning. DCI Linda Small has that case. I'll be liaising with her later to confirm the identification.'

Fifteen. Piper kept his countenance all the way back to his office, now he paced and racked his hair back.

Fifteen!

Charlie had said she looked young, but he'd thought she was age of consent. Piper paced as best he could in his office, but it didn't help. For a moment it felt like a prison cell. Hell, it wasn't much bigger. And thanks to the security risks, there were even bars on the windows.

Oh for Christ's sake, how do these things happen around Charlie?
Nothing for it now.

144

* * *

Small flexed her feet and looked down at her brogues. She could feel too much of the cold floor through their increasingly thin soles. Time to repair or replace. Given the ripping seams, the three previous re-soles and the fact that she had another pair unused in the box at home, it was time to admit defeat and finally throw these away. The prospect was much like the burial of a family pet, but as her other half would keep reminding her, if she kept them much longer, they'd walk themselves to the rubbish dump. She smiled, Ralph had promised to cook Salmon en Croute tonight, her favourite.

Right that's it, five minutes up back to it.

She was just about to hit the paperwork when the office door opened, and she was surprised to see her visitor. Somehow, she was less surprised by his worried expression. With a DS and two DCs in the office, she'd try for a lighter tone.

'Matthew,' she greeted with a smile. 'Am I to be visited by all of CID today?' Langdon hadn't long since left.

'I hope not, Linda, I've got work enough for all of them, and more. But I would appreciate a quick word if you have a moment?'

If she hadn't, for this she'd make one. Piper wasn't the sort to waste time and he'd already provided some valuable insights. She sensed this was not a conversation for the open office.

Raising a hand, she indicated the corner of the otherwise open plan area and then led the way. Small didn't keep a private office; instead she had turned the space that was supposed to be hers into a reasonable facsimile of a cosy living room; it put her visitors more at their ease, which they tended to need when a family member had gone missing. She stepped straight to the sofa and indicated Piper should take the chair. It was taller than the sofa and that put his head the higher. It wasn't something that bothered her, but she was aware that far too many people found her height intimidating, so she gave this small ground to win the bigger prize.

'Well,' she said when he seemed disinclined to speak. 'Neither Pearson not Stolz investigations have moved on, even with your help.'

'Nothing came of the Bodine Street house to house?' Stalling was probably a mistake.

'A cannabis farm and some uncomfortable feelings, but only the first was worth an arrest.' She shrugged, there was always more investigation than easy solutions. There was still some cross checking to do on the houses with uncomfortable feelings too, that was why her DS was still here and not out on the patch. It was obvious Piper didn't know how to start, she'd try for him. 'You look like a worried man, my friend, and that question was just time wasting. What can I do for you?'

He swallowed and rested his hands on the arms of the chair. His hands looked relaxed, but they were so still she knew it was an illusion of concentrated relaxation.

'Langdon came to see you about Marie Gallo a few minutes ago.'

She frowned but confirmed it.

'I have information that may be relevant.'

That was interesting. Another case, another Piper connection. They'd hardly ever had to work together before and how Broughton wanted her liaising with him on two cases and here he was to mention a third. *He's my own equivalent in CID, if one of my guys was teaming up with him, I'd go calling just in case.* 'Langdon and I agreed to work together on the Gallo case, but he'll be SIO. Don't you think that you should talk to him?'

'Oh,' the surprised tone matched the look. 'I thought, since she had the pre-existing case, you'd take that role.'

Normally, but Pearson and Stolz were too important to her. 'It's a murder enquiry now, Matthew. More his remit than mine. I do have to deal with them sometimes, but thankfully not often. And as far as I'm concerned, the less often the better. So, what is it that you don't want to tell him?'

Those still hands curled a little more in and up. Tension was so obvious it vibrated off him like the tone of a top C tuning fork.

'Your insight is unnerving. Let me run this by you first, then we'll figure out if it's relevant enough to reveal.'

Attentively listening, Small didn't say a word as he told her about Charlie's taxi job. After he'd finished she sat quietly letting all the implications sink in.

'Last Saturday, you say?'

He agreed.

'And Charlie hasn't seen or heard of her since?'

'Not to my knowledge.'

She watched his eyes. Little wonder he was a worried man. 'I am going to have to speak with him about this.'

'On or off the record?'

Unlike most of their colleagues, she wasn't that keen on throwing the book at the ex-sergeant, but she wasn't entirely ready to let him off the hook either. 'Off to start, but I'll have to wait and see what develops.'

Piper nodded, it wasn't the best answer she could have given, but he understood and though she paused to given him chance, he wasn't about to push her.

'Langdon will have to be told.' That was the way she worked, open and honest. Small sat forward. 'But I'll tell him. We all run our own informants, but if you go to him, he'll know it's Charlie and we don't want that blinding everyone to the information.'

He nodded and a little of the tension easing out of his frame.

'I'll tell Langdon I found the reference on the CHIS report. But I'll keep quiet about who provided it. You did record it, didn't you?'

Piper nodded. She should never have doubted that he was do any less than his best.

'Of course. It's dated Sunday, which was when I found out about it. Thanks for doing this.'

She pressed her tongue to the roof of her mouth as she weighed the wisdom of what she wanted to say. Given how stressed Piper seemed, she knew she had to give the issue room to breeze. 'You do know you're a bloody idiot for taking him on as an informant, don't you?'

Eyes that hadn't been able to quite meet hers suddenly snapped to and pinned her, challenged her. 'He had information we needed and registering him was the only way I could officially act on that information.'

'Yeah, I get that. And, no offence, but it looks to the rest of the world that you're more prepared to take his word on face value, a man we know is a murderer, than you are to listen to your own people.'

He was watching her intently. 'Are you sorry that Phillip Mansel-Jones is gone?'

'Hell no.'

'Well, there was no other way of getting him off the scene. Trust me, I tried everything I could.'

She nodded and smiled. She remembered the effort he had gone to, they all had. 'I know. That bastard just had too many connections; we were never going to stop him legally. Still, what Charlie did crossed a line the rest of us can't contemplate.'

Piper glanced away. He'd contemplated it. 'Charlie's a good fu-ella.' Perhaps he'd miss her slip. 'I miss him.'

'How many times did you sleep with him?'

Typical of Piper to ask the question she didn't want him to. 'Just the once.' Long before Ralph. 'I think I frightened him.'

'No offence, Linda, but you frighten most of us.'

Chapter 29

Hours later, Piper left the fraud squad office, wound far too tightly. The fraudsters were happy, they were going through the account books and were making progress but wouldn't reveal anything until they were sure exactly what they had. He felt like every move just took him down another blind alley.

Inside the incident room a knot of officers crowded around one screen. The low buzz of conversation stopped dead when Piper walked in. The looks he got were chill, a couple of the assembled staff couldn't meet his eye. Dread flowed through him.

Numb, he only just caught the door he was about to let go. It would have slammed into Langdon's face as he rushed in from the other way.

'What's going on?'

Wish I knew.

The crowd around the computer spread out, and with slow careful steps that intensified the gnawing at Piper's bones, Langdon moved across. He looked at the screen, then he looked back at Piper. Storm clouds had gathered in the younger man's eyes. The ache in his knuckles grew now there was no way to release the door.

Running feet pounded towards him. Suddenly Linda Small was at his side in the doorway.

'What is it?'

Struck mute, all Piper could do was shrug.

'Picture of Marie Gallo,' Langdon intoned. 'Taken Saturday afternoon.'

'That could be the last ever picture taken of her.'

'Yeah, and she's with Charlie fucking Bell.' DI Langdon shot Piper a look that could curdle milk as he marched from behind the row of desk.

'Well, that's not unexpected.' Small's words stopped Langdon in his tracks.

'What?'

How she could shrug so calmly when Piper's insides were in all at sea in a hurricane, he did not know.

'The informant who gave the initial report of Marie Gallo being taken to the marina was Charlie Bell. This isn't actually new information.'

But it was news to Langdon, whose look to Piper said words would be had, which was, frankly, fair enough.

'I'll go with-'

'No you won't,' Small refused Piper's offer. 'Langdon has the lead on this. He and I are more than capable of dealing with one interview.'

She didn't have to be quite so harsh about it.

* * *

Charlie was in the warehouse, checking the manifest when one of the gang tapped him on the shoulder and pointed. There was little point trying to shout over the noise of the factory; the machines, rollers, cutters, stackers, folders, the forklifts, or past the ear defenders they were both wearing. Charlie saw the pair, initialled the last item he'd checked and passed the checklist over.

They were obviously police, from their sour looks, flat shoes, and high street suits. The fact that he recognised them both didn't argue against the fact either. He rushed over to stop them moving further into the big open space. The man whose name he was struggling to remember tried to resist.

'You can't be in here without ear defenders and hi-viz,' he had to shout over the noise as he herded them out towards the roller door. The man said something, Charlie tapped his ear defenders, moved to a door inside the warehouse and led them through. As soon as the door closed behind Small, the noise level dropped dramatically. He removed the cups over his ears and left them in the resting position against the hard hat they were part of.

'Sorry about that, but I have to be mindful of health and safety. Take it this isn't a social call DCI Small, DS... Langdon?'

'It's DI now and, no. This is business.'

'In that case, congratulations, let's go to the office.' Because if they went to the canteen they'd have an audience he didn't need.

'You've done well to get your own office so quick.'

The stairs creaked as usual, three times now.

'Not my office, there are three shift supervisors, one for each team, we share the same space.' And it wasn't always easy - opening the door at the top of stairs led them into the small office. It was cramped, but at least it was private. He took off the hard hat and hung it on the hook, ruffling his hair where it had got sweaty under the plastic band. There was only one seat, the stool he used since being in the office wasn't a full-time thing. With a slight movement of a hand, he offered it to Small. An equally small shake of the head declined.

Given he was easily the tallest in the room, he decided to make life easier from their point of view and sat, bringing his head below theirs. Langdon's features were tight, there was resentment and something else he wasn't sure how to define. Small was looking around; he guessed the mess didn't impress her.

'It's dusty in here.'

'We make and cut paper. There's a lot of dust. And it gets dry in here, for the same reason. If you get thirsty, help yourselves.' He indicated the pack of a dozen small bottles he'd brought in with him just that morning and grabbed the half-drunk bottle on the side. 'So what can I do for you?'

'Tell us about last Saturday,' Langdon asked.

The way the younger man looked at him, Charlie knew that this wasn't good, that there was more to it. He also knew what the only thing was that he'd done last Saturday that would be of interest to the police.

'No.'

Langdon blinked, his head rearing in reaction.

'Charlie,' Small's voice was warning.

'You don't want to know about my Saturday, you want to know about the taxi job I did. I don't want to waste your time, or miss my time in work, so let's be clear on what's needed, and we can all get away from this quicker.' He took a deep breath. 'Everything that you need to know is in the report I gave to Piper, which I'm assuming you read before you rushed down here?'

Langdon looked momentarily away.

'I have,' Small announced. 'So, you tell me, when did you start working for a creep like Mansel-Jones?'

'God, you really did turn to the dark side.'

Charlie understood the disgust he heard in both voices.

'I did what I had to do. Then and now. Piper knows the details.'

'Piper's not here to protect you.'

And he wouldn't if he were. Charlie knew he didn't deserve any protection anyway. He didn't deserve a lot of things; the thing he really didn't deserve was waiting at home for him and kept warming his bed, making him dream of a better life.

'When did you get the call?'

At least he could rely on Linda Small to be professional.

'Friday, 7:12.'

'From Rhys Mansel-Jones?'

He nodded.

'What did you say back?'

'Nothing.' Charlie shrugged. 'I wasn't given the chance.'

'What did he say?' Small drew his attention back to her.

'Marriot. Three pm. She'll come to you. Drop at the Marina like before.' Charlie thought back to the call. 'The phone line was cut as soon as he'd finished.'

'Lucky you weren't on shift for the drop.'

'Not really, this place closes at two on a Saturday.'

The two officers held their silence. It wasn't a new technique. Charlie listened to his overactive pulse. The last thing he needed was to get arrested again. This was a job, not a vocation, but it was a reasonable job, he liked the people he worked with, felt a certain satisfaction at a job well done. And then he got to go home to Ari. He hadn't had that before, and he hadn't had it long, but he wouldn't want to be without it now. He had to figure out what these two wanted.

'I did was I was told, I picked up the girl, dropped her off. I handed the car back to Frank Beard, just like last time.'

'The last time?'

Charlie shrugged. 'The week before I did a similar job, an older woman. It's all in the records, a report I gave Piper.'

Small was nodding, it seemed she knew the details. Langdon didn't.

'It was all the same as when you dropped the older woman the week before?' Langdon asked.

'Ye -' Charlie stopped himself, remembering. 'No, not exactly.' He tried to think of how best to describe it. 'With the older woman, I drew up, she got in, I drove, she didn't say a word, when I parked at the Marina, she got out before I could get out to open the door for her.' It was all very cold and clinical. 'With the girl, she tripped on her way to the car. Stupid high heels. I got out and helped her up, showed her to the car, opened the door for her. She was shaking like a lamb, but she wasn't wearing much to keep her warm. I got her in the back of the car and got in the driver's seat and drove. I could see her in the rear-view mirror, she was pale and nervous. I guessed because she'd fallen or because maybe it was her first time.'

Small frowned. 'First time?'

Charlie shrugged. 'She was dressed like... well she was hardly dressed; Hem line to her hip, neckline to the naval. I've seen swimming costumes with more coverage. She was young, seventeen I guess. So I asked if she was okay, I asked her name. Marie Ann, she said. I took her to the Marina. I didn't especially want to, but I know what the Mansel-Jones family is like; if she didn't turn up, if I didn't do what I was told, we were both dead. So I drove. And when I got to the Marina, I got out of the car and I opened the back door, offered her a hand out. She looked around, said she didn't know where she was supposed to go.' Charlie hung his head and closed his eyes. *Should have told her to run.* 'I told her where the other woman went. Then closed the door, dropped the car with Frank and called Piper.'

'Then you're an accessory to her murder.'

Charlie looked up, slack-jawed at Langdon. It didn't compute. 'What?'

'We found Marie Ann Gallo's body yesterday,' Small explained quietly. 'Today we were sent this.' Small handed over a printout of the picture they'd been sent.

Charlie took it and stared at the grainy CCTV image of him standing with the girl at the marina. Since she was no more than five six even with the heels she'd been wearing, he seemed to loom over her. Almost like he was trying to intimidate her. This didn't look good.

'Oh and she was fifteen.'

The paper dropped. Charlie seemed to lose control over his muscles. It was a good thing he was sitting down. *Fifteen.* 'It was just a taxi job.'

'And it was two days before she died,' Small pointed out. Then she glared at Charlie. 'But don't think we won't be back if we find probable cause.'

Chapter 30

'It's a good offer.'

'It's a very good offer.'

The way Rhys relaxed back was more than just the comfort of ownership, it was triumph. This was his domain and he was enjoying it. Showing that he was lord and master of it all. His office was in a large area above the club, an area that could probably be put to better use, Rhys had his office. But what an office. Individually the furnishings were all high quality, but the mahogany desk didn't work with the chrome and white sofa, or the cowhide cushions on it. The Greek marble miniature Venus standing on a clear Perspex occasional table looked out of place. Like the man it was more money than taste. With his hair starting to need a comb over and thickening waistline, Rhys appeared older than he was. He kept himself fit but lacked the natural inclination to the youthful looks he so desperately desired. Phillip hadn't looked so old though he was more than a decade older.

For a moment Charlie looked away, revolted by his connection to the men.

The room was an ugly shade of... he wasn't sure what to call it. An unflattering beige-grey that somehow managed to remind him of the time one of the Whitewalk inmates had decided to go on a dirty protest. His nose twitched involuntarily. That fetid smell wasn't here, yet it was with him. One of the walls was covered in pictures, and not a necessarily happy mix. There were family photos, a couple of celebrity photos, a couple of photographs of women that were better suited to a dirty mag than a wall display, and Victorian etchings of African tribes and five images of mechanical exploded view diagrams. On the side board was a small, layered anatomical model of a human torso, it was all fixed, only the heart lay by the stand. There was another, this time of a human knee, next to it.

'The human body is really quite amazing when you look beneath the skin.' Rhys said. 'There are some that believe consuming human body parts can bring eternal youth.'

The beat of the overloud music from the club below was bouncing through Charlie's feet and ankles, up into his knees. The sensation was every bit as unpleasant as the ideas Rhys espoused. Even as he'd walked through the already packed club, the reek was sweat and desperation with an overtone of that unpleasant sweetness of cannabis smoke. Charlie wasn't comfortable. He felt trapped, as though he were in a dungeon and a maze of corridors stood between him and clean, fresh light and air. He wanted out of this place, and now. Once he'd considered clubs like this as prime hunting ground, his natural territory. But now there was Ari, he wasn't interested in hunting any more. It wasn't the only thing he was prepared to give up for her.

'I can't accept your offer.' *Because if you keep double-crossing me by sending photos of me with murder victims, I really can't afford to do anything else.*

Rhys looked neither pleased nor impressed.

'Look, Rhys, I'm sorry, I really do appreciate what you're offering.' *Degradation and the chance to parade to the world just how far I've fallen.* 'Only, the dates you're talking about actually clash with shifts I'm working, and though my job's not much, it's mine and it's starting to work out for me.'

'With me, you'll earn double what you earn there.'

'More than.' Charlie shrugged. 'But not everything is about money.' It wasn't even all about the exhaustion he felt after a heavy afternoon shift.

The smile had slid from Rhys' face. 'Money helps.'

Charlie smiled and looked away, having been refused a credit card only that morning despite the now steady income. 'It sure does.'

'Is this why you were talking to Detective Chief Inspector Piper on Sunday?'

That surprised Charlie, but he knew better than to show it. 'No. I spoke with him because he's a friend. Pretty much the only one I've got left from my life before prison.' A sad fact he'd rather not think about, but there was another one too. 'Look, I brought you back that watch because it felt like stealing even though I'd bought it in good faith, because I figured it was something you wouldn't have given up willingly.'

'You were just returning stolen property?'

Charlie shrugged. 'That sounds overly procedural, but if you want to put it that way, yeah. When you contacted me again, offered me that job, it felt like the old days, back when I was a cop. Same game, I expected the same feel. Only it didn't feel the same. I didn't come out of prison the same way I went it. I'm a murderer. Can't wash that stain away. Can't change what I did, can't make up for it. It would be stupid of me to try.'

Rhys' lip curled, as though Charlie had become a bad smell. 'Are you saying you're too good to work for me?'

'No. If anything, I'm not good enough. I have to face facts, face what I am. You think, or at least your brother thought, that I was hell bent on breaking him.'

'Well, you did shoot him.'

For a moment Charlie looked away, a bitter huff of self-loathing escaped. 'Yeah, I did. So I have no right being anywhere near you. To be honest, when I walked in here the first time, I was expecting you have your boys kick seven shades of shit out of me. I still haven't figured out how I feel about the fact that they haven't.'

'Kickings can be arranged.'

'True. The fact is, Piper *is* the only one from the old days who'll still talk to me, the rest hate me more then they hate villains, more than they hate you. My being anywhere near you is likely to drag you down, get the kind of people you don't want anywhere near you poking their noses where you don't want them.'

'Noses can be cut off.'

'Why bother with that mess when it can be avoided?'

* * *

Even as he walked away, Charlie wasn't sure what the calculating look on Rhys' face meant. Maybe Rhys figured he was right, that having Charlie around was more trouble than it was worth. Maybe he was just letting Charlie think that was the case, which was a much more worrying thought. Did Rhys think he had something to use against him?

Ari.

Suddenly the need to be home, the need to be with her was all-consuming, but a mosh pit was a bubbling barrier to be battled. Stepping into the melee, Charlie was repelled by the throbbing throng, even as he squeezed through the crowd. Eyes on the door, he tried to push through. The gyrations and overt enticement were repulsive, the last gasp of sobriety and spontaneity before drunken stupidity. Not inviting at all. He was approaching the edge of the pit when he realised the weight on his head was coming from the glares of others.

Two he recognised by face, the other, the one who was too old to be here really, was Covington. He and Charlie had at one time been sociable enough. Covington was a guy he would go down the pub and have a drink with, usually a dive of a pub where the conversation was sport and birds, but it would be friendly enough.

There was nothing friendly in the way Covington and co were looking at him now. Without a pause, he headed straight for the exit and Covington and crew were off to the side, all he had to do was keep going in a straight line.

Getting out of the mire of the dance floor was a blessed relief, and two long strides took him closer to the door before he was pulled up short by a grip on his arm that turned him to face one of the men he didn't recognise. Covington moved to the other side, the third man behind him.

Surrounded.

The one in front of him – Pearce, he recalled - was huffing like a bull about to charge. Muscles coiled, he calculated that he might just about be able to better the three of them, but it would be a bloody close-run thing.

'What's going on?'

The question was bellowed over the music by a blocky guy who spent too much time in the gym. The black t-shirt seemed to be spray painted on the Mr Universe upper body that was so sculpted it looked inhuman. The band around the guy's bicep declared him SIA licensed. Security Industry Approved. Or Sorry Inadequate Applicants, as he remembered one colleague ungracefully redefining it when he saw a failed police candidate on a door. Charlie remembered his name was Clyde, like the ape in *Every Which Way But Loose,* which he someone managed to resemble and why the name stuck in Charlie's head.

'What's going on here?'

'Just a friendly chat.' Covington smiled.

Clyde looked at him. 'This kind of friendly should be taken outside.'

'Hey, we paid to get in here,' Pearce shouted. 'We want to stay, we will.'

'I'm going anyway,' Charlie declared, and pushed past the third guy he didn't know. Any reaction was lost in the general throng, but Charlie wasn't worried, Clyde clearly knew what he was doing, and the troublesome trio wouldn't be stupid enough to make a move past that.

The evening was warm, the collection of heat from the day radiating off the concrete, but Charlie started to shiver as he strode for home. He'd been doubly lucky tonight. Rhys had let him go and Covington's coven got blocked. It could have been very different and so much worse.

Quickly, his desire to get home turned the striding into a jog, and he reached the house at full pelt.

'Oh God, is everything alright?' Ari asked, standing in the lounge door as he stepped in, automatically locking the door behind him. She looked truly worried for him. That was only one reason why he loved her. 'You ran up the street like the hounds of Hell were on your heels.'

'Just in a hurry to see you.' He picked her up, kissing her hard, keeping the contact as he started taking her willingly up to his room.

Smiling, she broke the kiss, but still frowned at him. 'What do you think you're doing?'

'Being grateful for being a lucky man.'

Chapter 31

When the switchboard put the call through on Monday morning, Piper really wasn't sure what to think.

'Hello?'

'DCI Piper?'

A man's voice. One that wasn't quite as assured as it could be. And it sounded odd, muffled. Like the man was trying to hide who he was.

'I am, yes. How can I help you?'

'You can't,' the man said. 'You can't help me, and I can't really help you. Not until he's arrested. It's not safe. I'm not safe now. But listen. The underground is going underground. They kept saying it. The underground is going underground.'

The phone was pressed to his ear, but the ringing was just the dead line tone.

The underground is going underground.

That rang a bell with Piper. A dim memory that he couldn't quite reach. He pushed back his chair and went to the incident room. Siddig was at a terminal.

'Siddig, what are you working on?'

As she told him, he moved around to look over her shoulder.

'Search for "the underground,"' he said, close to her ear. There was sufficient background noise for it not to overheard.

Frowning she turned to look at him. 'It's not exactly an unusual phrase.'

'I know. But there's... there's something in the back of my mind. Just run the search, will you?'

With a raise of her eyebrows, Siddig returned to the search page of HOLMES and searched the word "underground". Not surprisingly, there were a lot of references.

'Match it with "child".'

Siddig did, the total searches reduced, but didn't help much.

'Reduce to a local search.'

There were still more references than anyone could read through with any speed. Piper took over the mouse and started to scroll through the list, speed reading through the short description.

'There!'

He pointed to the screen. The Underground. The name of a paedophile ring which first came to light in the 1990s.

'See if you can find me anything more on this lot. Quietly.'

He patted Siddig on the shoulder and walked away.

* * *

Piper sat at his desk, desperately trying to figure it all out into some semblance of sense. Nothing was happening. He had taken to tapping his pen on the desk in frustration.

'Well, that's annoying.'

Piper looked up to see Malcolm Goodman, the forensic accountant, standing in his doorway.

'Tell me you're bringing good news.'

'Depends on your point of view.' Goodman stepped in and put the file on Piper's desk. 'I've put the books back into evidence. What this report says is that several companies are clearly laundering money. Problem is, all those businesses are now closed, and all answered to Phillip Mansel-Jones. We can, and the fraud squad will, follow this though. But frankly, it's not going to do you any good.'

'Thanks, just what I need. Another dead end, ending at a dead man.'

* * *

It was the end of the day and Piper felt no nearer a solution than he had at the start. He stared at the incident board and wondered if anything was ever going to break. He understood why Broughton had put him on this, even accepted that he had to do his time like a good little subordinate. But cold cases tended to be slower and tougher to crack. A juicy murder and he'd lay odds that they met the murderer in the first 36 hours.

Across the way, Langdon was looking over his own developing board. There wasn't a great deal on it right now. The draw was just too great.

'How's it going?'

Langdon looked over his shoulder. Piper moved over to stand beside him.

'Depends, have you anything pertinent to add that you're keeping hidden?'

That wasn't like Langdon. 'There was nothing pertinent ever hidden, and that is your one shot, Langdon. Don't forget I am still the ranking officer here and if you can't deal with that, I can find you somewhere else to work.'

Langdon looked away, mumbling an apology.

Then they both turned their concentration to the board. The picture of Marie from her parents, happy and healthy by some river that was just too wide and sumptuous to be in the UK. Then there was the image of her in the alley where she had been found.

'Slowly. It's going slowly,' Langdon answered Piper's question. 'Nothing from the door to door. What CCTV there is in the area is so poor as to be worthless. Still got a couple of teams still to report, but I'm not that hopeful. DCI Small is speaking to the parents, see if they can give us any idea who she might have been with.'

'PM?'

'Report confirms she was raped, anally as well as vaginally. That wasn't the cause of death. She asphyxiated. We're waiting on various tests for the fibres the doc pulled out of her throat, and the semen found in her bowel. Doc said that might be a bit questionable. Apparently, the guy used a prophylactic which must have failed, but the spermicide may affect the quality of results.'

'Those aren't the only questionable results.'

Both men turned to see Linda Small moving swiftly into the room on her usual long-legged stride. She had a file in her hand, but that was exactly where it stayed as she stepped up to the board and followed the timeline that Langdon had set out.

'Right, we know from our informant that Marie was taken to the Marina early Saturday afternoon, but her parents didn't report her missing until Wednesday and she was found in the early hours of Thursday.'

This was nothing new and Piper had to wonder why she was going over it.

'During the interview, Mrs Gallo did a lot of talking in Romanian. Now I don't understand a word of it myself, but I know a contradiction when I hear one. Men and women sound the same arguing in any language. They know more than they're telling.'

Which is useless until we know it too.

'Damn it, why are people always so scared to tell the police the truth?' Langdon grouched.

Small looked at him. 'It's not necessarily us that they're afraid of.'

Piper smiled at Linda. 'It might be you.'

The eye roll was almost audible. 'The more likely scenario is that whoever took the girl has some hold over the Gallo family. It wouldn't be unusual, the Gallos own a small shop on Frith Street.'

Frith Street. A side street going nowhere special. A small row of shops that either belonged to Mansel-Jones or paid him for protection. People might think the time of gangsters and protection rackets was 1950s New York; they didn't *want* to know such things existed everywhere, every time. Bullies always did what bullies could. And scared people covered for them.

'I've been talking to some of Marie's school friends. They were difficult to find. In fact, I didn't find one that wanted to admit being a friend. So I asked anyway, and no one has seen her for two weeks.' Linda put a possible addition to the timeline. 'From what the informant said of her when she was left in the Marina, I doubt that was her first day under control. Not the way she was dressed.'

Langdon considered the point. 'There was no mention that she'd been bruised earlier than during the rapes.'

'Beatings aren't the only way to coerce a person.'

Chapter 32

With a sigh, Piper switched off the car engine and headlights. *Home.* The absolute relief was welcome. Yesterday had been tough, and today nothing more than an unproductive slog. It was difficult to switch off, but after the day he'd had, he needed to. Looking into the lives and losses of kids and the crimes surrounding them, the people who committed crimes; that was shit no one should have to wade through. Yet he'd spent his day wading hip-deep in that filth. Now he had to let it go, not take it into the house where his family lived.

In the dark and the quiet, he sat back, head against the rest and closed his eyes. Breathe in deep. Breathe out.

In, two, three, four, five.

Out, two, three, four, five.

He repeated the exercise until the tension flowed out from between his shoulder blades and the children he was thinking about were those he'd given life to. Ashley, off loving university. Shauna, happy at home and enjoying studying locally. It never ceased to amaze him how identical twins could be so different. Then there was the baby of the family – oh how he'd hate being called that. Josh, resentfully finishing his GCSEs even though he was going to be in *the band* and be famous and rich and what did he need algebra for anyway? Huh? Piper let the smile spread slowly. The truth was, Josh was such a good guitarist, that maybe one day he *would* be rich and famous. In the meantime, Piper was going to stay on his back to get the algebra done right. Settled, Piper opened the car door and stepped out into the evening.

Walking past the living room window, he glanced inside to see Sheila and Shauna sitting in the adjoining dining room, looking over various papers spread over the table. The joy of two bookworm family members. Even as he put the key in the lock, the thump of music Piper didn't recognise flowed from Josh's room. As he closed the door, he pulled his phone from his pocket and sent a short text. The house smelled of roast chicken dinner. The family would have eaten earlier, but there would be a plated meal ready for him. Just a few vegetables to steam, since he hated when they went mushy.

He went through the lounge to lean on the edge of the arch between it and the dining room to look at his wife and daughter. Shauna was like her mother, but had taken on his own darker hair, only she had dip-dyed the bottom a gorgeous royal blue. Of course, he'd had to do the stern father thing because she could hardly rebel, or might even rebel too much more, if he told her that he actually really liked the way it looked. One thick strand of blue was bobbing over the paper as if she were writing with it and not the pen. The additional unrhythmic thumping was Josh coming down the stairs.

'What d'ya want?' he demanded as he slouched down to the other side of the arch, his response to Piper's text to come down.

Smiling as he looked the boy over, more of the cares of the day left him. 'For you to stand up straight for a start.' It was a familiar conversation. 'You're too tall to keep hunching down all the time.'

'I hunch because the rest of you are so short.'

He wondered how many times they'd had this exchange. It didn't matter though, Josh stood that little bit taller anyway.

'I just wanted you down here so I could tell you all I love you.'

'Oh God, what's happened?'

'Who died?'

'Are you dying?'

His breath caught, his jaw dropped. That was not the reaction he'd been expecting. 'I don't say it that rarely, do I?' He looked at each of them, ending on Sheila.

'Not to me,' she assured him. 'But you're not exactly free with those words generally.'

'Besides,' Shauna added, 'you show us every day.'

'Oh God, would be better if you were dying.' Josh punched him lightly on the shoulder. The boy didn't know his own strength yet; it hurt. 'You're just to embarrassing, Da-argh!'

'Down!'

The sound of gunfire caught Piper by surprise, but training kicked in. The sound of fracturing glass underscored Josh's yelp as Piper grabbed his son and dragged him behind what little shelter the arch could give. Something thudded on the carpet in the front room. Sheila had followed his lead and was hugging the now-crying Shauna to her.

'What's going on?' Sheila asked in a whisper.

All Piper could do was shrug and listen. He could hear the squeal of tyres as someone pulled away too fast. Beyond that was only a dog barking, the big Alsatian from next door. Yapping then suggested that the Pekingese across the street was getting in on the act.

'Oh my God!'

Piper recognised that voice. Dave Bova from number 14. With no other sounds of threat other than the verbal assault from the thrash Josh had left playing, Piper looked around the arch. A brick with something bound to it with an elastic band lay in the middle of the carpet with a million shards of what used to be their front window. The gunshots had been to break the glass or the brick would like as not have bounced off the double glazing.

His grip on Josh eased and he looked at the boy. 'Ok?'

He was white as a sheet, but he nodded.

Carefully Piper stood up, saw Dave approaching across the garden. He was wet with sweat, clearly coming back from a run. Jogging, something Piper felt he should do more often, but never enough to actually do it.

'Don't come any closer, Dave,' Piper called and held up his hand. 'Don't want to risk damaging any evidence out there.' Because given how far into the room the brick was, the person who threw it had probably been on their front lawn. *Bloody covenant*, Piper thought: the clause in the deed didn't allow them to put up any kind of barrier between them and the street. *Sod it, I'm planting a hedge.* Satisfied that Dave wasn't moving, Piper pulled his phone from his pocket.

With a direct line he didn't have to go through the palaver of the call centre; he put the incident straight through to someone who could deal with it efficiently and without fuss.

Ending the call, he looked up at Dave. Even from this distance, Piper could see the shivering. 'Dave, retrace your steps back as best you can and head home. Someone will be over in a little while to take a statement from you.'

'What about Sheila and the kids? Do they want to come with me?'

'That's a good idea.'

'I'm not going anywhere!'

Piper turned to Sheila. She was standing now, they all were, the three of them standing closer than they usually would. He smiled at his wife, dragged her to him and hugged her close. 'I love you, you brave woman.' One more squeeze then he pushed her away, hands on her shoulders. 'But even I can feel the temperature drop with that window gone. If you go to

Dave's, I'll know you're safe and that the scene isn't getting tampered with. Come on.'

'This isn't a *scene*, it's our home.' Her brow was furrowed and her chin up. His brave little warrior woman.

'And the sooner we deal with it *as* a scene, the quicker we can get it back to being our home.'

'We'll be fine here, Dad,' Josh assured him.

'But you'll be safer with Dave, and I'll be less worried.' Josh's lips were compressed too. He was only 15, but he was getting to understand that responsibility wasn't always easy.

'Okay.'

'Thank you.'

He looked at Sheila; she still wanted to argue. 'Please.' He felt the tension drop from her shoulders as she sighed. It was reluctant, but it was acceptance. He eased her towards the kitchen, herding them all towards the hall and back to the front door. There he checked around before opening up and nodding to Dave, who had gone back through his own footsteps. He pointed towards the edge of the lawn to keep the family out of the area of potential interest. The kids went first.

'Take care of them,' he whispered with one last hug for Sheila.

'You owe me for having to put up with him for an evening.'

He knew she was right. Dave was nice enough, but something of a bore, and that had only got worse since his wife had left.

'I know. I'll make it up to you.' Though as he watched the four of them heading down the road, he wasn't exactly sure how.

Chapter 33

'Sir, I—' Siddig cut herself off as she laid eyes on Piper, eyes that went very wide and showed very white against her darker skin. Quickly, she closed his office door and stepped towards his desk. 'Are you okay? You look like—' This time her hand went to her mouth. 'Sorry, sir.'

He waved the apology away. 'It's okay Siddig, I know I look like crap. Honestly, I feel like crap too.' With a sigh he sat back, unable to avoid the comparison between his smart, fresh-faced companion and his unshaven, exhausted, still-wearing-yesterday's-suit self.

'Anything I can help with?'

The glazier had replaced the front window; Forensics had the projectile and the note; Sheila, Shauna and Josh were back home, safe, calm and supporting each other; they hadn't called Ashley last night because two days ago, they'd chatted about the heavy-duty assignment she had on at university and he didn't want her distracted. Only this morning, he'd had to call her - thankfully the assignment was already handed in. He was just trying to carry on as normal. Which was particularly difficult after skipping a night of sleep and while jumping at the slightest thing. 'Not really. What have you got for me?'

'Well I was reading through the transcripts of your interview with DC Watson, what he said about the Don.'

He scratched at his chin, there was a reason he was usually clean-shaven, and he'd wished he'd taken the time to bother this morning. The Watson case was an open and shut one, not much to do, but the reference to the Don was still interesting. Shame Watson wasn't talking about that angle. 'And?'

'And his comment that it would take a virtual miracle might not be the dismissal it seemed.'

He couldn't see how, but... 'Go on.'

'Piper!' They both jumped at Broughton's voice as he stepped into the office. 'What are you doing in?'

'My job.'

Broughton, smart as ever in his immaculate uniform, strode forward, stopping next to Siddig, who looked just a touch cowed by the DCS's presence.

'Right now, your job is to go home and be a husband and father. After what happened last night, this is not the place for you.'

Now Piper was scowling. 'After what happened last night, this is exactly where I need to be.'

'What happened last night?'

Broughton wasn't answering that any more than he was. 'You can't risk an accusation of interfering with the investigation. Go home.'

Piper could feel the heat rising. How dare a man twice divorced with four kids, none of whom spoke to him, try to give lectures on what he should do with his family. 'I've still other investigations to conduct.'

'Not today you haven't. Go home.'

Muscles tensed to rise -

'Erm, excuse me.' Siddig shouldered lightly between them. 'What did happen last night?'

He didn't want to say, but he didn't want Broughton giving the wrong impression either. 'My front window was broken by hooligans.'

Broughton tutted. 'It was more than that and we both know it.' For a moment, that rigid stance eased. 'Okay I can see giving you a direct order isn't going to work. Right. Siddig, sit.'

As the young woman took one chair, Broughton closed the office door and took the other seat. The claustrophobic feel of the office increased, even if the tension dissipated a little. Broughton efficiently briefed Siddig on what had happened, silencing Piper with a look when he tried to downplay it.

'Do we have any idea who or why?'

That Siddig didn't waste time with pleasantries actually pleased Piper. It wasn't because she didn't care; she'd already proved she did. She was simply putting business first.

'Not officially.'

Siddig turned to Piper. 'Unofficially?'

'Rhys Mansel-Jones.'

'Now we can't go bandying names around like that.' Broughton cowed Piper with a hard look before turning to Siddig. 'It is, however, the most likely answer. He's the most likely to have guns in the area, and if not, the one with the easiest access to them. The car the perpetrators used was stolen half an hour before the incident, but from a street with no CCTV. The other cameras are being checked to see if we can get any images of the driver. If we can identify who was there, we might be able to establish a link. But we need more to go on than a vague suspicion.'

There was nothing vague about his suspicion, but Broughton was right about the lack of concrete evidence and without evidence, there was no way they could move on Mansel-Jones.

'Are we actually getting anywhere with anything?'

That was exactly the kind of question that Piper could do without Broughton asking. 'Yes and no. We know Watson has contact with the Don.'

'Had,' Broughton clarified. 'And he's not saying who that contact, or the Don is.'

Clearly no quarter would be given. 'We've traced one of the boys, Vince Long, he's alive and well and living in Worcester. Their local force is going to have a word, get the details of why he went, see if there is any connection with the rest of it. And Teddington is coming in tomorrow morning for an identify parade.'

'Who are you looking to get IDed?'

'The men who stopped her when Terry was taken.'

'Allegedly taken.'

'I think it's more likely than not.'

'I think an ID twenty years after the event is less than likely.'

Another thing he didn't want to hear.

'Besides didn't she already identify Dion Searlotti?'

'She did, and he's one of the men in the line-up.'

'Then do you really need to go through this?'

'Yes. At the moment he's being far from helpful, says we can't touch him, can't prove anything from a faded memory or a crappy photo.' And he had a point.

'You think that a face to face identification will push him harder?'

Piper nodded. 'I'm hoping that he won't be the only one Teddington recognises. There are two of Dion's former associates in the line-up, one may be the second man.'

'Do you really think her memory will be up to that?'

Piper shrugged. 'She said their faces are etched indelibly in her mind, so it might work, it might not. We'll have to wait and see.'

'Apparently, it's all we can do,' Broughton agreed.

'Not necessarily.'

Both men turned to Siddig. Her spine was straight, but from practice and comfort rather than the regimentation she felt the current company necessitated. Her knees were together, and her legs crossed only at the ankles. Elegance and comfort. Piper wondered if she'd trained to dance; she had the shape and flexibility of a dancer, though she was probably a bit too tall for most partners.

'As I was saying, I was going through Watson's statement, and that comment he made about needing a virtual miracle to stop the Don. I don't think he was being dismissive. I think he was telling you to look at the virtual records, the database. The DNA records might not be there, but it's just possible the record of who deleted them is. The same is true of records on HOLMES. I called the IT guys, they said I didn't have the authorisation to ask for those checks, but I figure one or both of you might. There's also the question of Watson's phone.'

'Watson didn't have a phone on him when he was arrested,' Broughton pointed out.

'Which is the point.' Piper refocused on Siddig, thinking he might know where she was going with this. 'Isn't it?'

She nodded. 'It's unusual. Most of the time when we bring someone in, the things you can virtually guarantee will have to be collected off them are some form of money and at least one phone. No one goes out without their phone these days.'

'Unless they're hiding or have something to hide,' Piper pondered.

'Exactly.'

'Or he ditched it,' Broughton suggested.

'True, sir, but that's still an attempt at concealment. I was thinking that if we can get hold of Watson's mobile, we might just be able to trace the calls back. There could well be a number of layers of links, but we'd get there eventually.'

'If we can get hold of the phone.' Broughton tried to put a dampener on the idea.

'Actually, no sir. I checked on that as well. The phone is great for finding out what text messages actually said, it'll have any photos, sometimes emails, but apparently, we don't need the actual phone. We just need to get to the phone records and we have Watson's number.'

'Then-'

'Then-' Broughton cut Piper off '-you can go home safe in the knowledge that Siddig seems to be very good at her job and I'll give her the backup she needs.'

The objection was on the tip of his tongue, but the idea of relaxing at home with the family right now was just too welcome. Still, perhaps it would be politic to let Broughton think he was just capitulating. 'If you insist, sir.'

Chapter 34

'Hi.'

Piper's stomach sank as he returned the greeting. It was a surprise, he hadn't thought his gut could get any lower. He just wanted to get home now he could. There was something about the tone of Charlie's voice that told him this wasn't just a social call.

'How's the family?'

The frown stopped him in his tracks. *What has he heard?* 'Why?'

Charlie's pause could have been surprise. 'Just asking.'

'They're fine.'

'Good. Shauna okay?'

For a second Piper took the phone from his ear and looked at it. Telephone conversations were useful, but he had the feeling a face to face would be better right now. 'She's fine. Still asks to see you every now and again.'

'I could pop over one evening.'

'No, you really couldn't.' Not with everything else that was going on. Besides Charlie was an informant now, that would be crossing a line he didn't want to cross. 'But I get the feeling we do need to meet and talk. Are you working?'

'Afternoons. I can come to the station if that suits you.'

Wouldn't be much point right now, would there? He had gained a new appreciation for how victims of stalking felt. He certainly felt he was being watched at every move, station or not. Even now he was constantly checking the mirrors, watching for a tail though he'd parked up to answer the call. 'Does Teddington know you want to speak to me?' *Must check how Ariadne is getting on.*

'Actually, yes. How about the coffee shop round the corner from the station?'

He looked at the turning to his own road. *So near and yet so far.* 'No. The independent one on Martin Street. Fifteen minutes?'

The aroma of coffee was so strong it attacked his nose before Piper even opened the door. The day was bright and warm enough that the tables outside were already filling up. Inside there was a blast of hot air as he stepped through the door, but the room was a more pleasant temperature. He got into the queue, which seemed to consist of already stressed-looking business types, several of whom were checking their watches. Seemed to Piper that the last thing this lot needed was coffee. He got in line. A quick scan showed Charlie hadn't arrived. Just as well he remembered Charlie's usual order.

The smell turned bitter. Coffee, yes, but burnt. He looked behind the counter. The two baristas were both fiddling with the coffee machine. Red faces and the way the younger boy looked ready to burst into tears suggested that something pretty major had gone wrong with the machine.

'Is this going to take much longer?' the woman at the head of the queue demanded.

The youngster's chin puckered, his lips quaked. The older guy clapped him on the shoulder and turned to the customer. Not much older. Twenties instead of teens, Piper judged.

'I'm very sorry, I can't sort this out immediately. I can offer you a full refund or an Americano.'

'I want a macchiato.'

The teeth behind his smile were clenched. 'Refund it is then.'

She and two other grumbling customers took refunds, others accepted the Americano and a free cookie. When the time came to step up, Piper stopped the barista apologising and ordered two Americanos. They were just being passed across when Charlie came in. With a nod, Piper invited the younger man to follow him.

The corner was shielded from the front by the counter, sat in greater shadow and wouldn't be easily watched. Piper put his back to the rear wall to watch out, and Charlie sat at the other wall.

'What is it?'

Charlie was frowning at him. 'You alright?'

'Why shouldn't I be?' He didn't like the defensiveness he heard in his own tone.

'Dunno, but when did you last not shave?'

He took a deep breath and sighed it out. 'I pulled an all-nighter and was just on my way home when you called. So, why did you call?'

'RMJ asked me to do a new job for him.'

Piper leant forward. 'What job?'

'Working the door at the Den.'

'When?'

The way Charlie shook his head told Piper he wasn't going to be happy. 'I said no.'

Piper felt sick. That was no way to infiltrate an organisation. It was no way to stay healthy either. 'Why?'

'He knew that you and I had been talking. He's been watching me, and he's already threatened Ari.'

The sound of those shots echoed through Piper's mind. The look on his family's faces. He'd never seen them so scared and hoped he'd never see them that way again. 'How did she react to that?'

Charlie looked away, hands on the edge of the bench seat and shoulders hunched. 'I haven't told her.'

His relationship, his call. Though Piper thought it was a mistake. Ari needed to know this sort of thing. There again, Charlie needed to know about the pictures and she wasn't talking about that either. That was their problem, they both wanted to wear the white hat, to be the hero. 'What happened when you refused RMJ?'

'He took it well. Worryingly well.'

That wasn't like the Mansel-Joneses. Refusing them tended to be injurious to your health.

'When did this happen?'

'Sunday.'

'And you're only telling me this now because?'

The hung head and the lack of answer were worrying. Could Charlie's refusal be connected to the attack on his own home? 'Any contact since?'

Charlie shook his head. A thump, strong swearwords, a hissing expulsion of steam. The clap of a high five. Piper looked to the counter, the baristas seemed to have managed to get something sorted on the coffee machine.

He sipped his own still hot drink. Nothing wrong with a good flat white. 'Should I take this as you telling me you're coming off CHIS?'

'Just that I'm not going to get in with you know who. I've thrown away too much in my life already, I can't risk Ari.'

My God, he's grown up at last. Mentally kicking himself for the sarcasm, Piper tried to readjust his thinking. 'No, you shouldn't. She's too good a woman. Too good for you.' He hoped the smile didn't look as forced as it felt.

'Yeah, she is. She might even be beginning to work that out.'

'What do you mean?'

His head shook, emphasising the fact that he needed a haircut. 'She's just been a bit weird of late. Reticent. A bit remote. The fact that Enzo seems to be underfoot all the time isn't exactly helping either.'

'The fact that I suspect you're not exactly getting on with her best friend is probably not helping either.'

Charlie flinched at that rebuke.

'Look, I think you're doing the right thing. And I think you need to leave the area.'

The brought Charlie's head up sharply. 'What? Why?'

Tell him the harsh truth or let him figure it out? 'You know the Lone Ranger had to take the mask off some time, right?'

Charlie frowned at him. 'So?'

So Charlie needed to stop trying to be the hero and actually be the hero Ari could go home to.

'Ari was telling me the company she's seconded to is based in Edinburgh. So, get her to transfer there. Take her and Mrs Whittaker and move. Get right away, a clean break. A new start for all of you.'

For a moment, hope shone in Charlie's eyes, then it died, and he looked away. 'They won't move for me.'

'You don't know that until you ask them.'

Again, Charlie shook his head. 'Mrs W is too attached to the place she lost her husband and son.'

'But she'll do anything for her daughter. So would you if you'd stop being a prat and think about it.'

'Thanks.' Charlie laughed at himself. 'I'll think about it. And in the meantime, I think you should know that when I was in the Den, I saw a couple of your lads. They were ready to attack I think, but one of the club's bouncers, Clyde Davis, got in the way.'

'Who?'

'Covington and Pearce. The other one's name I don't remember. But I think he's still Uniform, or at least he was when I was last working.'

Piper looked away, nodded absently. There was nothing he could do to stop Covington going to the Den of Angels, that was no evidence that the man was doing anything wrong.

It was no guarantee he wasn't, either.

'Piper?'

He refocused on Charlie, who was frowning at him.

'What's wrong?'

'Nothing.'

'Really? You just phased out. All-nighter or not, I know something's up with you. What's happened?'

'Haven't seen the papers this morning, have you?'

'No.'

Piper reached out to the one that had been left on the adjacent table. Ignoring the headline begging for information on Madeline Stolz, he turned to page 4, folded the tabloid and placed it in front of Charlie. Pointed to the two inches given over to reporting the smashed window and some wild speculation. So much in fact that that was the reason he'd phoned Ashley even though he didn't want to, because he really didn't want her finding out about it from anyone else. Charlie scanned it.

'Jesus. But everyone's alright? Sheila, the twins, Josh?'

'We're all fine.'

Hopefully Charlie would understand that that was the end of the conversation too.

'Did you find anything on the Don yet?'

The look should tell Charlie everything he needed to know. Like not to ask about ongoing investigations. But there might be something he could help with. 'What does "going underground" mean to you?'

Charlie frowned. 'Going undercover, I guess. Or the lyrics of a song.'

'Of course.' Piper huffed. 'That's why it sounded familiar. *Going Underground* by The Jam. Great, now I've got that stuck in my head all day.'

'What's a 1980s song got to do with anything?'

Piper looked around. 'Probably nothing, but I heard someone say, "the underground is going underground" and the phrase kind of stuck. God knows why I didn't remember the song straightaway. Workload probably. And it was a 1980s song, March 1980.' He knew that because he remembered where he was and what he was doing when it was on Top of The Pops, but he'd never told Sheila about that, so he wasn't going to share with Charlie.

'It was a phrase in Hall's book too. Part of anyway.'

Piper focused back on the other man. 'Go home.' *Oh God, I'm turning into Broughton.* 'Take care of Ari. Do whatever you need to. Let me know if anything happens, but whatever you do, don't come back to the station.'

Chapter 35

At ten to ten next morning, Wednesday, a much-refreshed Piper got the call. Teddington had arrived. Pulling himself together as he pulled on his jacket, he breathed out the stress and did his best to present a normal neutral persona. Reception was quiet, two people were by the desk, talking to the uniformed officer behind. Teddington waited to one side on a bank of screwed-down unpadded chairs. He was pleased to note she was wearing a long skirt, a lightweight jacket, and a corset. While he appreciated the sexiness, what he preferred was the indication that she was getting back to her old self.

'Good morning.'

Her smile was broad. 'Yes, it is.'

He unexpectedly found himself returning the smile; her apparent joy was infectious, reminding him that not everything in the world was doom and gloom. 'You're positively glowing this morning,' he noted and watched her blush. 'You're feeling better then?'

'Much.'

'No more photographs?'

'Oh at least one a day, but I'm trying not to let that get to me.'

'How's that working out for you?'

'Better when people don't ask about it. Shall we get on?'

Typical woman. He rolled his eyes and led her into the heart of the station. 'So is there something particularly good to counter the questions I'm not allowed to ask?' He prodded as they walked side by side down the corridor, though he suspected he knew the answer.

'Things are going great with Charlie. I'm a bit worried about him and the whole CHIS thing, but it's his choice and I have to respect that. Anyway, things between him and I are fab right now and I'm going to enjoy that.'

'Good. Good.' It was great to know that they had finally figured it out and got together, Charlie hadn't exactly been clear on that point. The thought ran through his mind that he could reassure her on the CHIS front, but that wasn't his place. Still, the pair of them deserved to be happy and their being happy together was just about the best thing for either of them. If Charlie could now learn to be totally honest with her, Piper would give them the best of chances for a long and happy relationship. He led her into the viewing room and gave Siddig the nod to start bringing the suspects in.

'No more trouble with Sanchez then?'

She looked at him; her lips were smiling, but her eyes were hard. 'Don't ask.'

'Okay.' Leave off the potentially painful topics. That wasn't going to be easy, given what she was here to do, but he could try. 'So, how's the new job going, back in IT? If I'm allowed to ask about that?' Piper said as they waited. It was his custom to try to put people at their ease and he had to still try, even when it was a minefield.

'Yes, you can ask about that. And it's good. Sort of. It's a new assignment, though technically I'm on secondment from the prison service, so it's the same job in a way. But it'll be different and at least it means that I get more recovery time before we all have to admit that I'm no longer fit for wing duty.'

'Will you miss it?'

'I already do.' She looked at him and he could see there were regrets. 'And I already don't.'

He almost understood what she meant as he watched the side door beyond the two-way glass open. 'Right, there'll be six men brought in, take your ti—'

'One.'

Caught in mid-word, Piper had to redirect his thoughts. 'Well, you can take your time but —'

'And number three.'

Mouth still open as she'd cut him off, he looked at her with raised brows. 'You can take your time. You should take your time.'

She turned to him. 'I know. I just don't need to. I thought I would, but the second I saw them, I knew. Both of them.' She looked back at the line-up. 'It was Number One and Number Three.' A nod. 'Definitely.'

He looked across. Number One. Dion Searlotti. Number Three. Ian Kinsley. Three convictions for sexual assault, multiple unproven complaints, and only fifteen months out of jail, but he'd been held in London, not locally in HMP Blackmarch.

'I wasn't expecting to see both of them,' she said. 'Number One is the guy from the photo, he was the first to grab me. But Number Three was the other one. I got a good look at both of them at the time. I know twenty years have gone by and in fairness, it hasn't treated either one particularly well, but it was definitely those two. If I remember right, that Number Three has a tattoo on his neck.' Her own hand went up and she was doing the directional thing to work out which side she was talking about. 'An anchor, possibly with a short length of chain. On the right-hand side, his right.'

Piper said nothing but looked at Kinsley. He was wearing a polo neck jumper, so there was no way to see what was on his neck. But Piper knew there was an anchor tattooed on the right side of his neck. And the only way Teddington could know that now was if she saw it back when she encountered these two. Piper allowed himself a moment of smug satisfaction. He was going to nail the pair of them and with a bit of luck close more unsolved cases.

Chapter 36

Piper sat opposite Dion Searlotti. The interview wasn't going as well at he'd have liked.

'So what?' Searlotti finally demanded. 'So what if some woman now claims me and Kins grabbed her twenty years ago? You can't prove anything. Just her word against ours.'

'But you know what the courts are like these days, and you have previous. Both of you.'

'Which is inadmissible,' the duty solicitor reminded Piper.

He shrugged. 'The way things have swung against men these days, that won't make much difference. Especially when we start to connect it to the disappearance of the girl's sibling.'

'Never saw the boy.'

'I never said it was a boy.'

Dion looked up sharply. 'You did.'

Piper shook his head. 'No, I really didn't. Never mentioned it.'

And the way the solicitor had reacted meant she knew he hadn't said anything too. The tape would be the final evidence.

'Someone told me.'

'Who?' Piper pushed.

'Don't know.'

'Where did you hear it?'

'Don't know.'

'But you do know it was a boy that was taken.'

Searlotti shifted in his seat. 'Didn't say that.'

'Yes, you did.'

'It's like fifty-fifty, anyway. Had to be a boy or a girl. I guess I just guessed right.'

'I guess you know more than you're saying,' Piper said. 'So start talking.'

'I'm no grass.'

'Then there is something to grass about?'

'Didn't say that.'

'You're not saying much of anything, are you?'

'You've got nothing for me to talk about.'

'How about sexual assault -'

'Grabbing a tit's hardly sexual assault.'

'Actually,' Piper rolled the word around a little, 'that is one of the definitions. Interestingly however, I never told you that that is one of the accusations made against you. So that's sexual assault against a minor. Would you like to talk about that?'

Apparently not.

Piper raised his brows. 'Nothing to say?'

Searlotti sat back, all pinched features and folded arms.

'For the tape, Searlotti has sat back with folded arms. So, you admit that you sexually assaulted an eleven-year-old girl by, and I quote, "grabbing her tit"?'

Searlotti moved his head from side to side.

'Searlotti shakes his head.' Piper said. 'So you are contradicting yourself, then? You didn't grab her tit?'

The man now looked up and glared at him.

'Which was it?'

Still nothing.

'Let's go with your first statement. It's her word against yours because grabbing a tit isn't sexual assault. That is what you said, isn't it?' Piper waited, though with little expectation that he would get an answer. 'You admit you were thereby aiding and abetting the abduction of a nine-year-old boy?'

Piper waited and got no response. 'Can I remind you that your failure to answer will be reported in court and is likely to be taken against you?' He waited and still nothing was said. He had to push Searlotti. Here was a man who had a string of offences, he'd been in and out of various prisons. But only for short periods. 'That nine-year-old boy was never seen alive again. That makes you an accessory to murder.'

'I never murdered anyone.'

'I said accessory. It still carries a much longer sentence than the three months or so you've ever done at a stretch. So do you want to start talking to me now?'

'Nothing to talk about.'

'Think that's what Kinsley will tell me?'

Searlotti looked around him. His mouth twisted as he considered, then he sat up. 'Look, Kins and I, we were just there. Pretty girl, the footie was on. We'd 'ad a couple. It was just a bit of fun. That's all. If that makes it sexual assault, I'm sorry, but I had nothing to do with any kid being taken.'

* * *

Piper steeled himself for facing Ian Kinsley. If he turned out to be as reticent as his partner in crime, this was going nowhere.

'Yeah, we did,' Kinsley admitted in answer to Piper's very first question.

That caught and stopped Piper. It took a heartbeat or two for him to process the response. 'You're freely admitting to sexually assaulting Ariadne Whittaker when she was only eleven years old?'

'Yep.' Blackened teeth appeared behind a sickly confident smile.

Piper, eyes on Kinsley, turned his head to Siddig, moving his eyes only at the last second. Siddig looked surprised too. Then she opened the buff file she had brought with her. From it, she pulled two photographs, one of twelve-year-old Ariadne with a girlfriend and a boy Piper was pretty sure was Enzo Sanchez. It was the only picture she could find from around that time.

'Can you identify which of these two girls we are talking about?' Siddig asked as she laid the picture down in front of Kinsley.

'That one.' One nicotine-stained digit landed unerringly on Ariadne Whittaker as she would have been back then. 'She was a bit of all right for a kid. Got the impression her tits hadn't quite come in yet, but they were still a decent handful.'

'Why did you assault her?'

Kinsley shrugged. 'Mansel-Jones bunged us a twenty each to do so.'

'Mansel-Jones?'

The old-looking head nodded. 'Phillip Mansel-Jones.'

This was all turning out too easy and pointing in the direction he was expecting, but not necessarily hoping for. 'Why?'

'Coz he wanted the boy.'

Sometimes the way criminals were so matter of fact floored Piper. This was one of those times.

'Okay.' He dragged in a deep breath. 'Let's start from the beginning. Can you tell me exactly what happened that day?'

'Well, one of Mansel-Jones' spotters-'

'His what?' Siddig asked.

'Spotters. Mansel-Jones had a network of spotters, well kiddy fiddlers. They kept an eye out for any available desirables. He got a call, there was a boy he'd like, but there was also a girl to keep out the way. We were told to keep 'er busy so someone else could grab the boy. We'd just got out of the car, were walking over the road, when the kid came out of park, and started to show an interest in the car.'

'The Roller?' Piper asked. Phillip Mansel-Jones had owned a range of beautiful classic cars. Amazingly, none were ever seen near any crime scenes, until the Roller was caught on CCTV – allegedly. That recording had disappeared too.

'Bentley, actually. Roomier in the rear. 'Spect the kid hadn't seen a real one before. So Mansel-Jones saw him heading for the car, but still nodded to us to see to the girl. So we did. Felt like going a bit further, little cow didn't half kick my shins. Bruised for weeks I were. Would have too, but I heard the Bentley leave and there was this dog and walker came on to the park, so we let the kid go and went down the pub.'

'So you were drinking after the assault?'

'Yeah.'

'Searlotti says you were drinking beforehand.'

The guy shrugged. 'We were in the pub when Mansel-Jones grabbed us. He was there before me, so I guess so. I 'adn't had that much, but 'e might have.'

The news was so prosaically given that Piper didn't actually doubt a word of it. 'Do you know who the spotter was?'

'Nah.' He shook his grey head. 'Not my area.'

'Do you know what happened to the boy?'

Kinsley shrugged. 'Not really, like I said, not my thing. I heard that Mansel-Jones had a place for 'em like though. It was said you could get anything for a price at the Tick Tock Shop. Not sure where but there were rooms, and those honoured enough to be allowed in got to sample whatever delights they wanted. For a price.'

'He charged?'

Again the shrug. 'I guess, but got the impression that it was more about some way of his controlling them. But I dun much know. It not being my bag an' all.'

'Who would know?'

A shrug. 'Not my bag.'

'What about other contacts.'

'Not-'

'-Your bag, yes I get that. There must be something more you can tell me.'

He huffed out fetid breath. 'Nah. You going to charge me then? With this assault thing?'

'Yes.'

Kinsley smiled. 'So I'll be remanded then, right?'

It wasn't usual for any man to seem so happy when facing the prospect of jail. He certainly wasn't in the business of giving the scum what they wanted, but there was a procedure to follow. 'You just admitted assault and being an accessory to an abduction, and conspiracy to protect a paedophile ring. Yes, you'll be remanded. Then tried. Then, hopefully, jailed. Interview terminated.' Sickened, Piper stood.

'Well, I'll be remanded.' Kinsley sat comfortable in his chair. 'But I won't live long enough to be tried.'

Piper stopped and looked at the old man. 'What do you mean? Has someone made threats?'

Kinsley's chuckle was bitter. 'Only the doc.'

'The Don?'

This time the laughter was longer and ended in a coughing fit. 'The doctor. The cancer's spread. Reckons I'll be dead in a fortnight, month at most.'

That explained the hollow cheeks and sunken eyes. 'Sorry to hear that.' It was a lie, but the thing to say. He turned to leave again.

'One thing I did hear.' Kinsley's announcement called Piper back. 'The Don's reign is coming to the end. In Costa I 'eard.'

* * *

'What are we supposed to do, then?' Covington asked at they sat in the incident room. 'Stake out all the coffee houses and wait for someone to croak?'

Piper looked at the new updates written up in Siddig's hand. At least it was one case closed. That Kinsley would spend his final days in greater comfort behind bars than if he were a free man left Piper mystified as to how to name his own reactions. That was one case solved, something that was significant to the statistics, but not especially the victim, because unfortunately it wasn't significant to the victim's brother.

'I don't know what it means,' he answered with a sigh. He checked that there was no one else in the room before he pinned Covington with a hard look. 'What were you doing at the Den of Angels on Sunday night.'

'Having a night off,' said Covington with just a little too much aggression. 'It's still allowed.'

'There are better places to do it than the Den.'

'It's my time off, it's my choice. Besides, it's pretty much the only club left in the town centre.'

The unspoken suspicion that that was because Rhys Mansel-Jones had got the rest of them closed down was a spectre in the shadows.

'And whose choice was confronting Charlie Bell? Just because he was in there?'

Covington sneered at the name. 'I didn't confront him.'

'You, Pearce and one other he didn't recognise surrounded him. Bell says if it hadn't been for the bouncer, he's not sure he'd have got out of there unscathed.'

'Maybe you should ask Bell what he was doing there in the first place.'

'I'm asking what you were doing there.'

Covington's teeth were gritted, and his folded arms couldn't cover the fact that his hands were fisted. 'I was taking some well-earned R&R. I can do what I want on my time off. What's Bell's excuse. You should have seen him, cosying up to Mansel-Jones. He was a good cop once, I'll grant you, but it looks like your old protégé has turned to the dark side. I wouldn't be in the least bit surprised to find that turncoat was working for the other side now.'

Piper seethed to put the man in his place, but bit back the truth. He wasn't sure who he could trust in the station and he couldn't risk Charlie's position.

'What Bell does now is his own business. He's not a member of my team - you are. We all know who runs the Den and we all know that it's not an entirely legit business. I don't want you or any other members of this department going there.'

'It's the best, pretty much only place to pick up girls around here.'

'They aren't the kind of girls you want to pick up. You can do better than that. And what if you pick one of the wrong girls? I don't want you risking being caught in one of Mansel-Jones' traps. Understand?'

Covington bowed his head, tension oozing from every pore. When he looked up, his eyes were blazing. 'Yes. Sir.'

It wasn't much but it was as good as he was going to get. 'Good. Now it's late. Go home. I am.'

Chapter 37

'Very active fifteen to twenty years ago, but never really closed down, just not so heard about any more.' Siddig reported on The Underground.

The Underground is going underground. It didn't make any sense. And the earworm was starting to bug him. Of course the underground was underground. That's how underground things worked, especially paedophile rings, they stayed hidden to get away with things no normal person would countenance.

'Can you check out Tick Tock Shop too?' He asked Siddig. 'No idea how it relates, but Kinsey's reference is really bugging me. Like I should know but don't.'

Siddig nodded. 'It's not obvious, but I'll look into it, sir. Thanks.'

That last stopped him. 'What for?'

'Trusting me. Giving me these opportunities.'

'I'm dumping a lot of research on you that I don't want to get bogged down in.'

'Yes, sir.' Her grin was wide. 'You're trusting me to help you find the pieces of the puzzle and I love that. Thank you.'

Piper stared at the empty door in Siddig's wake. If she was serious about being a career copper, she was certainly going the right way about it. He'd had to look into getting her on the fast track. It wasn't beyond possibility that she would out rank him one day.

Grantham appeared at Piper's door like the spectre at the feast. His bulk almost filled the width, and Piper spotted what he'd been too preoccupied to notice before; Grantham didn't smell of sweat, even though it was warm today. He didn't *expect* bigger to mean less interested in personal hygiene, it was just his experience that the two coincided.

'Would you come with me, please?'

Acid burned in Piper's stomach. He would eventually get to the doctors and find out if he had an actual ulcer. He needed a moment for the jelly in his knees to solidify. 'Why?'

'You'll find out.'

Grantham stepped back and walked away. Piper didn't feel any urgency to follow him or find out. A call from PSD was the last thing he needed. *Yellow slip ahoy?* On the other hand, he'd spoken to Sheila when he'd got home on Tuesday, about retiring early. After she'd finished laughing at the idea that he actually wanted to, she had very seriously told him that she'd love for him to give up, to be at home more. They'd even discussed a few possible things he could do as an alternative career. Not least of which was to actually write the book he'd been threatening her with for years. He might have to. Retiring might be less a matter of him wanting to and more a matter of whether he was allowed to. If he lost his police pension, he'd have to earn something some other way and he doubted he could restart from the bottom the way Charlie had.

Dry-throated and accepting that he couldn't put it off forever, he resolved to move. Demons dragged him down as he tried to stand. Every step was a Herculean effort. Following Grantham, the one thing that didn't take any effort at all to work out was where they were heading. Detective Chief Superintendent Broughton's office.

Bile rose in Piper's throat as he stepped inside. Broughton was the solid block figure behind his desk. Not a happy block figure, either. Grantham stood to one side, Kevin Shelley, local representative of the Police Federation, on the other.

Oh dear God, this is it.

He'd have to resign. It was the only good way out. The Police Federation, PSD, all in one room. That meant only one thing. A Reg 15 was about to be served.

'Matthew.'

First name terms. Serious serious.

'I think you know everyone here.'

Numbly he nodded. The walls were crowding in.

'Good. We've arranged a home visit with Carlisle, I thought that you would be a good fit to stay with Carlisle and Shelley after Grantham gives him the Reg 15.'

Not him - *Yes!*

No.

Wait.

They were investigating Carlisle? Giving Carlisle the Regulation 15 papers?

He should be elated. He should at least be relieved. But he wasn't either. Because any investigation into Carlisle was, by extension, an investigation into him. After what Siddig had found, and given what had happened with Bell, his profile was hardly the best, and rather too high even for his own comfort.

Nothing was going the way he needed it to. His investigations were all dead ends, his only lead was a man about to die who any good lawyer would destroy under cross examination, assuming he lived that long.

Would he survive? Would his career? He only cared this much because he loved his job. Was that a mistake? With bullets and a brick through his window he knew he was scaring all the right people, but what right did he have to put his family at risk? Screw his career, they mattered more.

He squared his shoulders. He'd joined the Force for a reason. He was staying for the same reason. And he was going to continue with that reasoning for as long as he was allowed to. *Keep the peace, prevent offence.*

Chapter 38

'How was yesterday afternoon?'

Piper and Siddig sat in the canteen. For a change they were the only two in there. 'An experience I never want to repeat.'

Carlisle's one-bedroom house was just the right sort of immaculate, it showed someone lived there, but was cleaner than a bachelor pad had a right to be, none of that unwashed, takeout and beer smell that often musted up around single men. Carlisle had been washing up when they arrived. He looked totally poleaxed when the notice was served. For the first time, Piper had reason to actually admire Grantham. The man was all business, but careful and considerate in the way he presented the notice and explained what would happen next. He and Shelley had stayed after Grantham made his swift and inevitable exit. They had had to go over Carlisle's legal rights, his possible moves, what could and couldn't be done. They asked him multiple times if he was alright. He said yes and went back to the washing up. Piper followed, watched the automaton moves, even as Carlisle washed the same plate five times. That was when he moved Carlisle back to the lounge area and finished the washing up himself. He stood there looking over the kitchen island to see Carlisle, sitting in the one armchair staring dead ahead, vacant and lost. It was the first time Piper really questioned Carlisle's guilt. From the first time the possibility had been suggested, he'd not seriously questioned it. It made too much sense. But Carlisle sat like a man lost. Adrift.

'Do you think I was wrong in taking what I found to PSD?'

'God, no.' That was one thing Piper was certain of. 'Any time any officer finds something questionable, they have to go to PSD. Just as Broughton told you to do with what you found against me.'

Siddig looked away. 'Sorry about that.'

'Don't be. I just said, it was the right thing to do. Besides, Grantham already told me it's not worth their while pursuing, but they'll keep it on file just in case there is ever any question of me screwing up, like pursuing a vendetta against Rhys Mansel-Jones.' *Like giving vital evidence to a non-officer.* He pushed the thought away, he had the book back well before anyone noted it was gone.

'Is that likely?'

'Well I'm not about to not investigate some toe rag on my patch, so potentially, yes.'

Siddig closed her eyes and tipped her head up. 'I'm so sorry.'

'Siddig, you said you want to be a career copper, so listen up. The thin blue line is just that. Thin. We have to be beyond reproach as we wade through a world of shite. And we're all human, we all make mistakes. I despise the Mansel-Joneses of this world. Rhys and Phillip Mansel-Jones most of all. I am not going to go out of my way to find a way to stop him, I won't fit him up, that really would cost me my job. And after what Charlie did on my watch, I have to tread very carefully. But I will not stop an investigation if it happens to go in that direction. That's why I need people like you around me. People who will stand up and be counted if they think I've done something wrong. It's very easy to fall off that thin blue line. It's the people we work with that keep us safe in that respect. Never be afraid to do the right thing, Siddig. Never.'

'Well, that's the best piece of advice you're ever going to get.'

They both looked around in surprise to see Broughton in the canteen. It wasn't unknown, but it was unusual. He pulled out the chair beside Piper and sat down.

'Right, catch me up.'

'Of the six cases, we've got DNA from the Halls, the Whitakers, the Cassidys, and the Butlers, they will be checked against what we have from the Joskins Field find. As yet they haven't turned up anything, but the full results aren't expected until tomorrow. We've got statements from Searlotti and Kinsley that are being cross-checked, but at the moment they are pointing only at Phillip Mansel-Jones. We are looking at anyone who might have acted as the spotter Kinsley mentioned, just in case. I've kept DCI Linda Small advised and she's checking the Bodine Street residents again to see if any of them have lived there 20 years.'

'So a lot of work and not much progress.'

Piper looked down at his cooling coffee. Didn't matter how he swirled it, he wouldn't find any answers in there. 'No, not much.'

'What about Hall's diary?'

'Some oddities about tunnels, no one was listening for children screaming one overly large scribbling of "Tick Tock Shop," which we can't find any other reference to. Other than that, it's great if we want to prosecute Phillip Mansel-Jones.'

'What about the smashing of your window? No ghost did that.'

'Ballistics have matched the bullets they dug out of my ceiling to ones used three weeks ago. They've linked up with the investigations. Forensics haven't given me a report on the brick or the note. The note was a Black Spot, nothing more and nothing more to go on.'

'The traditional pirate death curse,' Siddig mused. 'Well, traditional since *Treasure Island* anyway.'

Piper watched as the young woman's voice faded and she unfocused, her short, neatly manicured nails drumming against her coffee mug. Broughton looked at Siddig, then at Piper. Clearly he was thinking, as Piper was, of the other person they knew who had that same habit. Probably still had it.

'Let it run,' Broughton said softly to Piper. 'But not to the same conclusion.'

He watched the big man stand and walk away, when he looked back, Siddig was looking at him. 'What conclusion?'

Piper took in a breath before he could answer. 'He doesn't want you turning out like Charlie Bell.'

She looked slightly offended. 'I don't intend to.'

'Sir?'

Piper looked up and saw Lawson approaching.

'You've got a visitor, sir. Figured you wouldn't mind.' Lawson moved aside to reveal Ariadne Teddington following him. She was pale, leaning heavily on the walking stick she was using now.

The PC headed for the counter as Piper invited Teddington to sit. She was back to dressing as she used to, like the old her, but with less energy.

'I didn't get much sleep last night,' she admitted when he commented. 'I just wanted a quiet word.'

'Go on.'

Teddington glanced nervously at Siddig. Tired and nervous. This wasn't like her.

'Siddig can be trusted.' He forestalled the younger woman moving, thinking that he might just need the backup if Teddington did break down. 'She's fully conversant with the case.'

'Fully?'

The way Teddington tapped her finger drew Piper's attention to the phone she had carried in and placed on the table. He looked at Siddig. 'This is off the record. Understand?'

Siddig looked curious. 'Yes, sir.'

Teddington seemed all eyes until she swiftly looked down, flipped open her phone and tapped the screen, turning it to Piper. Not that the turn was needed. It was the same from whatever angle.

A black spot.

Piper felt his mouth go dry.

This wasn't a coincidence. It couldn't be. He pulled the phone to him and from a central point widened his fingers to zoom in on the paper behind the spot.

'I know it's just a literary reference.' Teddington was trying to sound normal, assured. It wasn't entirely working. 'But it kind of freaked me out.'

'When did you receive this?' He could check the message, but he was still concentrating on the writing.

'Monday night. Just before eight originally, then it seemed to disappear, and I wasn't sure I didn't just imagine it. Then that came through more clearly about ten, but the time stamp says it was sent at half seven.'

So about the same time that his window was being put through. He had to breathe carefully and control his own reaction, it wasn't for a civilian to know he had his own worries. He put the phone down and passed it back.

'Why did you delay coming to me till now?'

She swallowed. 'Because I didn't get a picture on Tuesday. I thought maybe it was done with. Then a couple of hours ago, this came through.' A couple more taps on her phone and she shared another picture. One of her with a black slash line through her neck. If the spot wasn't a threat, that definitely was.

'You do understand that now we have to make this official?'

Somehow, she managed to look both crestfallen and relieved at the same time. 'As long as you still don't tell Charlie.'

'*You* should tell Charlie. Apparently, you've gone, and I quote "weirdly reticent", he thinks you're pissed off with him over something.'

'Oh great.' She slumped and sighed. 'The great male ego needs reassurance.'

'Well, there's that,' Piper allowed. 'But I think you probably need some reassurance round about now too, and Charlie's best placed to offer that. He cares about you.'

'I love him too, but...'

'Then trust him.'

Locked Down

Chapter 39

Charlie might as well have been marching towards the guillotine as going to answer the phone. It was the second time it had rung in an hour and after the discomfort of the first call, he wasn't looking forward to this one. There was only one person it could be.

It's a phone not a viper.

He picked it up. 'Hello.'

'That took long enough.'

The grumbler was Rhys Mansel-Jones. 'I couldn't very well answer while I was on the bog,' he lied.

'This phone goes, you squeeze it off and you answer. Whatever you're doing. Understand?'

Rhys really did want to be alpha male, but Charlie was no lapdog and he wasn't giving in. 'You'll have the phone back tonight.'

'Oh, Charlie, I'm disappointed in you. It's a gift, me to you. You'll keep the phone and learn to do as you're told.'

Charlie took a steadying breath. 'Look, I don't care what you have to say to who, but just be clear that I don't work for you. Consider me too great a risk because of my friendship with a DCI.'

'Maybe that's what makes you an asset.'

A chilling thought. 'I'm not going to drag anyone else into this.'

'I understand that your "landlady" is actually your girlfriend.'

'Not quite.'

'Your girlfriend's mother, then. Do you really think pedantry is going to help you right now?'

'Do you really think being patronising is going to help you?' What had gotten into him, Charlie didn't know. He should just put the phone down and cut out.

'Ariadne Teddington took a bullet for you once. In the shoulder. She crashed a car to avoid another man putting a bullet in her skull.'

194

Now his pulse was up. He didn't want Rhys anywhere near Ari. Suddenly Edinburgh didn't look far enough away; he would talk to Ari about it when he saw her tomorrow. She wouldn't be back before he went on the afternoon shift and she'd asked him not to disturb her tonight, she needed to catch up on some sleep. His jaw was clenched as tightly as he held the phone. Nose breathing meant that Rhys probably knew he was getting to him. He had to counter that, and words were his only weapons right now. 'Your point being that she's a resourceful woman who can outwit and outlive many a threat?'

'My point being that you need an object lesson in obedience. You need to understand who's top dog here. Do the job.'

'No.'

'Ask your girlfriend about that.'

The line went dead.

* * *

The urgency of Charlie's phone call was a twist to the guts. Piper agreed to meet as soon as he could. Pub lunch. The Old Cock Horse on the road out of town, way out of town. It wasn't on a convenient bus route either, so Piper was surprised by Charlie's suggestion.

He was more surprised when he saw Charlie by the bar. Pausing a moment, he looked across at the younger man. He was slouched over the bar, swirling a tall glass. A dark liquid, apparently carbonated. Was he back to drinking shorts? Charlie's hair, which was getting ever more in need of a good cut, was tousled as if he'd been running his hand through it a lot. The swirling stopped and the long fingers of Charlie's right hand started to tap on the glass. Charlie slugged back the last of the drink as Piper stepped up to him.

'Another?'

Strain was clear in every feature. 'Please.'

'JD and coke?'

'Just coke.'

'Really? You look like you could use a stiff drink.'

'Could. But I drove.'

That was a surprise. 'You got a car?'

'It's Ari's. She put me on her insurance.'

Piper finally caught the eye of the disinterested girl behind the bar and ordered drinks and two ploughman's lunches. They took the drinks and the numbered wooden spoon to a table near the back. A draught cut across the table, which was probably why it had been empty. Piper looked around; they were near the rear door and someone had propped it open. At least it was private.

'What's happened?' Piper asked once they were settled.

'I had another call from one of RMJ's boys. Wanted me to do a job. I said no.'

'Good. Why?'

'Actually, because it clashed with the shift I'm on rota for.'

'Do you know what the job was?'

He shook his head. 'Only the timing, but that's not the problem. Then the man himself called, said he was most disappointed, like I'm some misbehaving child. He was patronising and I told him so. That didn't go down too well either.'

Piper could imagine. 'So why did you call me?'

'Because he said that what I need is an object lesson in obedience. That I need to understand just who the top dog is.'

That didn't sound good, but he couldn't delve further as the barmaid plonked their meals on the table. How the pickled onion didn't bounce right off, Piper wasn't sure. He had to move quickly to save his drink as she swiped the numbered spoon away.

'He spoke about Ari, clearly knows that we're living together.'

'Did he threaten her?'

'Not directly, but that's what he meant.'

Piper didn't doubt it. Charlie shifted in his seat and pulled something from his pocket that he lay on this table.

'This came through the door a few minutes after my call with Rhys.'

It was a small brown padded envelop, he opened it up and looked inside. Frowned over what he saw. A sausage in clingfilm. It was labelled "LONGPIG".

'Have you told Ari yet?'

Another headshake.

'Where is she?'

'Working.'

'At home?'

'I wish. No, she has meeting with her boss, arranging some training session I think. Then she's popping into town to get a prescription filled before going home.'

'Give her a call and tell her to go straight home.'

Charlie took a phone - two phones - from his pocket. One he found her contact on, tapped and put to his ear. He didn't look happy that he didn't get an answer. 'Shit. She warned me that she puts her phone on silent for meetings. She probably doesn't know that I'm ringing her.'

'Text her then.'

He waited while Charlie did just that.

'Please God, she reads that.'

'I'm sure she'll be fine.' He wasn't, but felt he had to say it anyway.

'She has to be.' Charlie pushed the second phone, a basic model, across the table. 'That's the burner phone I was given. Feel free to trace whatever you can from it.'

Piper pushed it back towards Charlie. 'Right now it's probably safest that you keep it. If he can't get hold of you, he may do worse that make vague threats.'

Charlie's own phone bleeped. He looked at it, his shoulders slumping in relief. He opened up the text and a smile spread across his face.

'What does she say?'

'"Just waiting on the prescription, then home. Intend to be asleep before you're back, please don't disturb me. We'll talk in the morning. Love you."' Charlie sighed and sat back. 'She's never said that before.' Smiling broadly, he typed something into the screen. Doubtless the return statement.

'About bloody time then.'

When he was done, he put the phones back in his pocket and looked at Piper. 'Am I worrying over nothing?'

'No. What's the issue with her sleeping?'

There was no stopping Charlie smiling now. Grinning like a fool in fact. 'I am. Well, that and she's still in some discomfort from her injuries. She tries to play it down, but it bothers her, especially at night and so she struggles sleeping, and has nightmares about the crash. She got a prescription for sleeping tablets, and she intends to take one early tonight, just to catch up.'

Piper nodded; an eminently sensible plan. 'How's she getting around if you've got her car?'

'Buses and taxis.'

'Pre-booked or ranks?'

'Ranks I think.'

'Good.' Made it less likely RMJ could get to her that way. 'Just text her later, make sure all's okay.'

Chapter 40

The day had clouded over. Ariadne looked up at the greying sky. She had so much to be grateful for; Charlie, the new job - an understanding boss. So why would fear and guilt not let her be happy with her lot? *Because you're lying to Charlie.* Not telling him everything wasn't *lying*, she told herself.

Then there was seeing those two men again, that had crowded the guilt in on her. She should have told the police all those years ago. Piper might say it wouldn't have made any difference, but she wasn't convinced.

Last night, after Charlie got home, she'd chickened out of telling him about the photographs, and he'd managed to take her mind off it all in the best way possible. But all the things she should have said and done were niggling. Today, she couldn't concentrate on her job and he was back in work. His text was slightly concerning, but she wasn't going to give into a life of fear. The first *I love you* really shouldn't be by text, but she couldn't stand that being one of the unsaid things a moment more.

With the luxury of being a consultant who had already been working overtime, she'd secured an agreement for the afternoon off not just to see Piper, but in the hope that a spot of retail therapy would help. It hadn't. Mostly because she hadn't done any; she didn't really have the spare cash and there wasn't anything she especially wanted. And she still had another hour to wait before she could pick up the prescription. Pain was starting to crowd too. The cast was gone, but her muscles weren't fully recovered yet and she'd been worn out before the window shopping, which was why she was leaning so heavy her walking stick. She hated that.

Hoping that the cloud would pass and in order to rest her leg, Ariadne headed into the nearest coffee bar. It was no great surprise that there was a queue, but thankfully there were more vacant tables than customers ahead of her. Aware that others had joined the line behind her, her mind was too occupied by thoughts of the future to be interested in what anyone else was up to.

She ordered her coffee, paid and moved on to wait. Seemed ages and no time at all before her order was presented. With her bag over one shoulder and leaning on the stick in her other hand, Ariadne realised that taking the cup and saucer was not going to easy.

'Let me.'

Ariadne jumped and turned her head to the man behind her. 'Carlisle! Can't turn around without seeing you these days.'

'The joys of being off work.'

His own coffee was pushed towards him and he took both in hand.

'Lead on.'

It would have been churlish to refuse, so Ariadne offered a smile and headed for a table further forward in the shop than she would usually pick, a choice based on more light and more people.

As she carefully placed her bag on an additional seat and slowly sat, Carlisle put the coffees down and chose the seat opposite her. The conversation began mundanely enough and Ariadne wondered how she would get away from it. Outside, the clouds grew darker and drizzle started to drip.

'So what did you find?'

Since she hadn't been really listening to Carlisle, she didn't have the vaguest idea what he was talking about.

'Find?'

'At the house. When Piper took you back there.'

Every nerve and fibre tensed. It was just like the first time she had met him. That instinctive feeling that something wasn't right. It was back and given the way DCI Piper had been reacting to the younger man during their last few encounters, it seemed her instincts were spot on.

'Nothing.'

'Seriously?'

Ariadne shrugged. 'I found nothing.' Well, that was true; the fact that she knew what the police had found was neither here nor there. 'Piper had me walk them through exactly what had happened, everything I saw, which we did time and time again, and then I left while they carried on doing whatever it is you guys do during operations like that. Looking unhappy, I presume. If they found anything, you'll just have to ask Piper about it.'

Outside, the drizzle had gathered into a shower. Ariadne finished the coffee faster than she enjoyed and moved to stand.

'If you'll excuse me, I'm going to head home before this gets any worse.'

Of course, Carlisle was on his feet, his coffee hardly touched before the bag was on her shoulder. 'I'll give you a lift home.'

'I wouldn't want to take you out of your way.'

'Like I said, I'm off work, nothing much to do. It's no bother.'

They were at the door now. Thankfully it had a press button opener, so Ariadne didn't have to thank him for opening the door.

'It's a kind offer -'

He grabbed her arm, talking breezily over her so there was little she could do but go with him a few steps.

'Let go of my arm, or I'm going to scre-'

He forced her sideways, his foot sweeping her good leg from under her. She fell to the side, passers-by gasped, but even as Carlisle shielded her and the syringe he plunged into her neck from their gaze, he was giving them some baloney about epileptic fits.

Chapter 41

The phone ringing made her jump, but she answered all the same.

'DCI Linda Small, Missing Persons.'

'It's Constable Lawson, ma'am.'

If ever there was a call she didn't want to take this was it, and the more she listened, the worse it got. The blood washed from her face. She wrote the name. 'Address?' She wrote it down. 'I'll be there in twenty minutes.' She tore the sticky note from the pad.

'Mike, call Family liaison, get someone to this address immediately. Then call DCI Piper, he'll want to know.' She grabbed her coat. 'Lucy, you're with me.'

* * *

'Sir!'

Siddig's breathless exclamation matched Piper's own grunt as they bounced off each other turning a corner in opposite directions.

'Siddig. Good. Come with me.'

Piper's difficulty breathing wasn't about the bump and he wasn't stopping even if he left Siddig behind. He couldn't hear any footsteps following him.

'But sir, I need to show you this.'

'Show me on the move then.' He'd reached the stairs and rushed down them. The echoes made it difficult to tell if there was someone behind him.

'Sir! Inspector Piper, sir!'

The urgency in most could be ignored, but Piper recognised Covington's voice and that man only got urgent when it really mattered. Piper stopped and leaned against the stair rail to look up to the higher floor. He was oddly grateful to see Siddig halfway down towards him. She had stopped too, waiting to see what happened.

'What is it, Covington?'

'DNA report, sir. Makes for interesting reading.'

'Pass it to Siddig, she'll tell me on the way.'

'Where we going, sir?' Siddig asked as he turned away.

'Another missing persons case.'

He knew that would raise questions, not least of which was why he wasn't letting Missing Persons look after it alone, but it was all he was prepared to give right now. And given the sound, clearly Siddig was curious enough to rush after him.

The pool car purred satisfactorily enough; Piper's fingers drumming on the steering wheel were a discordant note. Five hundred yards out of the station and straight into gridlock.

'Sir, since we have time, do you want to tell me what's going on?'

'Hopefully, panic over nothing. What's in the file?'

She was looking at the file Covington had handed over. 'Looks like some matches have been made. One of the feet that were found is a strong match for Gareth Halls. 97% certainty of sibling relationship. Another match for the Butlers, possible on the Cassidy, but the DNA of the Joskins Field sample was of poor quality. The pathologist points to the original sample quoting *freezer burn.*'

Piper nodded as he watched the traffic. 'Yeah, I remember a little about the case. Some of the body parts were blackened, like frostbite, some joker said they'd been left in the freezer too long and the pathologist at the time said that it wasn't a joke. Water crystals in the flesh suggested that the parts had actually been frozen.'

'Urgh.'

'Yeah, killing a kid is a horrible enough idea on its own. Can't imagine why anyone would want to freeze the corpses after. Or why there would only be parts left.' Some things didn't bear thinking about until he had to. 'Anything else interesting in there?'

She looked back at the file. 'Actually, yes. The overall accuracy is down on one point, whoever wrote this report has noted that the limb size that matches Butler's DNA suggests a boy at least four inches taller than Butler was at time of his disappearance.'

The traffic had started moving, but at under ten miles an hour it wasn't moving far. 'Could the science be wrong?'

Siddig closed the file and looked ahead. 'It's always possible I suppose, but extremely unlikely.'

Piper looked across at her. Her lips were pursed and her fingers were lightly tapping.

'What are you thinking?'

'Well, the foot that matched Hall was all but skeletal when it was recovered, but Hall disappeared after Butler, and that forearm was in advanced stages of decomposition, but it still had some flesh. And four inches at least is a big height difference.' Now she turned to look at Piper. 'What if the boys weren't killed quickly? What if Butler was held for a couple of years? You can't stop kids growing. If I remember right, Butler was one of the shorter kids taken, maybe they kept him alive until he got too big to be of interest anymore.'

Bile bubbled in his belly as Piper listened to the theory. It was as good a theory as any. And utterly sickening in its implications. 'Good thinking. Unpleasant outcome, but plausible.' He pulled his phone from his pocket, passed it across. 'Let DCI Small know.' He waited through the brief conversation. 'What were you in a rush for this morning? Ahh, that explains it.'

They had reached a set of traffic lights and now near the head of the queue, Piper could see two misshapen cars and drivers trying to sort out insurance details while those around gawked. As soon as they were past the accident, flow normalised.

'When you mentioned Black Spots, I had a vague memory of there being other cases where they featured, so I did a bit of digging yesterday afternoon. Found two other incidents of the Black Spot being used. Six and nine years ago. Both dead within a week. Both had links with the Mansel-Jones family and both were rumoured to have had negative dealings with Rhys Mansel-Jones just before the delivery of the pirate curse. In both cases, the paper the spot was sent on was a page of *Treasure Island*. A mass market 1980s version. So, I asked Forensics to check it out and they came back this morning to say that yes, the note to you was also a mass market 1980s version and they think it was the same book in all three cases.'

'1980 keeps cropping up lately, but I haven't had any dealings with Rhys Mansel-Jones.'

'You might not have to have had. The second death was Carl Holland. He never had any direct dealings with the Mansel-Joneses either. What he did do was offer support to a couple of the girls who wanted to stop working for them. If Rhys Mansel-Jones thinks Charlie Bell won't do what he wants because of you, that might be sufficient cause in his mind.'

Ice shuddered in his veins. When doing nothing or even the right thing became dangerous, every move had to be considered carefully.

'Did Rhys Mansel-Jones go after just the individuals, or their families too?'

'Individuals only.'

That was some comfort. Cold, but comfort nonetheless.

'Of course we can't guarantee this will be the same MO, it's been quite a gap.'

Not what he wanted to hear, but he couldn't fault her logic. The phone in he'd returned to his pocket felt like a lead weight. He had to call Sheila. He had to call Shauna and Josh, get them to go home. Or maybe not. He didn't want them worried over what might be nothing and if they were all together, they were just an easier target. He'd taught the kids well, they were practically adults now anyway. They could look after themselves. Sheila was better at hand to hand combat than the rest of them, being a judo black belt. He was overreacting. He hoped.

'You didn't say,' Siddig said, breaking the silence. 'Who's gone missing?'

Given that he had just turned into the relevant street and the police car was parked right in front of the house they were interested in, Piper didn't think he needed to answer. Instead he parked behind the patrol vehicle.

'Bell?'

'No.' The handbrake clicked as he pulled it up.

'Teddington?'

They were out of the vehicle and rushing towards the house.

'Yes.'

'Poor Mrs Whittaker.'

That didn't even begin to cover it.

At the door, Piper took a moment to compose himself before knocking. He didn't want to hammer on the door. He need not have worried. He had hardly got through the first knock when the door was opened and he was faced with the solid and reassuring presence of one of the most respected and capable officers the station had in uniform.

'Lawson.'

A grey head nodded in respect. 'Chief Inspector. Siddig.' Although Siddig had once worked with Lawson, there was no animosity that she had rather quickly overstepped him. Lawson liked being a beat officer, he wasn't looking to change roles. The man stepped back to let them into the wide hallway and closed the door behind them.

'What's our response been?'

'MisPers are still here taking details. Mrs Whittaker is in a bit of a state. Bell is looking after her but the mood he's in, I'd say he'd rather be out there bashing heads right now.'

It was a feeling Piper understood all too well. A decade ago, Shauna had gone missing, and Charlie had forced Piper to stay home while he went searching. That inactivity had been torture at the time, but now he understood that he hadn't been thinking clearly enough to do any good. At home with the rest of the family was exactly where he had needed to be then. Hopefully Charlie would see the same was true for him now.

Nodding his thanks, Piper turned and moved into the sitting room. The smell of paint had gone and more knick-knacks had appeared, including the silver framed picture of Terry, and another of Ariadne. Mrs Whitaker was on her chair, a handkerchief in her hand, her face pale. When she turned to him, her eyes were wide, too large in her face. Devastated. Again. Piper hated that this was the way he usually got to see the woman.

Linda Small and her colleague, one Piper didn't know, were earnestly asking questions. He hadn't realised that Linda was here, or he wouldn't have had Siddig make that call. Charlie was with Mrs Whitaker but was on his feet the second he saw Piper. Another worried man.

'Tell me you know where she is,' Mrs Whittaker pleaded. 'Tell me you can get to her.'

If only he could. 'We'll do everything we can. I'll do everything I can. But first, I need some information from you.'

Chapter 42

It was dark.

Pitch.

Ariadne blinked just to make sure that she was opening her eyes. She was, physically at least. But there was no light. Nothing. Her heart rate ramped up. Why couldn't she see? Was she blind? *Calm down.*

She tried to move her hand - only to find she was bound tight to... Taking a deep bre - *No.*

Deep breath wasn't even possible because there was something across her chest restricting how much she could expand her lungs.

Calm down and think.

She couldn't take deep breaths but with concentration she could avoid hyperventilation.

Take stock.

Gravity told her she was sitting up. She tried to move her head, found there was a little give, but something was keeping her head still as well. The air was cool, but not cold, that meant that there was some form of heating in here or had been at some point. The thing across her chest was also holding her upper arms in place. The edge her fingers curled around was smooth, but not painfully cold, so probably a natural material. Wood, most likely. She explored the profile with her fingers. Even the bits she hadn't warmed with her body heat weren't very cold, there was a slight grain. Almost definitely wood. Trying to move each leg told her that not only were her ankles bound, she was actually still wearing her boots. And, in fact, the rest of her clothes. That had to be a positive.

She licked her dry lips. The fact that she hadn't been gagged told her that screaming wasn't going to do her any good. In fact, it was all together possible that screaming was part of what her captor wanted.

The blackness around her worried her. She didn't think she was blind, but there was no echo of light. Usually some ray would show through.

The edge of a window or door. And there had to be at least one, she must have been put in here somehow. The air was... odd. It was dry but there was an earthy, acrid scent that Ariadne couldn't place.

At least she wasn't buried, if she was it was the weirdest grave she'd ever heard of, sitting up, no sense of walls inches from her. Besides, just because something was light-tight, didn't necessarily mean it was air tight. She was on a chair not in a coffin. She was breathing okay, so there was air. That also suggested a room of some reasonable size, not that there was any way she could actually check.

Bodily, there was pain. The ache in her leg and shoulder was no more than what had become normal. The unnatural position forced on her by the restraints meant that there were other aches and pains. Her backside was numb too. She flexed her muscles to get the blood flowing again. The pins and needles that started didn't exactly help.

As far as she could tell, there were no new injuries. Her head was hurting and there was a bit of bruising on her neck. She remembered the needle in her neck after Carlisle knocked her down.

Carlisle. Bastard.

If she could get her hands on him, she'd rip him limb from limb. Of course there was a chance that Carlisle wasn't working alone. How would he have moved her off that street? She remembered going down, she remembered the pricking of her skin and the tingling sensation that followed, but that was all. After that it was all blackness till now. Which was still blackness. But at least it was now an external blackness. Hopefully.

Had she been able to, she would have hung her head. She wouldn't get her hands on him, not unless he was stupid enough to let her out of these restraints. However depressing the thought, that was highly unlikely. The reality was, the only way she was going to get out of this was if someone else got her out. Charlie would be frantic, he'd be looking for her. How long had she been here? He could be on the way here now. Only how would be know where here was?

Tied up. Alone. In the dark.

She'd like to think she'd been in worse situations. Truth was, she actually hadn't.

I am not going to die here. I have too much to live for.

* * *

Arms crossed across that broad chest and face hard as granite, Broughton looked less than impressed that Piper had dragged him away from his lunch on an "urgent matter" he had yet to define.

Piper's heart was battering itself stupid, and it still didn't compete with the burning in his stomach. 'Ariadne Teddington is missing.'

The arms were uncrossed.

'Since when?'

'Some time yesterday afternoon. Her mother had access to her banking records and she called the bank, managed to find that Ari last used her debit card in the Costa in town at 14:07. Siddig is calling the CCTV guys, seeing if they can spot her and where she might have gone, what might have happened to her. Importantly, we know she had her phone on her because she texted Charlie at 13:18. I need your authorisation to trace that phone.'

'And we're sure that this is something that the poli-'

'Oh for fuck sake, sir! This is Ariadne Teddington we're talking about! Do you think for one second that she'd intentionally leave her mother wondering?' Piper pushed his hair back, paced the office. 'Jesus, if Mansel-Jones has her, what chance do you think she has?'

'We've no reason to think Rhys Mansel-Jones would have kidnapped her.'

Piper stopped in front of the desk, leant over it. 'He warned Charlie he had a girlfriend to lose.'

'I've read the transcripts, it wasn't that clear cut.'

'You want clear cut? What about the photos? The Black Spot? You want to see what the bullets did to my home?'

'Do you want to see past your own involvement?'

That brought Piper up short. He looked down at the hands on Broughton's desk. His hands. Straightening his spine, he took a careful breath and pushed down the red mist rising before his eyes. Careful not to let his hands slap together behind him, Piper clasped them together. 'Sorry, sir.'

'Don't be to sorry, Matthew.' One slab-like hand indicated the chair in front of the desk. 'Sit down.'

Controlling every move, Piper did. Broughton sat too. Both were a little too stiff to be comfortable.

'You have to understand Matthew, I agree your assessment is the most likely scenario, but we cannot afford any hint of impropriety, not with PSD breathing down the department's neck. Now, can you give any me any solid evidence that this actually is an abduction case?'

The sound of his swallow was too loud. If he hadn't had an ulcer before, he probably had one now. 'No, sir. Neither Charlie nor Mrs Whitaker have received any kind of direct contact to suggest a kidnapping.'

'Then we have to deal with this the same way we would any other missing persons case. Now, Linda Small is a good officer, she'll make a good job of things. However, given the potential implications of this incident, I want you to work closely with her.'

There was no power on Earth that was going to stop Piper doing that anyway. Something Broughton doubtless knew.

'What about the phone?'

'Give me a reason to.'

'Her life is in danger.'

'We don't know that.'

'With all due-'

The knock was cursory, the door opening was explosive. Piper and Broughton twisted to find Siddig rushing forward, newly printed sheets in her hands.

'Sorry, sirs. I know it's not the done thing, but you need to see these.'

She offered each man, both now on their feet, a sheet. Piper felt sick. Four screen shots on the page. Ariadne stepping out of the coffee shop. Carlisle stepping out right behind her. Ariadne on the ground and Carlisle over her. Carlisle with some unknown man assisting Ariadne out of town and towards the car park.

'I'll get the phone traced,' Broughton announced.

Piper handed over the number as he continued, directing his next comment at Siddig.

'You get onto ANPR, see if we can find Carlisle's car.'

Siddig was moving as Broughton turned to Piper. 'Get a warrant for Carlisle's place, Judge Deacon is on duty. Take Grantham with you if possible. I want every inch of that bastard's house searched.'

Chapter 43

The light went on.

Blinded, Ari scrunched her eyes closed, gripping hard on the edge of the chair arms. The switch from extreme dark to extreme light caused a pain she hadn't expected. Now with her eyes scrunched she was back to being blind, but she had other senses. The only sound was her pulse and her breathing. No one was coming. And she was alive.

She swallowed the copper in her throat.

Carefully controlling her breathing, she relaxed her eyes, but didn't yet open them. For a moment she took a juddering breath, pushed down the terror she was feeling and carefully squinted through her right eye. The light was out there, and in truth it wasn't actually that bright. Now she squinted with both eyes. Frowning under the band holding her head back, Ari slowly opened her eyes.

Eyes that went wide as her breath caught in her throat.

Terry!

Don't hyperventilate!

Her breath was shallow and too fast. Breathe, breathe, breathe.

No!

Stop!

Finally her brain kicked in and she scrunched up her eyes again.

Control it, control the breathing. In. Out. In. Out. In, two. Out, two. In, two, three. Out, two, three.

It was coming back. She was getting herself under control, but even before she opened her eyes, she could feel the hot streaks of tears running down her face. She opened her eyes, blinking and taking the time to clear her vision. She wasn't ready to see that dear lost face again, so she looked down.

She could see her knees. And her lower arms. The chair was definitely wood, and the restraints were sheepskin under leather and buckle. Bloodstained sheepskin and leather.

Victorian asylum restraint chair?

Not that it really mattered, but the bloodstains worried her. She'd take any bet that *they* weren't Victorian.

She swallowed the fear threatening to choke her and let her eyes drift forward. The floor was flat grey concrete. She was in a grey concrete box. She'd been in prefabs, they didn't have the same feel. That earthy scent was bothering her. The dampness of it. This had to be some kind of cellar. Was she under someone's house? Is that how they kept the police away?

There were too many possibilities, she had to keep with the facts. Floor and walls were grey concrete. With more stains. Could be blood. Certainly had urine in it, probably shit too, all part of the earthy smell. Probably all three if this was a torture chamber. Which was likely. Even looking at the floor she was aware of the squares pinned to the grey plaster walls. She didn't want to look at them, but she would have to. For now she stared at the joint between the floor and the wall.

Pictures. Photos.

Starting about halfway up the wall in a band she didn't think was quite a full meter in thickness. They weren't that tightly packed, but if they were what she thought they were, they were still too many of them. Taking one more breath she closed her lids, repositioned her eyeballs to look straight forward. Then she opened her eyes.

Terry looked back at her. His head was restrained by a sheepskin and leather band. His big brown eyes were wet, his face was red, tear tracks catching the light. His lip was broken and swollen. His chin dimpled where he was trying not to cry before the camera.

The squareness of the image told her that it was an instamatic shot that had been photocopied up in size. That picture had been picked and placed as a deliberate taunt. That told her something about her captor.

He's sick.

But she'd already known that.

He took my baby brother.

Only 'he' could not have been Carlisle. Carlisle was too young.

* * *

With a few bellows, Broughton had called a team together. Now DCI Small faced thirty men and women from across the division. The incident room was packed and they all paid attention as she led the briefing.

'The phone lost contact here.' She pointed to a large map they'd pinned up for the cold cases. The area she circled was a little way north of the town. 'The helicopter team is already in the air, there was an incident on the roads a little while ago they were called out for. They're going to fly the area and search with infrared as soon as they're done with their current response. With a little luck, they're already up there and spotting. Any news I'll report as soon as I have it.

'Whatever the eye in the sky may say, we're going to start here, Finnigan Way. We'll fan out for a fingertip search, road and fields. Any building, and there are a few, I want them opened and searched. Some of these fields are hop-growing, so you'll need to be extra vigilant between the canes, not only because the hop vines make for good cover but because I don't want any twisted ankles or broken legs. I don't like paying people to stay home with their feet up, understood?'

Thankfully, that was taken with the good grace with which she'd meant it. Broken bones didn't do anyone any favours. And Piper looked like he needed more than a favour as he stepped into the door and waited there, giving her the opportunity to finish the job she'd started.

'Now, I understand the reluctance some have shown in this case, but remember, Mrs Teddington is a member of the public - the people we are here to serve. And the people we suspect of snatching her are, firstly, a bunch of lowlife scum we all want off the streets, and secondly, one of the bastards is one of our own, and we've all had enough of getting tainted by association. Now I already split you into groups, Group A, you're with me to do the sweep of the area. Group B, you're going with DCI Piper to do the search of Carlisle's place. Any questions?'

'What about the current cases?'

She looked to DC Jamie Hussey, not so young, and not so keen as he had been before he'd found out who was missing. There was no need to hesitate.

'If you've got any idea where Stolz or Pearson or any of the others are, tell me – Please. But right now, I've got a missing woman I do have a lead on and that has to come first.'

'Are we looking for a connection between Teddington going missing and the disappearance of her brother?'

Small shifted her attention to the man who'd spoken, another one not happy when the names Teddington and Bell came up. He was CID and if she remembered right, that was DS Covington. It was a good question, she looked to the DCI by the door. 'Piper?'

'As far as I know, there's no connection between the two disappearances. I believe that this abduction has a completely separate motivation, but if you find anything that might help close the Terry Whittaker case, or the Joskins Field case, then do flag it.'

'And what are we looking for in Carlisle's place?'

She saw the frown flicker across Piper's forehead. Was he upset that Covington was going with him? The man was in his department why would Piper not want someone he knows on his team. There again she'd seen the man's attitude and was glad he wasn't on her team. Piper's gaze sat coldly on Covington and he took a breath to answer.

'Anything that links Carlisle to the destruction of evidence. Or shows him receiving payment for services, or blackmail to keep him in line. Anything that shows a connection with the criminal fraternity. And most importantly anything to indicate an order to snatch Teddington and where to take her. That includes syringes and liquid medications such as the CCTV images suggest were used. Anything else?'

A few shook their heads.

'Good. Group B, you're with me.'

She had assigned ten men to go with him, so he turned to walk away she was glad they followed.

Chapter 44

She didn't want to look at those photographs. But Ariadne couldn't resist.

Terry was her brother, and she had to know what had happened to him. And here were the answers she'd been waiting twenty years for. This was what had happened to him. All laid out in front of her, in faded colour and sickening clarity.

There was Terry presented so she couldn't be in any doubt. Terry being beaten, stripped, crying, starved. Being masturbated, masturbating a grown man as he cried. Other sex acts where he just looked numb. Often bruised. Forced to perform fellatio. Bent over and being buggered.

Oh dear God.

The worst of it all was that it was obvious that these abuses hadn't just happened over a short period of time. They took years. There was an obvious aging and growth difference between the little boy who she knew had gone missing and the terrified teenager who now stared back at her, eyes pleading for release. But what release could he have got from such a nightmare? Death would have been a mercy, though she suspected the poor kid had suffered terribly before that final moment.

Hot heavy tears ran down her face.

Her poor little brother. This was her fault, she should have kept a closer eye on him. Should have stopped reading that bloody book and just gone home with him. If only she'd told the police about those two damned men earlier, Terry would have been alive long enough that they could still have found him. Rescued him. Her fault.

I'm sorry. Really sorry. Oh Terry, I wish I'd done it all different.

The photographs extended beyond the limits of her ability to move her eyes and they weren't all Terry. These were pictures of so many different children, boys and girls, all ethnicities and all underage, at least in the first photos. These were images of abuse, beatings and bruisings, adult sexual perversions. The suffering screamed not just from the images, but from the fabric of the room. It echoed in the silent grey walls. It seeped from the wood of the chair into her pores, into her heart. No child should suffer like that, yet clearly so many had.

She jumped at the sound of metal scraping against metal. The sound was behind her. No wonder she couldn't detect any way in or out, she had her back to the door and was unable to turn. Carlisle had her trapped and there was nothing that she could do to defend herself. Her eyes automatically went forward.

Her heart was quivering, goose bumps covered her skin, she felt sick, she felt like she needed to pee. Her lurching stomach quivered all the way to her bowels. She couldn't fight, so her body was getting ready for flight, but she couldn't do that either. She couldn't control much, anything really. But she could at least try to control her body, manage her fear.

Concentrating on her breathing, she blinked away the tears and licked her lips.

Chapter 45

Piper looked at Carlisle's now familiar rabbit hutch on the tightly packed development. The footprint of the estate suggested that half the number of houses would have been a better fit. The police van pulled into the empty driveway and Piper parked behind. They weren't even all out of the vehicles and already Piper could see they were drawing a crowd.

Two of the hawking women were still in pyjamas at - he checked his watch - 13:26.

'There a problem, sir?'

He turned to find Siddig behind him, Covington behind her. 'No.' His eyes scanned the street behind the other officers. 'No problem.'

'This place just don't match what I know o' Carlisle.'

He winced at Covington's mangled grammar but couldn't fault the assessment. After all, the exact same thought had screamed in his own head when he'd arrived with Grantham. Even a sergeant's salary could afford better than this.

'Okay!' Time to take charge. He told the squad who was to take the lead, who was playing backstop, who had the ram, who was on crowd control. Then he set them off. Backstop jogged to the end of the next house, Piper watched him talk to the occupant and get access, so he could get into Carlisle's back garden.

Siddig hung back. As the others moved towards the front door, she moved to Piper's shoulder.

'Sir, is it me or is Covington acting, well...'

'Not quite the Covington we've come to know and love?' he whispered his sarcasm.

'Want me to shadow him?'

Piper nodded. 'Might be a good idea.'

He had no idea what she might catch Covington doing, but if it was hiding or falsifying evidence, then he wouldn't have to put up with having that miserable git around the office much longer. As per regulations, they knocked. They had to give the occupant the chance to open up and let them in. The knock thundered around the street. Grantham was not playing games. When he stood back to let the ram go, his gesture was sharp and commanding.

The door resisted, but not for long.

The squad rushed in, there were calls for anyone inside to be still and show hands. All the correct procedure. They would fan out inside, work their way through the house to make sure no one was there, then execute the search warrant.

For a minute Piper waited outside, let them all get on with it. The reality was that they were more likely to bust Grantham's case than his here. But he was more use here than in some field with DCI Small and her lot. She had his number; if they found anything, he'd hear about it.

Assured that none of the neighbours were about to intrude, and that the Uniform was on point if they tried, he paced to the front door. Beyond that was the living room. It was minimalist. Cool. The oversized television and untidy stack of DVDs were the only sign of life. DC Tyler was going through the merchant chest stowed under the stairs. He was just finding more DVDs. Tyler stood more upright and frowned over an open drawer. Then he pulled out a slim keep case and his frown deepened. He saw Piper in the doorway and caught his attention.

'Sir, does Carlisle speak Spanish?'

Piper shrugged. 'Not as far as I know.'

'Well most of these films are in Spanish.'

'It's probably just the packaging,' Piper said, stepping up to take a look. 'Likely cheap imports that can be played in English.' But as he took the keep case from the other officer, he saw that this was no multi-language blockbuster, it really was a Spanish movie. He looked in the drawer. All those movies were Spanish. He opened another drawer. All Spanish, all indigenous titles. Except perhaps 'Los Increíbles,' which Piper recognised as a Disney movie - those were always fairly distinctive. And they seemed unlikely for Carlisle to own, but who was he to judge another man's viewing habits? He passed the DVD back. 'You'll have to open every one. See if they hold any other surprises.'

The kitchen was through a wide pair of glassed doors. Three officers were in there, including backstop.

'Sir! You down there?'

Covington's yell pulled his attention upstairs. Even as he was going up, he saw Grantham coming out of the bedroom, Siddig in the bathroom, kneeling on the floor, Covington in the doorway, looking over his shoulder for Piper.

'What is it?' Grantham demanded.

Piper was beside him before Covington spoke.

'I think we found something.'

Piper looked down. The bath panel in the small space had been moved aside, exposing the void beneath the bath. From that Siddig had pulled a short Really Useful box. It looked a bit bigger than A4 and inside the clear plastic was cash. Stacks of £50 notes. He counted nine stacks. Christ.

Siddig pulled out another case. 'Twenties.'

And another.

'More twenties.'

'That's at least half a million,' Grantham estimated.

Siddig pulled out another box. 'More money and what looks like a document wallet.'

Siddig was already wearing gloves and Grantham was pulling an evidence bag from his own stock. Piper turned to Covington.

'How'd you find this so quick?'

Covington looked back over his shoulder. 'I remembered Carlisle was with us on the Tuddenham case.'

Six years ago. Jeff Tuddenham. Paedophile. They'd found thousands of images of child pornography in plastic bags under his bath. That was why they couldn't catch him on the internet, he was still using print. It had been Piper's case, but he remembered Covington and Carlisle had been there with him for the bust.

'Good call.'

This time Covington's lip curled. 'Yeah, well just cos I never liked your blue-eyed boy, don't mean I'm corrupt. That's why I let your latest favourite do the opening up, just so you can't accuse me of anything.'

'I never accused you of anything.' Though he would have done if he'd had the opportunity.

'Yeah well, I ain't giving you the chance.'

As Covington turned away and went back downstairs, Piper realised he had to reassess his own opinion. The man was right, Piper had judged him too harshly just because of the animosity he had seen between him and Bell. He'd have to spend a bit of time readjusting to this new view of himself and others in the station, only now wasn't the time.

Siddig was looking up at him, a passport open in front of her. 'Says Domingo Velez. It's Carlisle's photograph.' She flicked through the pages. 'Visa stamps for Mexico and Costa Rica.' She turned another page. 'Oh, and Ecuador. And Panama.'

'When?'

'All in the last four years.'

Since Bell had left the team. Piper had no idea that Carlisle had been taking such distant holidays. Siddig tipped the passport into Grantham's evidence bag and began looking through the other papers.

'This looks like some form of land sale. In Costa Rica.' Another document. 'And building plans. No wonder he lives so simply here.'

Piper nodded. 'He's spending all his money building a new life overseas.'

'Question still is, where's he getting all this money?' Grantham asked.

'No idea, but let's hope we find him in time to ask.' His phone was ringing. 'Piper.'

'It's Linda Small,' the voice told him. 'We've found Teddington's phone. It was still in her handbag. We're still in Finnigan Way.'

'She can't be far away then.'

'Hate to tell you this, Piper, but she could be anywhere.' The disembodied voice didn't exactly fill him with hope. 'The bag was found in a tree. Exactly at the trace point. The helicopter only found one heat trace and that was from a local gamekeeper. He led us to the tree because he said he saw a car stop in the area for a few seconds. A guy got out, threw something and then was away again. I think this is a decoy.'

Piper swore. 'Sorry.'

'Don't be, I said worse. We're getting a description of the car and anything else the gamekeeper can remember, but if she was driven away from here, the motorway's not far, they could literally be anywhere by now.'

'If you get anything, call me back.'

'Same goes for you.'

Piper swore again as he put the phone back in his pocket.

Chapter 46

'Pretty pictures, huh?'

The voice was behind her. She didn't recognise it.

'I'm sure you had fun making them.' Whoever it was, he didn't sound old enough. Only how old did he need to be? Twenty years ago, Terry was nine. History had shown that plenty of teenagers could torture and kill, even back then.

'Sometimes, they have their uses of course.'

'Pissing off relatives?'

He laughed. 'You're the first relative to see them. This way, anyway. Had parents, cousins and siblings actively down here, but that's different. This particular display was put up especially for you.'

'I'm honoured.'

'Yes, you are.'

Footsteps came closer, only three. So maybe two metres between her and the door back there. Not the biggest - hands appeared on her shoulders. She looked down but with her head trapped, she couldn't move her eyes far enough to see anything but the pale outline of fingers. Still the hands were just resting there, gentle. That wasn't especially reassuring when she was strapped to a chair and totally in his power.

'Why Terry? Why did you take him?'

'I didn't, but Phillip always had a taste for blond little boys. And he was on his own.'

'No he wasn't.'

He chuckled and stroked her neck, sending shivers of revulsion through her. 'Oh he was. You weren't giving him any attention. Too wrapped up in your own selfish little world.'

His fingers moved down her chest, pushing under the corset and kneading into her flesh. The grunt he gave was not terribly approving.

'Too much.' It was a grumble. 'You'd run to fat if you ever got old.'

Clearly it wasn't his intention that she was ever going to get out of here, but perhaps if she could stall him...

'So why me?' she asked as he pulled away. 'If you don't like busty women, why bring me here?'

'Bell. If he can't learn to do what he's told, he can learn what it is to lose someone he loves.'

Ariadne thought about how Charlie had been when he'd lost his son, Oscar. Devastated. He'd pretty much become comatose, willing to waste away in his pain. How would he react to losing her?

'He doesn't love me.'

Another of those little laughs. 'Yes, he does.'

'Well if he told you that, he never told me.' It wasn't exactly a lie.

'He didn't need to say it. He just needed to be with you. Constantly. And you let him. Despite everything. Despite his nearly getting you killed at least twice. Well, you know what?' The long fingers stroked her face again. 'Third time's a charm.'

Chapter 47

'Who are you?'

The man had taken his time to pace from the door to stand in front of the chair. He'd taken enough time for Ariadne's fears to rise and be quashed. Now she looked at a man far too old to be dressed as he was. Late thirties, possibly early forties, she couldn't be sure. His hair had thinned, and the beginnings of a comb-over were not attractive. His tan looked a bit on the orange side, though that could have been the yellowing of the bulb. It might also be the tanning agent he used, because he was starting to look like leather. He was lean, but there was a roundness above the belt of his slacks that suggested that wouldn't last long.

His sneer suggested that her question insulted him.

'I'm your worst nightmare.'

She hadn't meant to release the bark of laughter, it caught her as much by surprise at it did him. *Try hard.* A clear of the throat and she spoke. 'Nope, already lived through that.' Seeing what had happened to Terry, that was her worst nightmare, it was even worse than the things she had imagined, and after some of the things she'd heard from the Blackmarch inmates, they were bad enough.

'You won't live through this.'

Her heart was thumping, but there was heat in her cheeks. Nothing was as it should be. It wasn't right and there was bugger all she could do about it. Except go on a bitchfest.

'Maybe not. But you sure as fuck won't get away with it.'

He laughed. She rolled her eyes and tutted. He stopped.

'Pathetic,' she sneered. She was probably shortening her life, but she didn't reckon it was by much.

His jaw clamped, he huffed like a bull about to charge. 'I'll get away with it. I always do.'

'You always have, but the past is no judge of the future. I know Piper, he won't be stopped, not now. They'll trace that Black Spot back to you. He'll put you behind bars.'

'I'll never serve time.'

She chuckled at that. 'Oh, if I had a pound for every remand prisoner I've heard say that. They're all innocent inside, you know? Innocent as the day is long. Though in fairness, the days can be pretty short inside if you only measure the amount of time that the doors are unlocked. But you might be lucky. You might get an inmate you'll enjoy cuddling up to.' She deliberately looked at the pictures behind him. 'Though they'll be a little older that your usual tastes. Still, any arsehole in a pinch, right?'

He was sneering at her now. 'They won't find you and they won't touch me.'

'Ha! You do know who Charlie Bell is, don't you? He killed your big brother, who by all accounts was a fuck sight scarier than you. What do you think Charlie'll do to you when he gets his hands on you? You'll be lucky if he just shoots you.'

'She might just have a point.'

The door had been left open, but Teddington hadn't heard anyone coming, but she didn't have to see him to know it was Carlisle.

Rhys looked over her head. 'He can't prove anything.'

'He couldn't prove anything against your brother either,' Carlisle pointed out.

'Didn't stop him then,' Ariadne added. 'Won't stop him now.'

The kick stung her shin, Rhys moved faster and harder than Ariadne had expected. She went cold with the impact that rattled through her bones, followed by the heat of throbbing pain.

Rhys' attention was on Carlisle. 'Why are you here? Thought you were dashing off to wherever it is you were going to dash off to with all that money.'

'What money?' Ariadne asked. 'He's only a DS. How many backhanders have you given him over - urgh!'

The straggled cry didn't last long, the cold hand squeezed her throat and no amount of struggle would dislodge it. Her airways were so constricted, she couldn't waste the breath on speaking, she had to fight for every last scrap of oxygen. Racing harder than a workout, her heart pumped blood up, but it had no room to flow back down. The pressure in her head felt like it was going to burst through her eyes. With nowhere else to go, she closed her eyes and stopped fighting. At least this would be a quick way out. Not too much suffering. The instant she relaxed, the grip went. Deep automatic breaths pulled her back to the here and now. Her body doing what it needed to without the intervention of her brain. Finally as she managed to reduce her heart rate, she opened her eyes.

Rhys to her left.

Carlisle to her right.

Here I am, stuck in the middle with them. She pushed the inappropriate jingle away.

'Okay.' She noticed her voice was rougher than it had been. 'You're going to kill me. I get it. But seriously, you're only on a sergeant's wage, and that's recent. From what Charlie told me, you've only been in CID seven years. He —' she indicated Rhys as best she could, '— can't have paid you that much in that time to make it worth you disappearing yet.'

Carlisle rolled his eyes and looked over to Rhys. 'The bastards were going through my house. I can't get the cash or the papers.'

The crack of Carlisle's nose snapping was the first Ariadne knew that Rhys had moved. He really was that quick.

'If there's anything in there to link you to me, you're next in the chair.'

Carlisle leaned against the wall, sniffed and wiped his nose. 'There's not. If they do find a way of dragging you down, I'm not going to let them drag me down with you.'

'Oh so much honour among thieves,' Ariadne sneered.

This time Rhys only looked at her. 'I pay well, but you're right. I don't pay *that* well. But a bad copper can always find ways of picking up extra cash. After all, if you take the cash from a drug dealer, do you think the dealer's going to come back and ask for it? Or report the theft? Who to? The very police officers who would arrest him? The ones who committed the robbery? Take a package or two of the purer stuff. Sell it back to those who don't know or don't care where you got it.' Rhys shrugged. 'There's always ways to make money if you know where to look.'

Her sunken stomach shuddered in revulsion, knowing that she had just been told the truth. For the right person in the right position, taking untraceable money would be easy. And if Carlisle was also the one getting people off their convictions, he'd be able to get paid for that. And frame them just as quickly. A dangerous man. Certainly not someone who should be in the police force, but if they were already raiding his house, they already knew that. But if they were raiding his house, they weren't looking for her.

Since her eyes were about the only thing she could move, she moved them to look at Terry. His fear stared back at her. The same twisting, turning monster writhed in her guts. He'd survived down here for years. All she had to do was do the same until Charlie came to get her. If he - *Shut up!*

Chapter 48

Charlie knew Piper was right. He knew that following the instruction for him to stay home and wait for news was the absolute best thing he could be doing right now. He knew it, but he didn't feel it. When Piper's Shauna had gone missing, Charlie had had to virtually tie the old man down to stop him tearing around town looking for his daughter. Now he understood why it had been so difficult an instruction to follow. He didn't want to sit home and wait.

The urge to disobey, to go out, to search, to bash heads until someone squealed – just as he had to find Shauna – was almost overwhelming.

Shackled.

The scraping of a key in the front door had Charlie on his feet, hope springing high and shining in his eyes. He was at the lounge door as the front door opened.

'Ari-'

Sanchez.

As he stepped into the house, the big prison guard automatically closed the door. His eyes narrowed, lips compressed and his back went ramrod straight.

'Is it her?' Mrs W's tone was so full of hope it ripped a hole in Charlie's heart.

'It's just me,' Sanchez said as he strode into the house.

Charlie reckoned if he hadn't stepped out of the way, Sanchez would have walked right through him, stomping all the way. And he probably deserved it. Steeling himself for whatever was to come, he stepped back into the lounge and his heart sank further. Sanchez had his arm around Mrs W, reassuring her. Doing the things he, Charlie, should be doing for the woman he hoped would one day be his mother-in-law. Between his moving in and Ari coming home, he and Mrs W had made good progress on becoming friends and he had started to see her more as a mother figure. Shock shivered through him. How could he still need his mother? He was a full-grown man. After all he'd done, including telling his parents he never wanted to see them again after he was convicted, how could he need that familial bond now? Because people did. Everyone needed someone. He had Ari. Mrs W had Ari. Right now they should need each other. Only Mrs W had Sanchez, a man who had grown up under her nose, right next to Ariadne. The son some other woman bore.

Sagging against the door jamb, all he could do was envy the other man.

'She's missing?'

It was the second if not third time Sanchez had said that as Mrs W explained what was going on.

'Right!'

This time as Sanchez stormed towards the door, Charlie didn't get out of the way, he stayed deliberately in it. Catching Sanchez by the shoulders he found himself locked into a pushing contest. Thankfully they were evenly matched and going nowhere.

'Get out of my way.'

'No.'

'This is your fault.'

'Probably, yes.' Charlie realised that Sanchez would punch him now if he gave him a chance. He'd give that chance but for the fact he didn't want to upset Mrs W.

'I'm going to do what you should have done.' The words were pushed through gritted teeth exposed by lips pulled back in a feral snarl. 'I'm going to look for her.'

'Not like this.' With a mighty push, he propelled Sanchez a step backwards. 'Look, Officer Sanchez —' The form of address stopped the man in his tracks. '— I may not be good for much, but I know procedure and I know that the reason loved ones are asked to stay at home and wait is because love makes us all irrational. If either of us went haring out to tear up the town looking for her, all we'd be doing is putting ourselves in trouble. We've told the police all we can. They have all the information and will act on it rationally. They'll find her far faster than we could.'

'Please, Enzo.' The plaintive tone drew Sanchez's attention back to Mrs W. The younger man turned from Charlie and sank down on the sofa next to Mrs W.

Charlie ran his hand back through his hair, pausing to grip and pull. It was a small pain, not enough to divert from the sickening agony he was feeling. All he could see was his Ari, the way she'd looked. Horrified to see him in her home. Blissful to have him inside her. He couldn't lose her. He just couldn't. He turned to the front door.

'Bell.'

Charlie looked back at the warning tone. Constable Mary White, Family Liaison. Eyes and fists squeezed tight, Charlie struggled to regain control. When finally he felt he could release the clench, he took a breath and moved into the room properly, sitting in the nearest chair, overly aware that while Enzo was clearly worried about Ari and Mrs W, when his eyes flicked to him, they were hard as flint and cutting as steel.

The others, including White, were talking, subdued and concerned. He heard a barded comment or two flung in his direction by Enzo but he didn't react. The blame lay with him, so he took it. There were more important things to think about.

A hot mug was placed in his hand. Automatically he sipped. His fingers tapped the mug with slow repeating rhythm. All the points were playing in his head, he just had to piece them together. The puzzle would fit, but he didn't have the image to match it to yet.

* * *

There was no way to avoid it. Ari braced.

The baseball bat swung hard and the arm of the chair wasn't about to move. Her fingers crushed, bones shattering, skin splitting. The wail seemed a million miles away, but she knew it was hers. The constriction of the band around her chest stopped the wail, but nothing could stop the tears streaming down her face or the blood thumping in her head and out of her broken fingers.

'No more little love notes for you,' Carlisle sneered.

Bitchfest had been a mistake.

Rhys tutted, rolled his eyes. 'That's her left hand.'

The bat swung again to the accompaniment of her rapid breathing as she gritted her teeth and tried to control the rage and agony burning through her. Rhys reared as the bloodstained bulb of the bat stopped an inch short of his face.

'The bitch is left handed!'

Fuck bitchfest being a mistake, she wasn't going out quietly. 'Are you going to let him have all the fun? Not going to torture me yourself?'

Rhys just shrugged. 'Not really my thing. I like taking stuff apart. Especially people. I've become very proficient at it over the years. Makes them easier to store and dispose of.' He laughed. 'And in some cases, cook and serve up to unsuspecting dignitaries. Thinking I might keep a thigh or arse cheek from you, make a pie and send it to Police and Crime Commissioner Sheldrake.'

Sick bastard really doesn't cover it.

In that moment, he wasn't the problem. The bat struck her right knee, sending her kneecap out of the place and into more pieces than a patella ever should be. Sweat beaded as she gritted her teeth. The pain drowned her, tsunamis of unconscionable sensation washing her hot and cold and nearly insensible. She fought the inclination to pass out. *Think!* No more walking for her. Her left leg was screwed by the crash, now this, that was both knees forever disabled. *If I live long enough to see a wheelchair.*

Pushing through the pain as she'd been taught in Lamaze classes, she blinked past the sweat and tears and glared up at Carlisle. Sweat stood out on his brow too, his lips were pulled back, exposing teeth so white she knew they couldn't be natural. Possibly because they'd had a yellower tone when she'd first met him. When she'd first met him, there was something cold and calculating in his eyes that she simply hadn't trusted, now all she saw was pure insanity. He broke every rule and now the rules were biting him back, he had lost it. His blood was up, he could smell her blood, hell, he was as covered in it as the bat was.

I'm going to die.

Suddenly the thought didn't scare her anymore. It would be a release. She'd be with Sasha and Terry. She's miss out on Charlie, but he'd find someone. He deserved to.

The bat swung. She couldn't keep the scream in as her clavicle and shoulder shattered.

The pain was gone. She knew that meant that it was too much for her brain to contemplate. The bat had been drawn back again. She looked up at the pictures in front of her.

I'm coming, Terry. Be with you s–

The bat shattered her jaw. Red and white lights, stars danced before her eyes. For a moment she was aware of the blood spurting forward, flowing down her throat, the fractured mandible hanging from her torn cheek. She focused on Terry's terrified eyes as the world turned black.

Chapter 49

A lined pad and a pen appeared in front of Charlie. The middle unseen distance was replaced by White as she stood in front of him offering the items.

'That tap-tap-tapping is annoying, if you can't figure it out, write it down.'

The room smelt of coffee and concern. White looked down at him with the same disgust that was on Sanchez's face. Even Mrs W, who was worried but no longer crying, looked, well, miffed. When the rest of the officers were here, they'd done their jobs well and meticulously, Siddig taking notes as Piper took in the information. He remembered doing that when he was the rookie, and beyond. It helped. He took the pen and pad and when White held out her hand for the cold coffee, he gave the mug over.

'Another one?'

Mutely, he nodded. He hadn't drunk the first but a second would at least give White something to do. Resting the pad on the arm of the chair, he started to write. Whatever snippet came to him. Names, places, half-remembered phrases.

'Three times,' Mrs W said.

'Sorry?' Sanchez asked.

'Three times. In a year. That's how many times my Addy's been taken away from me.'

'We'll get her back.'

'DCI Piper didn't say that. Not this time. The other two times he was confident, absolutely assured that she'd be safe. Not this time.'

The other two times he, Charlie, had been with Ari, he'd kept her safe. As safe as he could. But there was no one to look out for her now.

'The police do everything in their power —'

'That's what he said.'

It was a fairly standard line, but it was also true.

'We'll get her back,' Charlie said. 'We will.'

Fear and sorrow were shining in Mrs W eyes as she looked at him. 'I can't lose her, Luke. I can't.'

He couldn't bear that thought either. The prospect of losing her, worse than the idea of losing his own life.

'It's just like Terry. All over again.'

He leaned across, covered her frail hand in his, not caring that the pad fell on the floor. 'Actually, Mrs W, it's not. I've not seen Terry's case file myself, but I know how MisPers - Missing Persons goes. Even for a kid.' Which always had a greater sense of urgency than a missing adult. 'They'd have taken the case seriously, but they would not have had the weight of a CID DCI behind them. This has escalated procedurally far faster than a standard missing persons case.'

'Because you're involved,' Sanchez sneered. 'Because she's not just missing, her life is in danger and that's your fault.'

Charlie looked at the man. 'You're not helping.'

'I'm not!' Sanchez shot to his feet. 'What about you? All you've done is sat on your arse and scribbled a few notes. We should be out there moving heaven and earth to find her.'

Charlie stood carefully to face him.

'Officer Sanchez, you would only be in the way,' White scolded as she came back into the room. 'Now sit down.' As Sanchez began to obey, she switched that warning look to Charlie. 'You too.'

Even as they both sank back to their respective places, there was a dark clash of looks, neither exactly comfortable with the other.

'Do you really think they'll find her?' The question wasn't directed at anyone in particular.

'Yes.' Charlie had to make himself sound more certain than he was.

'They didn't find Terry.'

'They will find Ari. They will.' *They will. Or I will.* Because despite Piper, despite White, the second he had something to go on, he was going. He was going to get her and bring her home and make sure she was never in trouble ever again.

'What's RMJ?'

Charlie looked up at Sanchez. For a moment not knowing what he was talking about. The man pointed to the fallen pad.

'You've written those letters all over the pad.'

Charlie glanced at it, but it was Mrs W that picked the pad up.

'Rhys Mansel-Jones,' he said.

'The man you killed.'

Sanchez was determined to put him in the worst light possible. Charlie couldn't blame him for that. 'Brother of the man I killed.'

'What would he want with my Addy?'

Again he switched his attention to the older woman. She deserved the truth. 'I took away someone he loved, maybe he's taken her because she's the someone I love.'

Her look was sharp, then calculating. His heart was in his mouth. It mattered to him that Ari cared about him, it mattered if her mother did too. If Mrs W took against him, that could drive a wedge between him and Ari. Mrs W's gaze slid away and so did his heart. He shouldn't need her approval, but he did.

'"They weren't meant for listening for children screaming."' Mrs W was frowning as she read from his notes. 'What's that mean?'

'It's a phrase I read in a similar case.' The Hall case. Mr Hall's notebook. 'It spoke of tunnels and...' He couldn't say torture that would only make Mrs W worry more. 'Stuff. "They weren't meant for listening for children screaming." It doesn't make any sense, but it stuck in my head. So I wrote it down.'

'You wrote down "listening" several times too,' White said, looking over the older woman's shoulder.

'Weren't you making tea?'

At Sanchez's snipe, White left the room, going through the arch into the kitchen. At least she seemed to be preparing the drinks.

'Tunnels. Listening.'

Mrs W's voice was very low, almost absent.

'Sorry?'

'Tunnels. Listening.' She looked up directly at Charlie. 'What if it's "listening tunnels"? There's an old World War Two listening station just outside town. There used to be some of those parabolic listening walls, so they could focus the sound and hear the planes sooner, but they were torn down in the seventies. The tunnels the listeners used though, they're still there underground. They weren't meant for listening to children scream.'

Charlie went cold. Could it be that simple? 'Where? Where are they?'

'South of town. In fields off Eight Mile Avenue. By the junction with Fools Road.'

Charlie's heart was racing. This was it, this was what he needed. He could sense the expectation in the air, knew Sanchez understood it too. Apparently, he wasn't going out alone after all.

'Do you know how we can get into those tunnels?' Charlie asked.

'Well, when I was a very little girl, there was a manhole in the copse at that junction. Outside the field itself. Some friends and I used to get in that way, there's a good half-dozen rooms down there. But the manhole was changed for a security cover years ago. All thick metal and heavy-duty padlocks.'

'I've got bolt cutters.'

Charlie and Sanchez were on their feet and running from the house before Mrs W knew what was going on.

Chapter 50

This had to be the most organised workspace Charlie had ever seen. Tools in marked spaces, all clean and two power packs in place, showing fully charged. There was something on the workbench, part-assembled. He moved closer.

'This looks like a music stand.'

'It is.' Enzo was taking the bolt cutter from the blue chest. 'It's for Ari. She plays the flute.'

Charlie had been about to touch the turned wood. It was one more thing he hadn't known about her. He really didn't deserve her. Enzo had what he needed in a bag. He held out his hand.

'Give me the bag and your car keys. If anyone asks, you can claim I stole them.'

The other man's jaw clamped. There was a sneer on his lips. A steely coldness burned in his eyes. 'I'm going with you.'

'If you do, you are crossing a line that you won't be able to come back from. Take it from someone who's already on the other side of that line, don't cross it.'

'You think you're the only one who cares about her?' Enzo snapped, stepped closer. 'I'm been in love with Ariadne since I was thirteen, if she's in trouble, I'm going to help.'

He understood that feeling too well, and knew time was too precious. 'Okay. I'll take the bag, you drive.'

The holdall was virtually thrown at him as Enzo led the way into the back garden and the garage. He was heaving up the garage door and remotely unlocking the car as Charlie entered. He moved straight to the front of the garage.

'You drive out, I'll close the door.'

'Like it matters.'

It mattered, but he wasn't going to argue since Enzo was going to the car anyway and he still had the door ready to close. Enzo had to drive out carefully, it wasn't the widest lane between the garages. As soon as he was clear, Charlie slammed the garage door and rushed to the passenger side of the car. As soon as he was in, Enzo hit the gas, throwing him sideways as they took the corner and he scrambled to get his seatbelt on.

'Slow down. We don't want to get arrested or dead before we get there!'

Enzo's head was down, like a charging bull, but his foot eased off the accelerator. Charlie wished his own heart would ease off, but he doubted that would happen. How Enzo felt about Ari was hardly a surprise, and it wasn't a threat either. Ari had made her choice and she'd chosen him. When he got her back, he was getting her and Mrs W out of here. They were going to go somewhere none of this would matter. They would be a family and they would be happy, free. He would never let anyone hurt his Ari again.

Chapter 51

'Yes!'

'Sir?'

Siddig looked worried when Piper turned to her. 'Come with me.' He was moving towards the front door but turned back to face the other men. 'Lawson!' He had the older man's attention, and everyone else's. He pointed to the fresh-faced Uniform next to him. 'You stay with Lawson. Get this place secured. Everyone else back in the van!'

'Sir?' Covington stepped down a few of the stairs. 'What's going on?'

'We have to go arrest Rhys Mansel-Jones.'

Not caring about the various shouts of triumph behind him, Piper was running forward to his car, Siddig hard on his heels. They were in the car and driving before she asked.

'What's happened?'

'The Gallo family broke their silence. Mansel-Jones was demanding money from them and Mrs Gallo was, unknown to her husband, keeping video evidence of that. In-store CCTV. The murder of their daughter was a step too far, she's given Broughton the evidence and he's got warrants for arrest and house search.'

His phone started ringing again. Slowing for traffic, he leaned towards the middle of the car, pulled it from his pocket and passed it to Siddig.

'Hello?' A pause. 'He's driving right now, this is Constable Siddig.' She listened. 'Oh hell. Hold on.' Siddig shifted in her seat to look at him more steadily. 'It's Linda Small, sir. Mary White called. Apparently, Charlie and Enzo Sanchez have raced off to Eight Mile Road.'

That didn't make a lot of sense. Piper frowned as he negotiated another corner. 'Why?'

'Hold on, let me put this on speakerphone.' She did and held the phone up between them.

'Linda?' Piper spoke loudly, knowing the speaker facility on the phone wasn't the best.

The voice crackled a little, but he heard well enough.

'Apparently Charlie was writing down things he knew about the case. Sometimes the same word over and over. Mrs Whittaker looked at it. He wrote something about tunnels that weren't built for listening to children scream. And Mrs Whittaker said there's a World War Two listening post on Eight Mile Road.'

Siddig just looked at him. He glanced across.

'Seriously?'

'Apparently. I didn't know about them either, we're all kind of the wrong generation, but it seems there are lots of tunnels under the fields around there. Tunnels and rooms. And according to Mrs Whittaker, only one-way in. An old grate that was replaced about 25 years ago. It's in a field owned by -'

'Mansel-Jones?' Piper didn't really need to ask. He also knew that Mansel-Jones owned several properties out that way, including a farm house that was neatly screened off by tall thick hedgerows. But he didn't own Joskins Field.

'Linda?'

'I'm already on my way.'

The call was cut and Piper stopped for a red light.

'Eight Mile Road is a pain in the butt to drive,' Siddig mused. 'Straight enough but too many rough edges, so everyone has to drive down the middle to avoid damaging their cars, and the hedgerows reduce visibility on most of it, making it extra dangerous. The whole thing is lined with tall fencing of some description. Everyone's asking why the council won't do anything about it.'

'Well, now I'm unofficially guessing the reason is Mansel-Jones.'

She nodded, making sense of it. 'Keep the traffic down and reduce the number of possible witnesses to any entry or exit.' She considered that for a second. 'Wouldn't it make more sense to just build over the entry, so no one could see anything?'

'Maybe, but on the other hand why make it look like there could be something of interest there?'

Siddig grabbed the dash as he went too fast around the corner and did a hand brake stop, turning the vehicle to face back out of the not-police car park that was actually right next to the station.

'Oy! You can't just leave that there!'

The car park attendant screamed as Piper jumped out. Siddig was suddenly in his way, her hand held out. 'Keys. You get the warrants, I'll be out front.'

Chapter 52

'You're sure this is the right place?'

Charlie understood Sanchez's uncertainty. Eight Mile Road was fairly featureless for a road that was eight miles long and ran through a bunch of fields. One field looked much like another, but he knew which one Joskins Field was. That had all happened while he was inside, but he'd read the papers, studied the map, searched his memory for any scrap that would provide evidence that this was the break they needed to shut the Mansel-Jones operation down once and for all. It had been a waste of effort. The obvious factor, however, was that the hedgerow there had been torn up in finding those body parts and it marked the start of a fenced area that eventually ran into a light industrial park that was usually entered from the other side at Larkin Way, about 300 metres south of Fools Lane, on which they were parked - which was to say that that was where the car looked abandoned.

He looked to Sanchez as he hefted the bolt cutters. 'I'm sure.'

The thick chain-link fencing was attached at the corner by a half-inch bar which was itself attached to the corner fence post by four more narrow connectors of the same material. He placed the bolt cutters over the bottom one and squeezed. When it didn't pop immediately, Sanchez added his strength and the holder sheared. The rest went the same way and Charlie pushed the fence aside, dashing through the gap and into the trees.

'There.'

Sanchez pointed and moved toward the just-about-visible plate. Charlie pulled him back from reaching for it.

'Wait.'

'What for?'

It was a struggle, but Charlie managed to stop him.

'Look at it!' They both did. 'It's covered in leaf droppings. If this has been opened any time in the last two months, I'd be surprised.'

He saw Sanchez's shoulder drop. 'So she's not here. Or we're in the wrong place. What now?'

Charlie stared at the plate, wishing for x-ray vision. 'This land is owned by Mansel-Jones. Loads of the property around here is.' He crouched down and looked at the lock. It was stainless steel, so no corrosion, but it hadn't been handled in a while. He faced Sanchez again. The defeat he saw in the other man's face was a surprise. 'Look, for all I know, this is a wild goose chase, but my instincts say not. It's possible there is another entrance that we don't know about, in which case, we have the element of surprise here.'

He pushed all the leaves aside.

'Shit.'

'Where's the padlock?'

There wasn't one. The metal sheet was solid and had no loop for a padlock. Charlie scrubbed more leaves away.

A smaller panel which he lifted.

'A fucking keypad?' Sanchez swore.

Charlie sat back on his heels. There was no way of knowing what the code was. He couldn't even be sure how many digits would be in the code. He felt the tears threatening and he pushed his hair back with both hands. Sanchez hefted the bolt cutters and with a cry of pure frustration, he threw them into the trees before he folded down to the ground.

'There has to be a way in. There has to be.'

It was the echo to Charlie's only thoughts. They had to find the way in. The idea that Ari was on the other side of that damned piece of metal was just too much. A part of him would smash the fucking thing open if he had to. He looked at the number pad. Research had to count for something.

He typed in Phillip Mansel-Jones' birthday.

Nothing.

He tried Rhys Mansel-Jones' birthday.

'What are you doing?'

'Trying.' Without success.

'Are you crazy? Do you know how many possible combinations there are for a lock like that?'

'If it's up to six digits, that would be one million.'

'And you've tried two,' Sanchez sneered. 'Ari hasn't got a decade to wait.'

'No, but it has to be something memorable. Something easy to remember.'

'Try the guy's birthday.'

'Just did.'

'Well we're not going underground unless we figure it out.'

Charlie stared at him. 'Going underground.' Couldn't really be that simple, could it. Could it?

He dialled in 1980.

Nothing.

'Bollocks.' What was it Piper had said? March? He tried 031980. Nothing. His teeth vibrated as he ground them. 198003. Nothing.

'We don't have time to try everything.'

He closed his eyes and wracked his brain. Time. Tick Tock.

Tick Tock Shop.

The conversation Piper had told him about. Kinsley's confession. *You could get anything for a price at the Tick Tock Shop.* Oh God could it be that horrific? Were the Mansel-Joneses offering a one stop shop for perversion? Mrs W said there were half a dozen rooms down there. Over time those rooms could be killed with whatever was necessary to fulfil whatever sick fantasy the man with the money could dream up. And Phillip would have given that to Rhys.

Charlie looked up at Sanchez and the image popped into his head. A frozen analogue timepiece. He looked at the number-pad. A cheapish watch that didn't tell the time. Three hands. Three numbers. 780. Nothing. 70800. Nothing.

Six numbers. One million combinations. That was the norm. On briefcases, security systems, six numbers; that was why too many people used their date of birth. Exactly eight minutes past seven. Not necessarily in the morning. 190800.

The sound of a pop surprised both him and Sanchez. One side of the cover popped up and he and Sanchez scrabbled to get their fingers under the sudden gap and force it up. Metal shrieked as they pulled up the plate. There was light below.

'So much for surprise.'

'I'll go first,' Charlie said as he moved to the ladder into the first room.

'Why?'

'I'm more expendable.' It wasn't the best answer, but it was honest. In the room, there was a smell of must and earth. That peculiar damp that was always below the soil. The walls were plan concrete, some brackets for instrumentation. This would have been one hell of a claustrophobic area to listen to anything in. What he could hear was a constant hum. Electrical. He looked at the exposed bulb, hearing Sanchez moving down the ladder. That hum was not a bulb. It was constant and engine-like. Like a pump on a fish tank. Or a fridge. Not that it mattered, he wasn't hearing Ari and that was what he was interested in.

'What-'

He stopped Sanchez with a raised finger.

Discounting the hum, he listened. Opposite where he stood was a corridor, the same corridor the hum was coming from. There was another sound. He couldn't place it, but he couldn't ignore it either. Any more than he could ignore the baseball bat propped against the wall. The business end was covered in dried blood. His stomach threatened rebellion.

Sanchez joined him, stepped around him and leaning slightly, took up the bat, weighing it in his hand to get a good grip. It wouldn't be Charlie's weapon of choice, but if it made Sanchez feel safer, he wasn't going to stop him.

Carefully choosing his steps, Charlie moved towards the opening to a corridor.

The corridor was maybe a metre wide. It had to run parallel to the road and six doors led off, all to the right-hand side. The first door was closed, but there was a small window, and was where the buzzing came from.

'Sounds like a fridge,' Sanchez whispered.

Charlie agreed, but his focus was elsewhere. The door to the next room was open. An empty square box. Concrete and stains. That smell he recognised from too many crime scenes. Someone had died in there. In fact the whole place stank like death. With an undertone of sex. His stomach roiled.

He moved to the next door. First, he saw the layer of photographs. Instamatic. Too small to make out at this angle. Lots of them though. As he moved into the doorway he saw the back of a large blocky chair. All square and blocky and screaming with the madness of years of torture.

Stopping facing the open door he realised that someone was in that chair, strapped to it. Someone with long brown hair and heeled black boots. He could see the royal blue of the corset she'd been wearing when he'd last seen her alive. Blood covered her, pooled around the chair.

Sanchez was beside him.

The bat clattered to the floor.

Sanchez rushed in, his hope still intact. Feet slipping in the gathered, not quite congealed pool of blood, he grabbed the chair itself to stop him falling, his gaze wide and fixed as he looked down at the occupant.

'Noooo!'

The elongated yell was anguish and pain. Every echo rattling around the shell that stood numb in the doorway unable to move, unable to articulate its grief, unable to do anything but stare at the back of the chair, at the back of Ariadne's trapped dead head.

Chapter 53

'Larkin Way.'

Siddig was already pulling off as Piper clicked his seatbelt on, and she drove. 'What?' She was going in the wrong direction for Larkin Way.

'Another team is already going through Mansel-Jones' home, he's not there. Given that Ariadne is missing, and Charlie's headed towards this Eight Mile Road listening post, I figure our best bet is the farm off Larkin Way that belongs to Mansel-Jones. I admit it's a wild shot, but I'm hoping my gut is right on this one because I've already called Covington. Jesus!'

Piper didn't see that gap as something that he'd ever have turned through, but Siddig did. Apparently, the guy she'd cut in front of shared his opinion, judging by the squeal of breaks and the blaring horn.

'I'll go with your gut on this one, sir.'

'Yeah, and I'd really like the contents of my guts to stay the contents of my gut! No more cutting across like that.'

'No, sir.'

But he could feel her acceleration all the same. The glint in her eyes suggested just a bit too much fun. She ran the junction faster than he ever would have.

'I'm never letting you drive again.'

* * *

'That's Carlisle's car,' Siddig said as she stopped behind the nine-year-old Toyota, effectively blocking it in.

'And that,' Piper pointed to the blue Audi A8, 'is Rhys Mansel-Jones' car. One of them, anyway.'

The van was already in front of them, as were the vehicles of DCI Small contingent.

Small stepped out of the house, saw Piper and walked directly to him, ignoring Covington who was talking to a man with a red face and a broken shotgun over his arm. He didn't look any more of a farmer than Covington did.

'Jesus Piper, you can pick 'em.' Small was intimidating enough when she was being fkneeriendly now she was scowling.

'What have we got?'

Before she could answer, their attention was drawn by a young man in ragged trousers almost falling out of a side door from the house door. He started pointing at the man with the gun, shouting in some quick-fire language Piper didn't have time to decipher.

The gun was on the move. Covington's fists moved faster, he had the barrel in his right and the red-faced man was stumbling back, blood flowing between his fingers from a nose broken by an impressive left uppercut.

Covington slapped the gun into the chest of the nearest Uniform and manhandled Red Face over the nearest item - a stone-cut horse trough - to cuff him.

He was yanking the man to his feet to face Piper. In a barrage of foreign language, the man in rags approached and Sergeant Kenneth Harris was a step behind. He stopped the man and barked orders in his face in the same language, the man quaked and moved away in the direction Harris pointed.

'There are half a dozen of them, ma'am, sir,' Harris announced as he moved towards the knot of officers. For the first time Piper saw the grey in his hair, and he was only mid-thirties. 'Cutters.'

Cutters. Those cutting the purer drugs in with whatever base they would be mixed with for selling on the streets.

'Polish?' Small asked.

'That one seems to be, the others are too scared to talk. Or even move.'

How Harris knew Polish was a question Piper was prepared to leave till later as he turned to the red-faced man. 'Where's the tunnel to the listening post?'

The way the man jerked away from the question confirmed that he knew exactly what Piper was talking about.

'Inspect!'

The call came from inside the house and cut off with a grunt. Piper rushed in, barking an order for Covington to bring the man with them. Inside, he rushed into a large, filthy front room, Small on his heels. The fireplace held ashes and half-burnt bits that looked like fag packets and food waste. The place stank of beer and curry. More worryingly, Constable Adams was on the floor, bleeding from the forehead.

Piper's eyes swept the walls, desperately looking for -

Thwack!

Piper turned in time to see Red Face ricochet off the wall.

'Where's the passage?' Covington snarled.

'Fuck you.'

'Don't you get it, moron?' Covington's lips were drawn back in a feral warning as Harris moved past him and Siddig looked to Adams. 'You're up to your pathetic neck in it. We -'

'Piper!' Small called his attention.

Piper swung back around and saw she'd found and opened a door next to the bricks of the hearth and directly where Adams' feet were pointing. The passage was low and led steeply down. There was light reflecting up and Piper could hear footfalls. Running. He rushed after them.

Crouching for the first ten metre rush was difficult in the half-light, but soon enough the tunnel flattened and grew into a straight corridor of bricks a couple of hundred yards long and he could run normally. Run after the two retreating figures. Aware that others were behind him, Piper still felt like a man alone. This was what he had to do. This was what he was meant to do.

'Carlisle!'

The bellow thumped off the walls, reverberated with venom. The man turned mid-run and looked with terrified eyes over his shoulder. Which was probably what made him trip.

Speed Piper didn't know he could achieve had him standing over the blood-spattered Carlisle, grabbing him by the shoulders as he tried to recover. He pushed the man head first into the wall. Satisfaction washed warmth through him as Carlisle slumped in a dazed heap. Heavy footfalls approached. Surprise replacing satisfaction as Small, Siddig and Covington bore down on them.

'Noooo!'

Anguish and sorrow reverberated around them.

Chapter 54

Something cold and hard sat where a heart used to be. The pounding of blood in his ears thundered out all other sound. But it was a false rumble, he was listening to the sound of running. Fleeing.

The only one who would be coming this way was the bastard behind all this.

Carlisle.

Bending his knees, Charlie reached down to pick up the bat, his resolve as cold as the concrete on which it lay.

There was no sense of feeling, no sense of vengeance, just the certainty that he had to stop this horror in its tracks. The footfalls were getting closer and it sounded like there was more than one person coming.

Bring on the hordes of Hell. I'll beat every bastard.

Each step deliberately taken, he moved towards the end of the corridor, which clearly wasn't the end. The running was close now. One runner ahead of the others. He spotted the shadow.

Raised the bat.

Stared directly at the wall.

Swung at the first thing to step into his path.

Thwap.

A body hit the wall.

Groaning.

He stepped across in preparation of the next attacker. The steps were getting closer. The man slumping on the floor was getting up. He swung the bat down, hit a shoulder. The man cowered away. One fluid motion from hit to recovery had the bat ready to be wielded again.

The man was moving again. He lifted the bat above his head, cracked it down on a thigh.

Screaming.

'Charlie!'

Raising the bat again. He aimed for the arm raised up against him.

'Charlie!'

Another figure was coming towards him, he repositioned to swing.

'Charlie!'

The warning in the tone, the voice, finally reached him. Blinking focused him.

'You are not the law here.'

'Piper?'

'Yeah.' He tugged the bat from Charlie's hand. 'And that's Rhys Mansel-Jones.'

The frown creased his forehead. He had to concentrate, translate the words into something meaningful. *Piper. Here.* Bodies moving around them. A keening gave the hum new melody.

'What?'

'It's alright, Charlie. We got them. Rhys Mansel-Jones and Carlisle. And a lot of other people. We got 'em and they won't be wriggling out of this one. It's alright, Charlie.'

Nothing was ever going to be right again.

'Sir. You need to see this.'

On automatic, Charlie turned to see a young woman, pale beneath the darker skin of her Middle Eastern looks. Piper followed her, he followed Piper.

Small was stepping in to a room, he heard a child's cry of fear, but it didn't touch him.

'Inspector!'

Piper stopping, stopped Charlie. Harris skidded to a halt as he rounded the corner. He wasn't expecting Piper.

'Small?'

'Here.'

Charlie looked into the room, Small was crouching beside a small girl. Madeline Stolz. Her hair was dark lank blond, skinny unclothed shoulders peaked over the wrapping of a stinking dirty blanket. The hard grey wool was covered in stains, blood, urine, spunk. When she saw him looking her large eyes were full of fear. She was too afraid to scream, but some reactions were instinctive, the woollen blanket darkened at the bottom, the smell and pool of urine started to spill out. He remembered another little girl to scared to do anything but wet herself. The image was instantly pushed out by the image of the woman in the next room.

As Small stood up and stepped out of the room, Charlie stepped aside, out of the girl's vision. Harris pulled Small to the far side of the corridor, talking in an urgent low tone.

'The guy with the gun started talking. Apparently, three young boys were taken out of here half an hour ago. If we move, we can still get to them before they get to the marina and out of the country.'

Clearly Small needed to go, and without instruction, Siddig stepped up and went to the little girl.

"Go," Charlie said in monotone. "Go save someone."

Piper confirmed he'd wrap everything up here. As Small rushed away, Siddig came to the door again pointed the two men to the far end of the corridor. Piper moved down, stopped at the next door, his hand went to his mouth. Inside, Sanchez was still sobbing. Ari was still dead.

'Not that, sir.' Siddig didn't move, she had to both protect the girl and do her job. 'Door at the end.'

Piper moved on. Part of Charlie never would. He stepped forward, followed Piper. The door was open. Piper looked inside.

'Jesus.'

Stepping up again, Charlie moved around his old boss. Another room, this one with two big chest freezers, and lots of shelves filled with... he supposed the word was mementos. Charlie stepped inside. Numbly he opened the first freezer. He wasn't surprised to see a frozen head inside a plastic bag looking back at him. He wasn't anything.

'Longpig.'

Piper stepped up beside him. 'Explains why the pathologist thought some of those parts in Joskins Field were ice-burned. Must have been the dumping ground when the meat went bad.'

Frozen body part lay on top of frozen body. Remains. There was a pink friendship bracelet around the tiny wrist of what would once have been a girl. These weren't whole bodies, they probably weren't even the parts to make up a whole body. The knee on Rhys's sideboard came to mind. The image of cannibals. He closed the lid again.

In front of them a shelf had been lined with a set of small hooks. From the hooks hung jewellery. A loveheart pendant on one. A gold cross on another. A cheap plastic bead necklace. A St Christopher. A diamante 'Mandy'. Too many others.

No.

Charlie looked again; the silver pendant drew him like a magnet. He pulled it towards him. Not St Christopher. St Jude.

'Terry.'

Chapter 55

DCI Small was out of the car before Harris quite stopped the vehicle, long legs and flat shoes meant that she was running full tilt towards the Harbour Master's office in a heartbeat, handbag across her torso flapping at her thigh. She was expecting to see Mike Penry, but only Carol Tynes was in sight.

Harris had filled her in on the way. Lawson in an unusual display of aggression that just about stayed the right side of the law, had persuaded the armed man they'd first met at the farm to talk. He'd said that three boys had been taken out of the tunnel and into a van. They were heading for the Marina and a boat out to somewhere. The man didn't know where.

'Carol,' Small greeted the constable as she skidded to a halt. 'What you got?'

'Five boats due to leave in the next hour, three gone in the last 30 minutes.' She passed across the list. 'Mike's gone to the first lot up that way.'

Small looked across, a list of boat names and their docking positions. She looked up at the marina. 'Isn't there a barrier on the way out to the estuary?'

'Yes, ma'am.'

'Did you get the Harbour Master to close it?'

Carol flushed, and her eyes dropped. Small stepped around the woman and stepped inside. She didn't have to ask who the Harbour Master was, it was obvious. Of the two guys in the cramped space only one looked like he understood what command meant. She pulled her warrant card from her back pocket and showed it about as she read the name on the man's shirt; he was Willis and the other was Maca. 'Close the barrier, no one goes out.'

Willis, a salty sea dog if ever there was one, nodded to the younger man who blasted the horn, and the Master started the mechanics.

'Thank you!' Small was halfway out of the room already.

Harris was directing Carol and two uniforms towards the middle of the marina; another uniform stood with him. As the others moved away, Harris indicated that they should be heading towards the end of the marina, the end nearest the barrier.

'Our first target is the *Daffy Rose*. Owner and skipper Nicholas Doty. Should be on board.'

'Any background?'

'Speeding, but that's all.'

The daily crime that people had largely become anaesthetised to. The *Daffy Rosa* was the third boat in. Small know nothing about boats and cared less, but at this point she couldn't really see how three boys could possibly be hidden on board. A man who looked about mid-forties was ducking out from the helm, and not looking happy.

'Mr Doty?'

He turned to her, scowling. 'What?'

'We'd like a word please sir, do you mind if we come on board?' She displayed her badge.

He paled. 'Do I have a choice?'

'Not really, no,' she said, taking the high step onto the deck, aware that Harris was behind her.

'What's this all about?' He was looking between the three of them. Looking up at her. This was one time when her height was a distinct advantage.

'Some very precious cargo is to be transported out of the county, possibly out of the country. From this marina.'

Doty swallowed, his ramping heartrate betrayed by the shaking of his hands. 'No-nothing to do with me.'

'Then you won't mind us looking around, will you?' Harris's tone was just the light side of heavy that brooked no argument but avoided being too threatening.

Doty's eyes widened, and he swallowed. 'Well, I, er, I-'

'You don't really have much choice Mr Doty,' Small assured him as Harris and the uniform disappeared inside the boat.

He hung his head and nodded, sitting down on the hard-plastic bench seat moulded into the edge of the deck. They were going to find something. He knew it and now she knew it.

'Should I just cuff you now?'

His head hung lower. If he knew they were going to find three kidnapped boys on this boat, he'd be reacting more violently than this.

'I didn't think it was that big a deal.' He was shaking his head. 'It's only skunk.'

Cannabis? Like she was interested in cannabis. 'How much?'

'Two pound.'

At fifty quid an eighth that was still a street value over twelve grand. And way too much for her to ignore. *Shit.* She didn't need this wasting her time.

'Inspector!'

She looked up to see Maca running down the marina. He was sporting a split lip that hadn't been there before and lump was forming on his forehead.

'Inspector!'

The gait was staggered. Maca was going to some effort to bring her this news, which meant it was important.

'They're getting away!'

The man was staggering now, that bump to the head really not helping. He stopped and grabbed a rail for support as he neared the boat. 'Some big bloke just stormed into control, whacked me one and forced Willis to open the barrier. The *Gemini* is going for it.'

She looked where the man was pointing and saw a larger, sleeker vessel moving purposely through the water, and it looked like the speed was going to cause it and other sailors problems. There was no way that they were getting to that boat without one of their own, and if they didn't, the boat and the boys would be long gone. It was moving from the far end of the marina, which meant the *Daffy Rose* was still closer to the barrier than they were. Her attention snapped to Doty.

'Help me intercept that boat and I'll forget about your confession to a custodial offence.'

Doty scrambled to his feet and started the engine. 'Cast off!'

Small only just turned in time to avoid the rope being thrown at her. 'We're free.' She had to grab the rail around the boat as they moved suddenly from the dock.

Harris was stumbling up from below decks as Small moved to stand behind Doty. 'What's going on?'

Small scanned the marina, tried to judge if they were going to be able to intercept the *Gemini*. She looked across to the larger vessel and felt her world shift.

DC Michael Penry was looking straight back at her.

No.

It could never be forgotten that too many paedophiles had jobs that brought them into direct contact with children, but the idea of one of her own being involved made her feel physically sick. It hardened her resolve like steel. Mike raised his arms, and the shot tore through the shelter around the pilot's area.

Doty swore and cowered.

Harris dragged Small down as another shot rang out.

'Keep going!' Small screamed as she felt the boat slow, but Doty was cowering on the floor.

Harris moved to the pilot's seat and took the controls. For all his ability surprised Small, she wasn't going to deny its potential. She looked at Doty.

'Flare gun?'

The snivelling coward was shaking like a quake as he pointed to the locker behind Harris, who himself was cringing against the fire he was not only approaching, but nearing. Small found the locker was padlocked. A bunch of keys slid across the plastic floor. Hands trembling, she concentrated on opening the locker. Inside, she found the flare gun and checked it was loaded. It wasn't much of a weapon, but it was better than nothing. She looked at Harris, he wasn't cringing anymore, there was no more gun fire. The uniformed officer appeared from below.

'What's your name?'

'George Robinson.'

'Okay, George. Do you know how to drive this thing?' Because if she was going to board the other ship, she'd rather be with Harris, who she knew she could depend on, than someone she'd never met before.

He nodded.

Small glanced at the *Gemini*. A couple of yards away. She adjusted her grip on the flare gun. Thank God sweaty palms weren't her problem, though she was fought to control her breathing, aware that her pulse was rapid. They were going to meet that boat and it sat about a foot higher in the water than them. 'Do you think you can get us in behind that boat?'

'What?' Doty demanded. 'The wash, the wake.'

'I can do it,' Robinson agreed, giving Doty no more attention than Small had. Harris stepped aside, Robinson took the wheel. Small stood, moved next to Harris. 'Ma'am, this is going to be dangerous.'

'Three scared kids.'

She didn't need to say anything more; Harris nodded. The barrier out of the marina was still rising. 'Why aren't they closing it?'

'Because it's got to go all the way up before it can start coming down,' Harris supplied.

That meant that there was no barrier to the *Gemini* leaving the marina but them. Robinson was getting them to the back of the other boat. The ride was getting choppy, unbalancing the boat. Small grabbed the rail to steady herself, and Harris did the same. The boat bucked and bounced - it was going to be in place behind the other in seconds. Harris moved, swung one leg over the rail, ready to jump. He glanced to Small, she was just as ready. Even though she had to swallow nerves as she stuffed the flare gun in the back of trousers, she was ready.

Three scared boys.

This - *they* - were why she did this job. She'd get those boys back and this was just the high water she was going to have to get through to do so.

'Now!' she yelled, and Harris jumped with her.

The flat soles of her brogues slid on the wet surface of the deck, but she caught hold of the rails and saved herself a dunking. A glance to her right told her that Harris was safely on board, twisting further, holding the rail for dear life. She looked behind her to see Robinson, nodded and he moved the boat away. Another glance at Harris. The silent question. He nodded his readiness.

Adrenaline copper-lined her throat as they moved from the lower stern area onto main deck, taking each step slowly, looking for signs of trouble. There had to be at least two men here. The person steering the boat and Michael bloody Penry. There could be any number of other men, but she was only worried about three little boys, and praying that they were here and alive, for them to be okay was a hope too far.

They got two steps before a figure appeared again.

Penry.

'Fuck!'

Harris's exclamation was evidence that he hadn't expected that one, but he didn't hesitate either. As Penry raised the gun again, Small assumed he had gone below decks for more ammo. Harris twisted, picked up a seat cushion from the nearest chair and chucked it like a ninja on a good day. The gun fired into the air and Penry was knocked unstable, Harris was on him in a second. Figuring the older man had more than enough skill to overwhelm the Penry's strength, Small headed for the helm. Stopping this boat was now the priority. She skirted the other side of the deck past the fighting men.

There was an open doorway into the heart of the boat, but the helm was ahead, the man at the wheel intent on getting out of here.

Pain slammed into the back of her knee.

Small fell onto that knee, but hands caught her, kept her upright. Hands at her neck, strangling her, robbing her of her of breath. Her breath, but not her senses. As he grappled with her throat, she groped into her bag and grabbed her small deodorant. Pepper spray would have been better, but she didn't routinely carry any. She popped the top, pulled it from the bag and sprayed it straight into the thug's eyes.

Dragging in a much-needed breath that tasted of Right Guard, she surged to her feet, ignoring the screaming in her knee, fishing in her bag again. He grabbed her. Now she had her lighter in her other hand. The marina barrier was coming down, but it would still take too long to close. As the man tried to drag her over the rail into the filthy-looking water of the marina, she didn't bother raising her hands. Instead, she struck the lighter and pressed the deodorant nozzle bringing flame and spray together, right over the man's crotch.

Screaming, his sex literally on fire, he stumbled back and crashed over the side. She slammed into the rail, breath punched out of her lungs. His hand was still wrapped around her purse strap. His weight nearly pulled her over. The stitching tore, she grabbed the purse as he fell away, and his hand simply slid off the broken end of the strap.

Limping now, pissed off to have damaged one of her favourite bags, she stumbled towards the helm.

'Stop this boat!' The man looked at her and reached for something. The pressure in the lower part of her spine reminded her of the flare gun, and she dropped the bag and pulled it out. Suddenly the flare gun and a Glock were virtually nose to nose.

'Drop it or I'll kill you!'

'Oi!'

Harris's shout from the other side of the boat surprised the helmsman, his arm started to move, Small fired the flare. She was reasonably sure she didn't hit him, but she and Harris ducked out for the worst of the flare as the pistol fired into the helm. When she ducked back in, the flare was flaring, the man was on the floor, coughing and screaming and holding his burnt chest. Harris stepped in, grabbed the fire extinguisher from beneath the helm and sprayed it over the man's burning clothes. Small had no idea how to drive a boat, but she figured that the lever the guy had been holding must be some kind of throttle and she yanked it down. The boat bounced to a halt, or at least to an unpowered drift as Harris emptied the cannister on the flare that just wouldn't give up.

He grabbed the man's hand, cuffed him to the foot bar of the pilot's chair.

'You okay here?' She squinted against the flare, breathing heavily. The pain radiating up from her side and her knee made her grit her teeth.

'I'll get us back. You okay?'

'Damaged knee. I'm going to see if I can find those boys.'

The ship listed as the engines returned to power and the direction changed. They were going back. The interior of the ship seemed too dark. For a second Small stopped, stood. Listened. Couldn't hear anything over her own breath, so she held it. There was nothing to compete with the sound of the engines or the pounding of her blood in her veins.

There were three doors. She went to the first. A tiny galley. The second was a cramped sitting area. The third...

She looked into a room barely bigger than a broom closet and thickly-lined. Orange insulation and that soundproofing foam that looked like eggboxes covered the walls, floor and ceiling. Inside, huddled together, chained together at the ankles, were three boys, Stephen Pearson on the left. She sagged against the door frame. *Thank God.*

* * *

Harris got them back to the dock, from where uniform and paramedics swarmed the boat. Small vaguely registered Carol telling her that they'd got the guy from the water. Clyde Baxley. One of Rhys Mansel-Jones's bouncers. There'd be no denying the connection now, although given that Mansel-Jones was already under guard, Small didn't think that was going to be an issue any more.

She heard her name being called. The frantic demand of a desperate man. She turned and saw Doty struggling between two uniforms and Robinson close by.

'You said you'd forget about this,' Doty whined.

'I said I'd forget your confession.' She pointed to the brown evidence bag and the transparent section that clearly showed her the large bag of leaf. 'That's undeniable evidence, can't forget about that.

Chapter 56

Piper was alone in the incident room. That mere fact was unusual, in itself some achievement. But Piper knew it was because he'd scared the rest of the team out. He was a bear with a sore head. Of course he was. He'd been on shift for thirty hours now and he'd lost someone. He carefully started taking pictures from the incident board and putting them in the archive box.

They'd found out what happened to Terry Whittaker. They'd saved Madeline Stolz, Stephen Pearson and two other boys. They'd also revealed Carlisle and Penry as working for Rhys Mansel-Jones. Either, indeed both, were the Don. It made him question if that title, that sickness could ever be cut from the heart of the station.

A crystal tumbler appeared on the desk beside the archive box. Then the bottle of Teachers -

'No.'

'Fuck that.' Broughton tipped the bottle and poured a finger of whiskey.

'This isn't a celebration.'

'No.' Broughton put down another tumbler, another finger of whiskey. 'But part of you should see that it should be. You identified and stopped the Don. You've resolved over twenty missing persons cases. The Fraud Squad are peeing their pants over the evidence that they're getting on a number of businesses because of the account books you found. The file Vince Talbot sent as soon as Rhys Manel-Jones' arrest went on the news seems to have enough detail to break a major paedophile ring, not that you hadn't got that on your own anyway. And you helped Small rescue four children, four children who would never have been found without you. That's not a bad day's work.'

'Do you think the Don is really gone?'

'For now,' Broughton was too realistic to lie. 'We'll do our best to ensure that another one doesn't arise, but there are no guarantees.'

Piper still stared into the box, unable to meet his superior's eye. 'It's not enough. I didn't get there quick enough.'

'Matthew, you can't blame yourself for everything, and certainly not for what you mean now. We all wish we'd got there sooner, solved it quicker. We did the best we could with the information we had. That's all any of us can ever do.'

'A woman is dead because I wasn't good enough.'

'No. A woman is dead because Rhys Mansel-Jones is a sick bastard. Because Carlisle was a turncoat. Because Charlie Bell wasn't good enough. And it wasn't just *a woman*, it was Ariadne Teddington. A good, brave woman who deserved a damn sight better than she got. She's why I'm here.' Broughton took up his glass. 'To Ariadne.'

The burning in his throat needed a reason. Piper picked up the glass and raised it. 'Ariadne.'

Chapter 57

Guilty. The verdict was three weeks ago, but today came the sentence. Life imprisonment. No parole for at least thirty years. Mansel-Jones and Carlisle both.

Piper stepped out of the courthouse and looked up at the sky. Solid white cloud. So much for a blazing summer. It had taken a year to get from arrest to trial to verdict. It was the right verdict, but Piper was unconvinced it was the right result. That bastard would still be alive. He might not be able to go far, but he would still be a living, breathing bastard. The scumbag surviving while the woman who deserved to be here right now was rotting in a cold grave. Life really wasn't fair at all.

'Inspector Piper?'

He turned to the older woman in black behind him. She had aged in the months since he'd last seen her. Her cheeks were more hollow, she appeared more fragile. She would mourn her daughter, and her son, for the rest of her life. Another unfair fact.

'Thank you for everything you did.'

The dryness at the back of his throat was in total contrast to the wetness pricking at his eyes. 'I'm sorry I didn't do more.'

'You didn't give up.' She placed a white shaking hand on his arm. 'And you brought my children back.' A tear escaped her eye and Piper had to blink back his own. 'You gave me answers. That matters.'

That was his job, though right now he wished he'd done it better. Suddenly, Mrs Whittaker's eye-line shifted.

'Luke!'

Piper turned and saw a suited Charlie Bell pause. He'd seen him in court, but the younger man refused to meet his eye. Charlie turned for a moment to face them and all Piper could see in that strained face was conflict. The war of what the younger man wanted to do, what he could do, and what he could stand the pain of. He'd barely seen Charlie since

Ariadne's funeral, but he knew what had happened. Bell's year hadn't been easy or fun. In fact, Piper would say that he'd had the year from hell. But it wasn't his call.

The rabbit in the headlights look switched to one of guilt. Charlie's eyes slid away from Piper and Mrs Whittaker, his head hung as he continued down the court's steps.

Mrs Whittaker had moved to Piper's side and they both watched as Charlie moved away.

'Will he be alright?'

Lying was an option. He turned to meet direct gaze of the woman who had been through far too much. 'No, Mrs Whittaker. I don't think he will.'

'Ha!'

Piper looked on in astonishment as Mrs Whittaker stepped past him.

'Lucas Charles Bell, you get back here.'

The call drew lots of attention, some curious looks watched, but they weren't of interest to Piper. The tall man stopped in his tracks. For the first time since the trial started, Bell actually straightened his spine. Piper watched Bell breathe in deep, he glanced at the determination carved on Mrs Whittaker's face. This was a clash he wasn't going to get between, but he wasn't going to miss a moment of it either.

'Well?' She called out.

Like a recalcitrant child, Bell hung his head and turned, walked back to stand before Mrs Whittaker, apparently unable to look her in the eye.

'Are you happy being miserable?'

Piper frowned, that wasn't what he'd expected, and apparently Charlie wasn't sure what to say either.

'Look at me,' Mrs Whittaker said softly.

Reluctantly, Charlie did. The redness of his eyes, the sallowness of his cheeks told their own story of what he'd been putting himself through.

'Do you think this is what Ari would want for you?'

Confusion clouded as he looked at the older woman. He swallowed. 'I loved Ari.'

'Yes,' Mrs Whittaker acknowledged. 'And she loved you. That's how I know the last thing she would want is for you to feel bad. Now stop hanging your head. You did nothing wrong. What happened is not your fault. I don't blame you, don't blame yourself.'

Charlie shook his head and looked to the heavens.

'Alright Luke, listen up.'

Mrs Whittaker got Charlie's attention back on her.

'I have buried my husband, both my children and my grandchild.' At that point she had to stop to swallow her own emotions. 'For two of those I had to stand by Ari's side and I can tell you that they broke her heart. You mended it. I believe she wanted to do the same for you after your own son died. Don't make her last act a failure. She loved you, and she'd want you to be happy.'

Mirroring tears escaped both Charlie and Mrs Whittaker, Piper swallowed the lump in his throat.

'So, you damn well find a way to do that. Understand?'

Charlie nodded, and for the first time, Piper felt a glimmer of hope for the man.

THE END

Locked Down

Acknowledgements

There are lots of people that I depend on to get any writing done, most obviously my family who never go without a mention. But Locked Down proved more difficult than most to get draft one done, and so there needs to be some special mentions. Here are just a few of the people that kept me going through the writing of Locked Down.

To Steve Jones for saying this was some of my best stuff when I was ready to delete the third rewrite of the start.

To Tony Fyler, who not only edited me remorselessly, but also had to do the "there-there neurotic writer, just get on with it" bit to keep me going.

To Doug Sinclair, who passed on some brilliant advice that really got me writing when I was struggling with the ending. The advice was, "just let rip and see where you end up". I'm paraphrasing here because there was more cursing in the actual advice.

To Dorian Lloyd, Steve Jones (a different one - it's a popular name around here) and Mike O'Shea, all of South Wales Police, who helped me get a lot of procedural details right for cold cases and professional standards, not to mention a lot of the effects that aren't noted in the procedures.

To the anonymous Twitterer who confirmed what Google Maps couldn't about Lewisham Police Station.

And thank you, of course – thank you for reading, because that really is the whole point of writing after all. If you like this book and you want to see more of what I'm up to, check out my website and social networks:

Website: www.gailbwilliams.com
Twitter: @GailBWilliams
Blog: thewriteroute.wordpress.com

Locked Down

Locked Down

Locked Down

Printed in Poland
by Amazon Fulfillment
Poland Sp. z o.o., Wrocław